MURDERERS AND NERDY GIRLS WORK LATE

by
Lisa Boero

ISBN: 0615762522

ISBN 13: 9780615762524

Library of Congress Control Number: 2013935071

Nerdy Girl Press

Marshfield, WI

For my mother - the best mother, friend, fan and editor an aspiring author could ever hope to have.

Murderers and Nerdy Girls Work Late

by Lisa Boero

CHAPTER 1

On the fourth stair down, I knew something was wrong. I sniffed and caught a whiff of sulfur and charcoal. The smell was familiar to me, but didn't belong in the garage of a prestigious law firm. I took a hesitant step and inhaled again. There was another scent below the first. Deeper. More pungent. A feral mix of iron and salt. And then, all of a sudden, I understood. It was blood.

I didn't set out to become a detective. The occupation found me that night in the stairwell. In fact, I'm wholly unsuited to the job. Some people say they never forget a face. I can say I never remember one. Never. As a child, I thought everyone was like me. Now I know better. I also know to guard my secret. Having an obscure neurological condition is not something you can mention unless your goal in life is to be the object of pity or freakish fascination. Neither appeals to me. To pass for normal, I notice everything else: the way people walk, talk, and move their hands. I memorize hairstyles, clothing choices, shoe sizes, jewelry and purse selections. I learn their habits and schedules so I know when I might expect to meet them. These tricks work pretty well. Most of the time.

I drove to work the Tuesday morning of the murder, one hand on the steering wheel, the other holding a waxy fruit pie I'd bought at the gas station. Breakfast of champions. I took a bite and the vaguely artificial apple taste filled my mouth. So much for all of my good intentions. I'd probably eat plastic if it had enough sugar on it. The light turned green and I inched forward. The traffic seemed to get worse the closer I got to the river.

I was a summer associate at Ghebish and Long, a large law firm located a couple of blocks from the St. Louis Arch. The firm leased the top six floors of the building. The offices had spectacular views of the river if you were one of the privileged few who got an office on that side. In sun and rain, you could see the barges moving slowly up and down the wide Mississippi. The view had a practical angle as well. G.L. had an admiralty law group that did nothing but manage barge accident litigation.

If a legal career were a marriage, the summer associate period would be the honeymoon. The partners were friendly, the lunches out were frequent, and the happy hours started early and ended late. Our real job was to get to know the partners and associates. In a boom time like 2005, we were likely to be hired after law school if we did a decent job, kept our tempers, and held our liquor.

Even so, law school is all about type A personalities climbing over each other to get to the top. We all noticed who worked for the big partners, who got the plum projects, and who billed the most hours. I was competitive too, but my goal that summer was to find a partner who had interesting work to give me, and who was decent to me when I did it. I'd found Janice Harrington in the estate planning group.

I got within sight of the building and looked at the clock on the dashboard. If the semi in front of me would just get a move on, I might actually make it in before 8:00. Sigh. I had tried so hard to get up early. Kelsey made a point of telling me that she was in by

7:30 every morning. And she had an office right by the managing partner, John Harding.

Kelsey was one of three petite blonde summer associates who all dressed in the big firm uniform – dark pantsuit with a bright colored blouse cut like a man's shirt. They also wore the same style and brand of black pumps, and had similar girlish voices with Midwestern accents. At first, these women gave my recognition strategies a real workout. To my poor brain, they were identical triplets. Luckily, Kelsey got a short haircut, Becca bought a Tiffany necklace she decided to wear every day, and Samantha adopted a verbena-scented body spray that I could smell at fifty paces. Crisis averted.

I pulled up to the garage and waved my card at the reader. No luck. I unbuckled my seatbelt. Still not close enough. I opened the door and lunged at it. Someone honked behind me. Great. I felt the sweat beading on my forehead and a trickle run down my back. Even better. I didn't have anything to change into if I sweated through my clothes. This early in the morning, I could already feel the heat radiating from the asphalt. The weatherman had said it would be cool today. Much he knew about St. Louis in August.

The bar finally went up, and I scrambled back into the car. Now onto the next trial. Finding a parking space. If only I were a partner, I'd have one reserved. And then a miracle occurred. Right there, in front of my eyes. A space on the first floor. It would be tight, but I didn't care. I maneuvered my ancient Chevy Corsica in between a Mercedes and an Accord. I could barely get out of the door, but that didn't dim my triumph.

I hummed as I took a short cut to my office.

"You're in a good mood," Sally said as I passed her cubicle.

The secretarial cubicles formed an inner ring beyond the attorney offices. The firm seemed to hire secretaries that fell into two categories: young, nubile and not too bright, or middle-aged, motherly and sharp as shark teeth. I got one of the sharp ones. On the first day, Sally told me that she would do what she could for me, but she had two partners and a senior associate already. I didn't have much to give her anyway. She had other uses. She was a good source of information if you got her going.

"Try to keep the happy thoughts. Tom Green stopped by. He wanted to know if you're done with the memo."

"I sent it down to word processing last night. It's not back yet?" I started to panic.

"Wasn't here when I got in. And Tom's on the warpath. His wife kicked him out again, so he's not what I'd call chipper."

"Wonderful. Let me drop my things and then I'll go investigate."

The lowest floor housed the information systems and the word processing. Word processing handled overnight dictation transcription and prepared large copying and printing jobs. There were also graphic arts professionals who helped prepare fancy computer presentations and exhibits for trials. And then there were the information systems personnel – an insular and odd group of people. They reminded me of the librarians I knew when I'd worked with government documents. My degree in history hadn't gotten me more than a job as a library assistant after graduation. But where librarians had merely dabbled in eccentricity, the computer people wallowed in it.

As I wended my way to word processing, I passed by the programmer who owned a complete suit of armor for jousting tournaments at Renaissance fairs. I said hello to him, and heard a soft shriek off in the distance. I didn't have to look. The systems analyst obsessed with whales. She listened to music played over whale vocalizations. Their high-pitched intonations floated out of her cube and over the department like ghostly echoes. Another turn and I was at the purse lady. She collected plastic purses from the 1950's and stacked them like children's blocks on her desk.

"Hello, Elizabeth," a voice said behind me.

I stopped and forced myself to turn around. It was Chester. Chester always stared without blinking. He also had a habit of showing up to my office unannounced. The last time, it was to replace the old roller ball mouse with a laser light one. He'd popped the rubber-coated ball out of the mouse and pitched it suddenly into my lap. "For luck," he said with a creepy smile. I nudged it into the trash as soon as he left.

"Um, hello Chester. Sorry I can't talk. Got to get something from word processing."

He continued to stare, and it was all I could do not to yell, "Blink!" I excused myself again and hurried along. Tom Green was on the management committee. I couldn't afford to tick him off.

The management committee consisted of ten of the most senior partners. Janice Harrington was still the only woman of this august body. John Harding ruled the committee and therefore the firm. He maintained tight control, but only two on the committee could say they worked closely with him: Blane Ford and Thomas Green. They were the heads of the mergers and acquisitions department and the corporate litigation department, respectively. Physically, they made an odd pair. Ford was tall and painfully thin with a Lincolnesque face – compelling and strange at the same time. Green was short and rotund, with a full dimpled face emerging from a thick double chin. Despite their physical differences, Ford and Green worked in unison to carry out Harding's wishes.

I'd asked Janice about Harding's influence with the management committee one night over drinks.

"Even if they think John's making a crazy decision, they won't oppose him. They're all afraid of Tom and Blane," Janice said.

"Why would anyone be afraid of them?"

She took another sip of her martini. "Beats me, but I can't mount a rebellion by myself."

It seemed odd to me that such a large firm could be run so auto-cratically. I wondered if the other members of the committee really trusted Janice, or if they kept certain things hidden from her. She was a pioneer – one of the first female equity partners at Ghebish and Long. Equity partners bought into the firm and shared the prof-its. Non-equity partners had the title but were salaried. Only equity partners could hold positions of power at G.L., so she should have been in the loop. They couldn't ask for anyone more dedicated to the work than Janice. She'd even sacrificed her marriage to the job.

It turned out that the memorandum I'd dictated was still waiting to be typed. I begged and pleaded and finally got them to promise that it would be done before 10:00. Summer associates didn't have the clout to ask for more. I wandered back to the elevator feeling defeated. I should really take the stairs, but I just didn't have the energy. A blonde woman stopped me as I got out of the elevator. Short hair, no necklace, no verbena. Must be Kelsey.

She wanted to catch up and asked all sorts of questions about my current projects. I tried to answer politely, but without detail.

No need to give Kelsey more of a leg up. Janice's throaty voice summoned me before Kelsey weaseled too much information. Janice had some research she wanted to discuss, so I followed her back into the elevator and up to her office.

After we went over her project, she said, "How is the summer going so far? Good I hope."

I responded positively. Janice may have been a workaholic, but she remained attentive to the people around her. She'd told me several times that she liked me because I didn't fit the summer associate mold. She was more right than she knew, but even discounting my neurological quirks, it had to be clear to everyone that I wasn't part of the social scene.

"And the other summer associates are okay to work with?" she said.

"Fine. There is always a little drama, but nothing out of the ordinary," I replied.

In truth, the happy hours produced more summer associate affairs than I could count. It was like a daytime soap – with less attractive actors. Except for Grant. His tattooed arms and dangerous swagger made many smart women act very stupid. Not me. Most of the single male associates were too egotistical for my taste. I wasn't their type either. It didn't help that I'd let the freshman fifteen sneak up on me in law school after avoiding it so carefully as an undergraduate. The dreaded trifecta: stress, sitting and snacks.

Still, some associates were more down-to-earth, and I counted them as friends. Vince, for example, was likable and funny. His family had emigrated from Colombia when he was a small child, so he knew the value of education and hard work. He told me about his older sisters, both doctors, who teased him that law school must be easy if he was in the top ten percent of his class. He also had a younger sister at college in town. His stories made me wish my own family lived closer. It was a day's drive to my parent's house in the wilds of Wisconsin.

And there was Stephanie, who seemed happy in her marriage and talked children. Of course, she was older than the rest of us, which didn't hurt.

"How's Beth Jones doing?" Janice asked.

Her question caught me off guard. "I think she's doing fine. Why?"

"I saw her talking to you yesterday. Normally, she's so quiet."

I smiled. "Not like the rest of us? She only asked me about a reference book she'd seen me with."

Janice nodded, her curiosity satisfied, and spoke a little about her own days as a summer associate. According to Janice, female summer associates in her day were forced to beat on the glass ceiling with pickaxes. I listened politely, but my mind wandered back to Beth. She stood out because she didn't put herself forward. She was small and blandly attractive, with a dark layered pageboy and a penchant for delicate gold jewelry. But how had she distinguished herself enough to get hired?

Law students are actually trained to talk. Like Olympic ice skaters, we're expected to prepare a "short" and a "long" program for interviews. We can then roll out our credentials to fit the occasion. Beth seemed to have missed this important lesson. All I knew about her was that she'd been born in Las Vegas – she let that slip at a gambling-themed firm party – that she went to Saint Louis University with Vince, and that she lived in an expensive apartment in Clayton. I figured her family must have money and a connection to the firm. Some people have all the luck.

When I finally got back to my office, a woman with straight blond hair sat in the chair in front of my desk. The verbena was even stronger than usual. "Hey, Samantha, what's up?"

She stood and shut my door. I wondered how long I would be able to stay in the closed office without a headache.

"You'll never believe what happened —"

I surreptitiously looked at my watch. This was sure to be some story about Grant, and I wanted to start Janice's project because it would take me a number of hours to complete. However, before Samantha could get any further, there was a knock. Grant opened the door.

"Hey Liz." He stopped. "Oh, Sam, umm, what are you doing here?"

Samantha blushed furiously and stood up. "I better go. I'll catch up with you later, okay, Liz?"

Grant watched her walk out the door and then shut it. Here we go again. He sat down, stretching his legs out in front of him.

"So what's going on?" I said innocently.

"With Sam? Oh nothing. She's okay." What damning praise. "Kelsey told me that Harding gave you a project."

Ugh. How had I let that slip?

Grant continued, "I wanted to know if you need help or anything. I'm doing some work on the Roswell deal, so if it's related to that —"

This was a new low. "No, it's something different. He gave it to me awhile back, so I'm pretty far along. Thanks anyway."

"Oh." Grant seemed deflated. Did he really think I was that gullible? I waited for him to get up, but he must have had something else to tell me.

Then there was another knock at the door. Sally stuck her head in. "Just got this from word processing." She held up a sheaf of papers. "They also sent you the memo by email. Do you need me to do anything with it?"

"No. I'll make the corrections myself. Thanks so much."

"Project for Janice Harrington?" Grant said.

"No. Tom Green." Grant's eyes got very big. The urge to gloat was almost too great to withstand, but I did. "If you don't mind, I really have to get this done."

"Yeah. No problem." He got up and slowly made his way to the door. "If you need anything, just let me know."

"Will do. Thanks again. Please close the door on your way out."

The next several hours flew by as I rushed to complete Tom's memorandum. He was still in a foul mood when I delivered it to him at 2:00. I hadn't eaten, so I wasn't feeling great myself. I thought about asking Vince to go for a coffee, but then remembered Janice's work. I didn't want to let her down. I grabbed a granola bar out of my desk drawer and got a Diet Coke from the machine.

As I ate my bar, I looked out the window. I had a view of the street. A thin blond woman was walking down the sidewalk. Cheri Harding? The walk seemed familiar, but I couldn't tell at that distance. The current Mrs. Harding – third in the line – was twenty years younger than her husband. Even so, it was obvious she spent a serious amount of time at the spa trying to hold back the sands of time. And the hairdresser. That perfect platinum could not have come cheap. There wasn't a root to be seen. But I usually recognized her by the gigantic diamond ring she wore. It was easily six carats and blinding under certain lights. If the rumors were true, she put up with a lot in exchange for that ring.

I heard the door open and Stephanie walked in looking flustered. Her long dark hair was pulled back in a ponytail. She had great hair. The kind you see being flipped around in shampoo commercials. "Do you have a minute?"

"Take a seat." I popped the rest of the granola bar in my mouth.

She closed the door and sat down. At this rate, I should have a "Free Psychiatric Help" sign on my desk.

"Have you had many projects with John Harding?" she said.

I swallowed and the granola bar caught in my throat. "Some. I've got one now," I wheezed.

"Well, I wouldn't tell this to anyone else, but he just called me into his office and, I swear to God, started taking off his clothes. Do you think that's odd?"

"How much of his clothing?" John Harding was in his mid-sixties and distinguished. He had clearly been very handsome in his youth. Even now, he maintained a trim, athletic physique. Still, the thought of a striptease was disturbing.

"First the coat. Then he loosened his tie and took it off. Finally, he unbuttoned his collar, far enough that I saw plenty of gray chest hairs. I mean, he was talking to me the whole time like nothing."

"What was he talking to you about?"

"Asking how my summer associate experience had been now that we're almost at the end. That sort of thing. I don't know, but I also had a strange feeling he wasn't really looking at me."

I nodded. "He always looks at my chest when he talks to me."

She started to giggle. "He does not."

"It's true. And you should be careful. Unless it was a hundred degrees in his office, he was stripping for a reason."

She frowned. "As if I'd ever —"

"I'm sure there are many who have."

"That's just gross." She paused. "And if you think that, why are you still here?"

I shrugged my shoulders. "I like working with Janice, and with my student loans, I've got to sell myself to the highest bidder. G.L. is it."

She sighed. "Isn't that the truth?"

I nodded.

But then again, murder changes your perspective.

CHAPTER 2

After I'd finally gotten her to leave, I settled in to work on Janice's project. I wasn't done by 5:00, so I grabbed a quick burger for dinner and then headed back to the office. When I finally finished, I looked at my computer screen. It was just after 10:00. I yawned. Maybe it was time to go home. Janice had also asked me to do some research for a lottery winner client. I didn't have anything better to do that night, so I decided to stay and finish it up. Plus, I had a strong feeling that that the client would call at any minute to demand an answer. Lottery winners don't have normal schedules.

The phone rang. I picked it up. It was the lottery winner. Surprise, surprise. I talked to him for 23 minutes exactly. Attorneys always keep detailed records of their time for billing purposes. I marked 0.4 on my time sheet and typed: Tel. conf. w/ client re: lang. of test. trust. doc. & title issue.

I considered going home then, but my lonely apartment seemed particularly unappealing that night. I had one more small project. I decided to go get a glass of water in the kitchen and then come back up and do it. I would fall asleep as soon as my head hit the pillow if I worked another hour. My legs were stiff from sitting too long, so I made a plan to take the internal stairs instead of the elevator. That's what I really needed, more exercise.

In addition to the elevators, the floors of Ghebish and Long were connected by a spiral staircase that ran up through the center of the building. As I walked to it, I saw only a couple of attorneys at their desks and a few other offices with their lights on, including Vince's. His door was partially closed so I walked on without saying hello. He was likely doing some last minute work to impress the partners. From what I could tell, they were impressed already. They would be lucky to keep him.

When I opened the door to the staircase, I heard footsteps in the distance below me. A woman's footsteps, I noticed, but I couldn't tell whose. They sounded like they were several floors down. By the time I reached the kitchen on the eleventh floor, I was winded. I needed to get myself to a gym. Stairs didn't used to bother me.

The kitchen was deserted. I filled a glass from the water cooler and drank. This is what it's come down to, I thought. I'm standing in an empty kitchen in the middle of the night because I have nothing better to do. Sad. My friend Holly told me that I needed to get out more. Maybe she was right. It was just that getting out for her meant going to someone's apartment for a potluck dinner where everyone spoke in code. Holly was a Ph.D. student in electrical engineering. That is a different crowd.

I washed and dried my glass and another that was already in the sink. As a Wisconsin girl, I couldn't overlook dirty dishes. A man's glass, I thought as I washed it, because there was no lipstick imprint. I put the glasses back in the cupboard and then paused. I felt a little strange standing alone in the silence of the kitchen. Goosebumps prickled up my arm.

I took a different door out of the kitchen and passed the smoking room. It looked like a glass enclosure at the zoo and held the rarest of all breeds – the smoker. Although the firm was non-smoking, several of the old partners still indulged. On any given afternoon, you could find one or two of them puffing away inside it. Now the door to the cubicle hung open and the stench of stale tobacco almost blew me over. I glanced in. John Harding must have been there. It took me a moment to identify how I got that. Then it clicked. I smelled this type of cigar on his clothes whenever I sat in his office to receive an assignment. There was half a cigar in the ashtray.

An assignment. I had that assignment due for him by the end of the week. I hadn't let on to Grant, but I had a couple of minor questions to ask before I turned it in. Harding was probably still at work. I'd go up to his office on the top floor and speak with him. It was the perfect solution. I got my questions answered, and I put in some valuable face time. It certainly couldn't hurt to show the managing partner that I stayed there till all hours. It didn't even occur to me that he might make a pass. Unlike the other female summer associates, I wasn't anyone's type. My suit completely covered my one asset. And I didn't have shampoo commercial hair.

I huffed my way back up the stairs. I really was going to do something about this out of shape business. I opened the door onto the eerily silent sixteenth floor. I started to feel the bumps prickle up my arm again. "Face time," I said to myself and walked out into the central reception area. The back wall had floor to ceiling windows. They opened up on breathtaking views of the city. The night was clear and radiant. The humid haze of the day had evaporated away, leaving the brilliant lights of the St. Louis skyline.

At the sight, my perverse brain felt homesick. The farmland stretches out in every direction from my small Wisconsin town, and the night is filled with a thousand twinkling stars. I looked again. Not a star visible in the sky even on a clear night, their radiance snuffed by the brilliance of electricity. Some things man cannot improve upon.

I walked toward John Harding's impressive corner office and saw that Kelsey's office was dark. Harding's door hung open but the office appeared empty. His lights were on and his briefcase sat beside his desk. I entered. It looked as if he could return at any moment. His computer seemed to be running through a reboot procedure.

I realized that I didn't really need to do another project and trudged back down the stairs to my office. My computer said it was 11:25. Who knew I could waste so much time just wandering around? That was talent. I tried to shut the computer down, but the shutdown sequence stalled. The network had been doing strange things lately. Something to do with a server crashing. I waited for a few minutes, then lost patience and manually turned the whole thing off.

I went to the elevator bay by habit, jangling my keys in my hand, and hit the down button. What about my new resolve to get some exercise? Hmm. I didn't think I could handle the stairs all the way down, so I decided to take the elevator to the sixth floor, which was the last floor of office space, and then take the separate garage stairs down to my car, which was parked in that sweet spot by the door on the first floor. It was a start.

A little voice reminded me that it wasn't a good idea for a woman to go alone into an isolated stairwell at night. But I was at the firm, I reminded the little voice. It had twenty-four hour security. Plus, it was only five flights. My car was right there. I opened the door to the garage stairs. What could happen?

CHAPTER 3

The hairs on the back of my neck stood on end. Now that I knew the smell was blood, I hesitated. I should go back up. But someone must be hurt and I couldn't just abandon them. Who else would find them this late at night?

I called down the stairwell, "Is anyone there? Anyone?"

The only sound I heard was a faint rattle off in the distance. I had to investigate.

I moved slowly and deliberately, feet apart and back against the wall. Down, down, to the fifth floor landing and then around the bend again to the fourth floor landing. There was nothing but the sound of my breathing now. In and out, in and out. I fought down the panic as I crept past the fourth floor landing. That's when I got my first glimpse of what was below me – somebody sprawled on the third floor landing. I could see the feet in a pair of black polished wingtips. Oh no!

I shouted, "I'm coming! I'm coming!" and flew down the last flight of stairs. Silence was the only response.

When I reached the step above the third floor landing, I knew why. The man laid out on the decking was covered with so much blood that it took a moment for my eyes to process the scene. I stood still, stunned and paralyzed. I couldn't breathe for several seconds. When I did breathe, I wished I hadn't. The smell of blood was so strong in the narrow stairwell that it took all my force of will not to be sick. I opened my mouth to scream. Nothing came out but the sound of my lungs sucking in air.

Get a hold of yourself, I kept thinking. Finally, my logical brain began to function. It told me I was in a crime scene. I willed myself to take stock of my surroundings. The body lay face up, with the left arm over the head and the right arm curled over the chest. The legs were bent and splayed apart. Most of the face, except the forehead, was nothing but a bloody pulp. The blood pooled under the head and oozed outward, although it had congealed a little, creating a sticky skin on the concrete. There were spatters of blood, and I didn't want to know what else, on the walls of the landing.

He was dressed in a suit. I looked at the fabric of the pant leg closest to me and then at the shoe. My heart sank. I knew that suit. I knew those shoes. John Harding wore them both two weeks ago when I went to his office to get a project from him. It was the same project I'd wanted to talk to him about tonight.

At that exact moment, my survival instinct kicked in. It suddenly occurred to me that whoever had done this to him might still be in the stairwell, ready to do the same to me. I had to get out of there. I sprinted up the stairs, panting so hard that my chest hurt. I got to the door of the sixth floor in record time and pulled on the knob. It didn't budge. Then I remembered – the pass card! I had to swipe it on this side to get back in.

I fumbled in my purse. My fingers seemed numb and unresponsive. I found and dropped the card twice before I was able to stick it in the reader.

I ran out into the sixth floor lobby. The silence only fed my panic. I banged on the elevator's down button until I heard the bell ding. I jumped back as the door opened. Empty! Thank goodness. I held the door close button the entire length of the ride. Just get me to the ground floor lobby, I chanted over and over. When the doors opened, I saw the security guard at the reception desk leaning back in his chair, eating a cup of yogurt. He glanced up and dropped the yogurt. I must have looked terrible.

"What's wrong?" he said, springing out of his chair. He came over and grabbed me around the shoulders.

"John Harding," I managed to say in a whisper.

"What?" I noticed that he had a marked St. Louis accent. Likely born and raised here.

"John Harding," I said again, my voice rising but still faint.

"What's wrong with John Harding?"

"He's in the stairwell." The guard looked confused.

"What stairwell? What are you talking about?"

"He's dead!" There, I'd said it.

"What?" He stared at me like I was mentally unstable.

"Call the police!" I felt like screaming, but my voice wouldn't go above a whisper.

The guard still didn't move. I began to feel faint. My stomach churned uncomfortably. I swayed and the guard gripped me even more tightly by the shoulders and forced me to walk to one of the couches scattered about the lobby. He pushed me gently down into a seat, and kept one hand on my shoulder to steady me.

"Okay, what's going on?" he said gently.

I pulled myself together enough to speak normally.

"John Harding is in the garage stairwell. Third floor landing. He's dead. Call the police. Now."

The guard's dark eyes widened in surprise, but he went to the reception desk and spoke quietly into the phone. I felt so woozy that I put my head between my knees. My head felt incredibly heavy, like it had its own gravitational pull.

I heard the man's voice calling me. "Miss. Miss! They want to talk to you."

I closed my eyes tightly. Why didn't they have a cordless phone around here?

"I don't think I can get up."

I heard footsteps and then felt him standing beside me. "I'll help you up." I opened my eyes and saw his extended hand. He had a big muscular hand. I put my hand in his, and he hauled me up to a standing position. I still wasn't steady on my feet, so he wrapped an arm around my waist and propped me up.

"Sorry," he said, looking at his hand around my waist.

"Don't worry."

"What's your name?" He propelled me to the desk.

"Liz. Liz Howe. Pleased to meet you, Louis." He looked surprised that I knew his name. "Your name tag," I said.

He nodded. "Good to meet you, Liz. They're sending the cops and an ambulance right now, but they wanted more info."

"What did you tell them?"

"That someone died and to come now." We got to the reception desk. "Say, he's dead, right? Did you try CPR or – I mean, maybe I should —"

"No," I said. "He's dead. Don't go down there."

"I probably should've asked before now," he said sheepishly, "but they don't tell you about this stuff."

"Don't worry." I picked up the phone. "CPR wouldn't have helped. He doesn't have a face." Louis gulped convulsively.

The voice on the other end asked me a series of questions about my identity and the identity of the injured. She asked me about signs of trauma and when I explained what I'd seen, she stopped. "Okay. Help is on the way. Just stay where you are."

I hung up the phone.

"You said third floor?" Louis asked.

"Yes."

"Damn. It'd have to be there."

"What?"

"I'm just thinking. The cameras don't get there."

"What about above or below?"

"There's one above and one below, but nothing for that."

"You'd still be able to see who went down or came up though, right?"

"Yeah, unless you knew where to walk. There are ways of getting round this place without nobody seeing nothing."

I couldn't think about that now. I concentrated and made it to the couch without assistance. I put my head on my knees and the room stopped spinning. Much better. I was holding up pretty well, all things considered. I hadn't thrown up yet.

I heard sirens and then the room filled with voices. I lifted my head up as paramedics and police ran in. I directed them as best I could from where I sat. Louis opened a "Staff Only" entrance to the garage and helped the police and paramedics get to the third floor landing. It must have been clear from the first sight that the paramedics were not necessary. I saw them trickle back out. The police cars continued to arrive.

Finally, an officer sat down beside me. She was a middle-aged African-American woman with short hair and a motherly demeanor. She radiated a certain peace and tranquility, and I wondered if she was specially designated to interview frightened witnesses. She told me her name was Pam Kingston and patted my hand.

"I know you're shook up right now, Ms. Howe, but I need you to tell me everything you remember about finding the body."

"Mr. Harding," I corrected.

"Yes," she replied. "Mr. Harding."

I told her as much as I could remember. She made encouraging noises and took notes. Whenever I got stuck, she urged me on with a combination of soft questions and rapt attention. I felt more relaxed the longer we talked. She was very good. The din around us lessened.

Officer Kingston looked up and said, "I think that is everything for now, thank you. You've been very helpful."

I nodded. She gave my knee a little pat and stood. "Take care of yourself, dear." She moved off to talk to another group of officers.

I looked around the room. Louis had obviously called the other building employees. He stood at the reception desk with a collection of security guards and maintenance personnel. Periodically, the phone at the desk rang and Louis answered – presumably to inform someone else about the situation.

I noticed a group of attorneys on the opposite side of the lobby. They must have been working late like me. A police officer had pulled Blane Ford aside and was talking to him intently. I knew it was Blane because of his tall gawky figure and the listless way he moved his long bony hands. I wondered what would happen to the firm now? It seemed impossible that John Harding was dead. And who was to succeed him? Blane Ford or Thomas Green? Or would they continue to work together? Given human nature, that didn't seem likely.

I saw Vince standing near a ficus in a ceramic planter. He had a very distinctive stance. He sat back on his heels and shifted his weight from foot to foot in a way that seemed out of character with his conservative suit and tie. I wondered if he wasn't much more comfortable in a slouchy pair of jeans and a tee shirt. I gave that mental image a try. He probably looked pretty good in jeans. Not the time or place, I scolded myself.

But I'd caught his eye. He ambled over to my couch and sat down beside me.

"Are you doing okay?" His voice sounded warm with concern.

"As well as can be expected, I guess." I tried to smile but was not entirely successful.

"You look grayish."

"I feel grayish." I pressed my fingers into my temples, trying to relieve a dull throb of pain that had started.

He put his arm around me. I stiffened in surprise, but then relaxed. His arm felt comforting.

He squeezed my shoulder. "It'll be okay, I promise."

"I don't think you can promise anything, but thanks for the sentiment."

"I'm glad to see you haven't lost the sarcasm."

"That never goes away." I smiled more successfully this time.

He moved his arm back down to his side and we sat there for an awkward moment.

"Do you think they will let us go home any time soon?" he asked.

"I don't know. I've never been in a situation like this before."

He nodded. "None of us could have seen this coming, that's for sure."

"Well, maybe one of us." He looked at me. "Whoever killed John Harding."

"You don't think anyone at the firm did it, do you?"

"Maybe."

"I think it will turn out to be a random killing just like every other murder in this city. A robbery gone wrong."

"You're probably right." I was too tired to argue anything.

He rubbed his eyes. "Do you think they'd mind if I took a little nap? I could just stretch out here and you could wake me if someone needs me to do something."

"If I'm still awake when they do. I wouldn't count on it."

"I'm going to ask when we can all go home," he said.

"Good idea." I just wanted the ordeal to end.

He wandered off to speak to the police officers still standing with Officer Kingston. I put my head in my hands again. The headache came on stronger. I was so lost in the pain that I jumped when someone tapped my shoulder.

I sat up and saw a tall, dark-haired man standing in front of me. Even though I didn't recognize faces, I knew from all my cues that he was a stranger.

"Are you Elizabeth Howe?" His voice was very fluid and pleasant. I wondered if he ever worked in broadcasting. He had the kind of voice you could listen to for an entire newscast without getting bored. I sat up a little straighter.

"Liz." I studied his face for a moment. Very attractive. Mid-thirties at most. Despite my fatigue, I gave him my full attention.

"Liz," he repeated, smiling. "Hello, Liz. I'm Detective Paperelli. James Paperelli." He extended his hand. I extended mine and he gave it a swift, firm handshake.

"Do you mind?" He indicated the spot on the sofa next to me.

"Of course not. Please sit down."

He sat and turned to face me. He seemed so at ease that I felt my shoulders relax. Perhaps, like Officer Kingston, they always sent him to deal with hysterical witnesses. It worked. His ease was contagious. I took another moment to study him closely. I noticed his clothes. He didn't dress like I thought a police detective would.

He wore jeans, a polo shirt, and a jacket. The polo shirt looked crisp and was tucked neatly into a pair of jeans that might actually have been ironed. The jacket was made of chocolate brown leather, tailored but soft. I realized the weather must have changed. He wore a pair of very elegant Ferragamo loafers – I could tell by the style of the buckle – and I wondered just how much of his salary went to clothing. Clearly a significant amount. Very unusual.

His manner didn't fit my stereotypes either. Where was the hard-bitten gruff exterior? Kindness radiated from his smile and his eyes, which were as blue as sapphires, with large black pupils and long black lashes. For all his ease of manner, however, his look was intense and perceptive.

"Okay." He smiled at me again, and I noticed that his teeth were very straight and white. His smile was dazzling, really. I looked down and watched as he flipped his pen with his fingers. He wasn't wearing a wedding ring.

Could he possibly be single? Married men didn't always wear a ring, sometimes because it wasn't practical at work, and sometimes for less honorable reasons. But how was anyone so desirable still wandering around unattached? Maybe he didn't want to be attached. Maybe he was gay. That might explain the obsession with clothes. I had a habit in college of attracting men who then promptly came out of the closet. I always knew before they did, but Detective Paperelli didn't give me that vibe. Perhaps my gaydar was off.

"So, Ms. Howe —"

"Liz," I said.

"So Liz, I know you've had a long night, and I know that Officer Kingston has already taken down the basic information, but there are a few ends that I'd like to tie up."

I nodded, and he smiled at me again. He certainly had charisma. I wondered a second time if he was specially trained to deal with skittish witnesses. Skittish female witnesses. It didn't hurt that he was so attractive. His thick dark hair waved over the right temple. He had a nick out of the side of his left ear, just above the earlobe. Paperelli. I'd heard the name before, but I couldn't place it at the moment. Italian-American clearly, but the eyes were so blue. His mother's family must be from somewhere else, or maybe from the north of Italy where people tended to be fairer.

"I see here that you are a summer associate at the firm?"

I brought my mind back into focus. "Yes."

"You were working late like the rest of the attorneys?" He gestured over to the group clustered around Blane Ford.

"I decided to stay late and work on a project for Attorney Janice Harrington." And to waste time because I don't have a life.

"Attorney Harrington?" He looked over at the attorneys questioningly.

"She's not here. She left early this evening for a dinner with clients. She's in estate planning."

"Okay." He scribbled a few things down on a small notepad. "So you were at work in your office, right? And then what?"

"I went downstairs to get a glass of water at about 10:30. I could tell you more precisely if I could look at my log."

He cocked a questioning eyebrow.

"Billable hours. We keep notes down to the minute."

He nodded. "Did you see anyone else on the fourteenth floor when you went downstairs?"

"A couple of people – I gave all of this information to Officer Kingston, by the way – and there were a few other offices with lights on."

"Did you see anyone on the stairs?"

"No, but I heard footsteps below me. I don't know who it was." I looked over at the group of attorneys. There were several female attorneys standing there.

He glanced down at his note pad. "You told Officer Kingston that they were 'female footsteps.'"

I nodded.

"Why?"

The question surprised me. "What do you mean, why? They were, and she told me to tell her every detail I remembered, so —"

"Sorry," he interrupted me gently. "I mean, how did you know they were the footsteps of a woman?"

I shrugged my shoulders. "I just did. It's something I notice."

He waited for a better answer.

"They were too light to be a man's footsteps, and I could tell that whoever it was wore high heels. Probably pumps, but without a strap across the instep."

He looked at me strangely, so I tried to explain it. "I could hear how the heel hit the stairs a second after the toe. If the shoe doesn't hold the instep, your foot is loose and so the back of the shoe slips off after you step down on the toe. It's a distinctive sound, even on carpet."

He stared at my face a long moment, his brow furrowed in concentration. "What?" he finally said.

I stared back at him. How hard was this concept? "What do you mean?"

"How do you do that?" He paused, searching for a better way to phrase the question. "Do you normally pay close attention to details?"

"Well —" I stalled for time. I certainly did not want to mention my diagnosis. He already had the beginning of that look people sometimes gave me when I knew too much for their comfort. Like I'd sprouted a second head or something. Anyway, that experience was never pleasant, and it certainly wasn't going to be any more so if the person who thought I was weird happened to be a very attractive man, even a married one. I had some pride after all.

"I'm very observant?"

"Very." He waited.

I waited longer.

Finally, he said, "So you went down to get a glass of water?"

"Yes. The kitchen is on the eleventh floor. I got my water and then went up to John Harding's office."

"Was there anyone down in the kitchen with you?"

"No, I was alone." I paused for a moment, wondering if I could confide in him. I looked into his blue, blue eyes and decided to go for it.

"That's why I came back up. The quiet started to frighten me." His eyes held mine too long, so I hurried on. "You know when the silence is too much and you realize how alone you are? It's silly, but —"

"I know just what you mean."

I gave him a quick smile in gratitude. "And then the smoke reminded me I needed to speak with John Harding about a project."

He held up his hand. "I think you're going to have to explain that one."

"What?"

"The smoke bit."

"Oh." Shoot! Did I have to appear like a freak of nature every two minutes? I usually didn't have this much trouble seeming normal. But I felt obligated to describe every detail, since anything might be important. Best to get this over with.

"There's a room for the partners who smoke. John Harding smokes a certain kind of cigar. You can smell it on his clothes if you stand close enough. Well, that and his aftershave."

Detective Paperelli looked at me oddly. His meaning dawned on me, and I hastened to add, "Not that close, of course. I mean, when you walked into his office. I have a good sense of smell. I'm not involved with him, if that's what you were thinking."

He shrugged noncommittally.

"He's old enough to be my father. Even grandfather. Maybe even great grandfather – but only in certain parts of Missouri."

He chuckled. "Yes, definitely your grandfather." He had a very nice throaty laugh. That must go along with the soothing voice. And he had a tiny dimple on his left cheek. Was it necessary to have a dimple, too? He was smiling at me again. His lips were nice. Outshone by the teeth, but well shaped. Maybe a little wide for his face, but that was hardly a terrible flaw. His lower lip had a little indent in the middle.

"So, back to the smoke," he said, trying to keep me on task.

"I smelled his cigar smoke when I walked past the open door of the smoking room. There was a partial cigar in the ashtray. That reminded me of the question I had on the project I was doing for him."

Detective Paperelli jotted down some notes and then he looked up. His gaze was sincere, but there seemed to be just a hint of mischief lurking at the back of his smile. "This is going to sound strange," he began, "but given everything you've said so far, I'm going to chance it. When you smelled the cigar, could you tell if he'd been in there recently or not? In other words, was it old smoke?"

"Actually, I remember thinking that it seemed about an hour old. The smoke starts out sweet but turns acrid, you know."

"I don't, but I'll take your word for it."

I nodded. Something about the smoking room bothered me. I could feel it nagging at the back of my brain, so I looked down and tried to concentrate. "I think he was suddenly called away."

"What makes you say that?"

"He didn't smoke the cigar to the end. It looked like there was about half of it left but, then again, I don't know anything about cigars. You smoke them most of the way down, right? I mean, it was likely an expensive cigar, so you would think he would finish it. He must have been called away."

Detective Paperelli regarded me. I couldn't tell if it was intrigue or the rubbernecking you see with terrible accidents. "Yes, that's logical. I'll make sure someone gets the cigar to verify." He noted this in his notebook and then said, "So you went back up to find him?"

"I wanted to talk to him about that project."

"It couldn't wait until morning?"

"I needed the face time."

He raised that eyebrow again.

"I wanted him to see that I was still at work late at night, that I would make a good associate. You have to think strategically about these things. He was the managing partner."

"So you went back up the stairs?"

"Right. His office is on the top floor, off the reception area."

"Did you see anyone when you went up?"

"No."

"And he was not in his office?"

"No, but the lights were on, his briefcase was still there and his computer was on. I didn't feel like trying to search for him, so I went to my office and got my things to go home."

"How long did that take?"

"Ten minutes or so."

"Did you see anyone, either on the stairs or walking back to your office?"

"Not on the stairs, but I noticed Vince Lopez's light was on when I passed by. His door was still partially closed, so I figured he must be hard at work."

"And then?"

"I took the elevator and got out on the sixth floor. There was no one in that lobby. I went to the garage stairwell and started down. My car is parked on the first floor."

"Why did you take the elevator and then the stairs?"

My cheeks flushed. "I thought I should get some exercise, but I didn't think I could manage so many flights. I was sure I could do the garage stairs."

"I appreciate your honesty." There was a twitch of a smile at the corner of his mouth. "Go on."

"I found the body on the third floor landing." My stomach turned over again just thinking about it. I swallowed hard.

"I know this is difficult, but I want to make sure I have the details right."

I nodded.

"When you opened the door to the garage stairs, did you notice anything or hear anything unusual?"

"Not at first. Wait, there was a faint rattling sound, but I couldn't tell where it came from. I called out, but no one answered. I continued down, but then I knew something was wrong, so I called out again and ran down the stairs."

"How did you know something was wrong?"

"I smelled the gunshot and then the blood."

Detective Paperelli sat back on the couch. He stared at me again with that look that could be fascination or repulsion. "You smelled the gunpowder? That long after the shots?"

"Yes, but I didn't see a gun."

I remained quiet for a moment, wondering if I should have told him. Maybe it would have been better to talk about feminine intuition or something. I looked down and noticed that he was playing with his pen while he digested this new information. His right thumbnail was ridged. I wondered if he'd injured it at some point or if it was a genetic marker of something. I looked up and realized that he was still regarding me.

"What?" I said.

"Nothing, nothing. Then you found the body —"

"I saw the feet first and then the whole body when I came around the bend. It's a narrow staircase. I stood there for maybe a minute or so. I think I was in shock. Then I fled back up the stairs and got out at the sixth floor lobby. I took the elevator down to the main lobby. I told the guard what happened and he called for help."

"So you didn't touch the body or approach it in any way?"

"No. He was dead. I knew there was nothing I could do."

"Something I've been wondering about. Given the state of things, I don't know how you identified the victim as John Harding."

"By the suit and the shoes."

"I beg your pardon?"

"The suit is an odd color – sort of gray and sort of brown – and it has a fine red pinstripe. He wore a maroon tie with it when I saw him before, and it harmonized nicely. I couldn't tell if he was wearing the same tie this time with all of the blood. Then, when I looked at the shoes, I knew it was him." Suddenly, fatigue threatened to overwhelm me. I shivered and crossed my arms, trying to remain sitting upright.

Detective Paperelli leaned over and put a friendly hand on my shoulder. "Don't worry, I'm almost done. I know you are exhausted."

I felt the warmth of his hand through my suit jacket. It made me feel a little better. "What else do you want to know?"

"What was it about the shoes?"

"John Harding had a strange walk. I think he must have injured his right leg at some point, because he carried it more stiffly than his left. He limped slightly. The heels of his shoes were unevenly worn. That confirmed it for me."

Detective Paperelli removed his hand from my shoulder. I looked up. He was closer to me than I had realized. I blinked in surprise. His eyes bore into mine as if trying to read my thoughts. My pulse quickened. There was electricity in his stare that made me feel lightheaded and strange. I couldn't look away.

"You are amazing," he said, and pulled something out of his jacket pocket. It was a business card with an embossed gold badge on it. "I'm going to give you my card because I have a feeling that I will need to talk to you again." Our fingers brushed briefly as I took the card. He smiled at me in a way that inspired confidence. "If you think of anything, any detail that would be helpful, please call or email me." He hesitated a moment. "Would you mind giving me your contact information?"

"Sure," I said, trying not to sound too enthusiastic. I gave him my cell phone number and my Hotmail account. Somehow this didn't seem like the kind of email I wanted sitting on the wustl.edu servers. He leaned back, and I knew that this was the cue for goodbye. He extended his hand, clasping mine in a firm grip.

"Ms. Howe, despite the circumstances, it has been a very real pleasure speaking with you this evening. Your memory for detail is phenomenal."

Detective Paperelli didn't know the half of it. I just smiled in reply. He got up and walked back to the group of his fellow officers. I watched him as I took my usual mental notes – his height, his gait, the way he shifted to his right foot as he stood, how he twirled his pen absentmindedly in his hand. I listened for his voice, trying to memorize its cadence. For one brief moment, I heard his laughter again, and I stored that away as well. Who knew if I might ever see him again? But if I did, I certainly didn't want him to be a stranger.

The fatigue I had pushed away came rushing back. I felt like I might collapse there and then.

"They told us we could go," Vince said, rousing me from my stupor. "Let me take you home. You look too tired to make it on your own."

I nodded silently and let him help me to the car.

Pizza. That was it.

CHAPTER 4

The fallout from the murder was swift. The owners closed the building while the police continued to muck around. The management committee told everyone to stay home while the firm tried to reorganize. The summer associate program abruptly ended. Blane Ford called us together at a local hotel and gave us a short but scrupulously written speech. It hit all the right notes – the firm valued us, the firm was committed to security, and the firm would get through this terrible time – but fell flat. The murder was not discussed, but the rumor mill supplied the details and then some. I could tell that the scramble to find other positions had already started. They cancelled the final happy hour.

Janice Harrington invited me out for lunch after the big speech. I wasn't sure if she wanted to reassure me or dig for information. Maybe both. We went to a restaurant in Clayton, away from the prying eyes of downtown. The restaurant bustled with the noon business traffic, and we squeezed into a small table in the corner. I looked at the menu. Some sort of fusion experiment. Clayton restaurants had caught the fusion bug and recklessly combined anything and everything. The menu mentioned, "the classic flavors of Baja California infused with the spice of Bombay."

Janice took a sip of water and then set the glass on the table, her mouth pursed the way it did when she tackled a thorny legal issue.

"I can imagine how you're feeling about the firm right now, but I want you to stay," she said.

Her bluntness took me off guard. "I have to say I'm flattered."

"You should be." She gave me a winning smile. "You're the best summer associate I've ever worked with, and I don't want you going somewhere else."

I drank water while I turned the problem over in my mind. I'd considered other firms, but I liked Janice, and I liked the work she did. I stalled for time.

"How could I refuse such a generous offer?" I said.

Janice's smile grew broader. "No, I'm serious about this. The management committee will send out letters this week offering positions to all of the summer associates. I know that most of you are already looking around. Frankly, I would too in your position. I'm sure that there are summer associates who won't set foot in the building again and some who will accept just because they know that they won't get anything better."

She leaned in closer. "You can get something else and you have the most reason to be frightened, so that's why I wanted to talk to you." She paused, pursing her lips. "So, I'm asking you to please come join us in estate planning – to join me as my associate."

I sat back in my chair, wondering how to respond. Part of me wanted to accept her on the spot, but I still hesitated. I drank more water.

"I don't need an answer today. You can have as much time as you want to think, unless of course you want to say 'yes' now and get it over with."

"To put you out of your misery?"

"Sure," she replied gamely. "Oh, and there is one other thing. I would like to hire you part-time during the year. Perhaps ten or fifteen hours a week of special research projects. As your schedule permits of course, and at the summer associate pay grade."

Janice certainly knew how to up the ante. I shuddered to think what my loans were. If I worked during the year, maybe I could keep them in the low six figures. But I would have to be strong enough to go to the office day after day and park in that garage. No one knew who might have murdered John Harding.

However, starting over at another firm, trying to find another partner like Janice – impossible. I wouldn't meet anyone like her again. I could always make other parking arrangements. I had a strong stomach. My nightmares weren't that bad. Besides, murder didn't scare me. Much.

"I would love to work for you," I said.

"Wonderful!" she clapped her hands together.

"My schedule this year is pretty full, so I may not be able to do many projects. I'm a notes editor for *Quarterly*." *Quarterly* was one of the journals published by Washington University School of Law.

She nodded in understanding. "You just let me know what you have time for. No strings attached." She picked up her menu. "What are you going to have?"

I scanned mine rapidly. "Curried chicken taco?"

"Well, it's the only thing on here that has a chance of tasting good." She gave the menu another critical glance. "I think I'll make it two. Wine?"

"I don't usually drink at lunch." I didn't drink at all in social situations. Alcohol dulled my already limited abilities.

"There is always a first time. It's been a hell of a week."

"I can drink to that," I said. Now was not a time for quibbles.

"Good girl. See, you and I are going to work together nicely."

I laughed.

"The question is, of course, what kind of wine do you order with a curried chicken taco?"

"White?" I said.

"Um." She surveyed the wine list. "Champagne."

"Champagne?"

"We are going to toast our future together. Celebrate everything. That's my new motto."

"Life is short," I agreed.

She nodded, more serious.

"How is everyone holding up?" I asked.

"Firm wise or people wise?"

"Both."

"Well, people wise I think Blane Ford has taken John's death the hardest. He's known John since he was a kid so that's hardly surprising."

"Really?"

"They grew up together in Poplar Bluff, went to school together, although John was a little older I think, and graduated the same year at SLU." Saint Louis University, or SLU, was a long standing and well respected Jesuit institution.

"I didn't know that they were so close."

"They go way back," she assured me. "He even introduced John to the current Mrs. Harding, well John's widow now." She looked down at her water glass. "It still seems strange to think that John is dead. He was such a fixture. The firm will go on, of course, but it won't be the same."

The waiter finally arrived to take our orders. He seemed surprised when Janice ordered champagne, but took it down with a surly efficiency. He left and I said, "So you were saying – about Mrs. Harding. I've only met her a couple of times."

"Blane introduced Cheri to John four or five years ago. She's a distant cousin of Blane's I think – younger cousin certainly. Cheri was divorced at the time – or soon to be divorced – it's hard to know. No kids. John was still married to Maddie, but things weren't going well. How could they?" She leaned in closer and lowered her voice. "I shouldn't speak ill of the dead, but John was a womanizer, plain and simple. Very few women would hold up under what he put Maddie through." She shook her head. "I wonder about Cheri. I mean, when you are the mistress, you have to know what kind of marriage you are signing up for."

I nodded. "That, or you think you are 'the one.'"

"You're never 'the one,'" she replied contemptuously.

"What happened to Maddie?"

"She stayed here, but didn't get as much in the divorce as you'd think after twenty years. You take your chances marrying a lawyer in this town. She went back to teaching to make ends meet, but didn't hold that against John. The kids live with her, of course. Cheri never got along with them."

"How old are they?"

"Let me think, John Jr. is 17 and Jennifer is 19." She paused. "I will say this, John loved the kids, even if he nickel and dimed Maddie.

I'm sure his death has been very hard on them. And Maddie, too, of course. She'd made her peace with him."

"Maddie sounds like a very forgiving person." I tried not to sound skeptical.

"Maddie is one of those incredible women who can put everything aside in the best interests of her children. The divorce got nasty, but she never used the kids against John. She could shut it all off somehow, and focus on what was important."

"She wasn't bitter? Even a little?"

"Just tired of the drama. I think she liked to talk to me because I could give her an idea of how the firm worked, and why John was so tenacious about little things – a view inside the head of a lawyer – that sort of thing."

"They didn't understand each other? Even after twenty years?"

She nodded her head. "Amazing, isn't it? They were opposites in so many ways. I've always wondered how they got together. Well, Maddie was – is – beautiful, aside from being a wonderful person, so I see why he married her. John was a widower when she met him, and I have to think she was drawn to him because he was grieving. She's very motherly. And John could be charming when he wanted to be."

"I'm sure he was handsome when he was young."

"He still thought he was."

"He was young to be a widower."

"His first wife died in a car crash on her way to do a television pilot in L.A."

"An actress? Was she in anything I would know?"

Janice shook her head. "Bit parts mostly – and before you were born."

"I've watched a lot of re-runs."

Janice smiled. "They wouldn't have re-run anything she was in. It wasn't good when it was first run."

"Is she the one in that photograph on his credenza?" John Harding had the usual collection of family photos lined up, but one stood out. It looked like a headshot from the lighting and the pose, and it had the orange cast that photos from the 1970's often have. The woman had long straight dark hair and bright green eyes. She was radiantly lovely. The hair was a dead ringer for Stephanie's.

"You noticed that?"

I shrugged my shoulders.

"Yes, that's her. Maddie told me that John was so devastated after her death that he went back home to Poplar Bluff for a time. He couldn't practice law or do anything. Maddie met him when he finally pulled himself together and resumed his practice in St. Louis."

The waiter reappeared with the champagne. "Your order will be out shortly," he grumbled. He struggled with the champagne cork, finally putting the bottle between his legs for support as he worked it free. I opened my mouth to warn him but he just glared in my direction. The cork came free with a loud pop and went sailing over Janice's head, barely missing a person at the next table.

"Sorry about that," he muttered. "I need to work on my aim."

I smiled at him in an encouraging way. He was roughly my age and had that angry look people have when they're putting in time at a job they hate. I noticed his hands as he poured the champagne. He had paint under his fingernails that scrubbing hadn't removed.

An aspiring artist. I caught a whiff of linseed as he leaned over the table to set my champagne flute in front of me. Oils. A very difficult medium to master. I looked at him with a rush of compassion. Maybe if he just had some encouragement, he wouldn't feel so bad.

Pity compelled me to ask, "So what do you paint?" I don't know that I've ever seen anyone so startled. He nearly dropped Janice's glass on the floor. If we had been anywhere else, I would have burst out laughing at his expression.

"What?" he said.

"Oils, I know, but what? Portraits? Still life? Landscapes? Or is it more about style and less about subject?"

"Urban landscapes," he said. "Hey, have I met you somewhere before? I've been in a couple of shows, mostly local."

I smiled mysteriously. "Maybe I just had a feeling that waiting tables was not your true calling."

He grinned. It was the first time I'd seen him smile, and it softened his entire face. He extended his hand saying, "Matt Crandall."

"Liz Howe." I returned his firm grip. "And this is Janice Harrington." He shook her hand as well.

"You're right about waiting tables, but please don't tell my boss. Until my work takes off, I have to live."

"Understood." I smiled up at him. "So tell me about your work. What interests you about urban landscapes?"

"There's so much beauty in decay, you know? The rusted metal, the crumbling brick, the way a broken door hangs off its hinges. I can't not paint that."

"Oils are difficult to work with —"

"Not if you know how to handle them." He would have said more, but the hostess signaled him from the front. "I'll be back in a minute with your food."

"Thanks." He walked quickly away. I looked up. Janice eyed me. She pursed her lips again.

"Okay, what was that all about?"

I opened my mouth, but she waved her hand. "Don't lie to me. I am a hundred percent sure that you've never met that boy before in your life, and I'm also sure that you didn't pull oil painting out of thin air. So, out with it."

I looked down at the table, unsure how to respond. I weighed the pros and cons.

"I've seen you do some strange things, Liz. You seem to know things you shouldn't know. I've been paying attention."

Busted. I racked my brain for some normal explanation.

"Out with it. How did you do that?"

"ESP?"

"Try again." She looked me in the eyes.

I decided that I had to trust her. "I can't recognize faces."

She sat back in surprise. "Come again?"

"Its called prosopagnosia. I've had it since I was young."

"But how does that explain the waiter? Wait." She held up her hand again. "When you say that you can't recognize faces, you mean that you can't remember people you meet?"

"It's more than that. I can't recognize them. Ever."

"Anyone?"

"Everyone. My own mother. Myself."

"You see her face – you see your own face – and don't know who it is?"

"Yes."

"Everyone is a stranger?"

"I am a stranger to myself," I said.

She thought about this. "I don't understand."

"Look, people are more than their faces. I notice everything else." I could tell that she was starting to comprehend. "Every person has a million little differences: a certain way of walking, or standing, an individual voice, a unique smell – many things. I have a very good sense of smell and that helps tremendously. Your favorite perfume is 'Red,' not to be confused with 'Red Door,' which smells completely different."

"I'm impressed," she said, "but anyone can wear 'Red.'"

"The perfume is only part of it. Body chemistry makes up the rest. 'Red' smells different on each person." I paused. "You're the only woman at the firm who wears it anyway. Women my age tend to use soaps and body sprays instead of perfume and none of the other female partners wear it. One wears 'Obsession.'" I wrinkled my nose. "I can barely walk in her office."

Janice laughed. "Even I can smell that." She looked thoughtful again. "So that is how you do it, by noticing the details that everyone else misses?"

"Other people may notice, but they don't rely on that information the way I do."

"You're a regular Sherlock Holmes."

"I'm not trying to solve a mystery, just trying not to appear strange." I sighed. "I hoped I'd succeeded with you."

She reached across the table and patted my hand reassuringly. "I thought you were the brightest summer associate I'd ever met, but I see I have completely underestimated your intelligence. And thank you for being honest with me, even if I forced you to."

"Just a little arm twisting."

She smiled in acknowledgment. "Drink some champagne and tell me about the waiter. You're sure you've never met him, right?"

"Yes. One eye is smaller than the other and he scrunches the small eye up when he talks. I wouldn't forget something like that."

"What told you our waiter is a painter?"

"He had paint under his fingernails, and I could smell the linseed oil when he leaned over the table. And he moved his hands like a painter – precise, delicate but firm. He wasn't meant to be a waiter."

"I noticed the not wanting to be a waiter part, but what if he'd painted in acrylics, or if he painted furniture? Would you have known?"

"Probably."

She looked skeptical.

"The hand movements would have been different if he painted furniture – that requires precision but more force. The acrylic I might have smelled even though it dries more quickly. Every kind of paint has a different smell. But even if it had dried and I couldn't smell it, I would have known."

"How?"

"It sticks to the hair differently than oils do."

"He had paint in his hair?"

"A little blue streak, on the right side, back behind his ear. I'm sure he couldn't see it when he got dressed for work. I noticed it when he bent over the table. The paint was clearly oil paint. Acrylics would have clung around the shafts of hair. They're a plastic, after all."

Matt reappeared with the food. He acted extremely friendly now and tried to loiter to talk with me about his work. Janice shooed him away as quickly as she could, but not before he'd slipped me a business card with his name and a picture of one of his paintings. I had to admit, rust did look quite beautiful when painted that way.

"You're very talented," I whispered to him as he set my plate down. "Keep at it. Don't get discouraged." He gave me a thumbs-up as he turned to leave.

Janice stabbed a bite of curried chicken taco and put it cautiously on her tongue. "Hmm." She chewed slowly and gingerly. "Not too bad. What do you think?"

I nodded, my mouth too full to talk.

She took a sip of champagne. "Well, this lunch has certainly been a revelation. A good one," she added hastily.

"I'm glad you think so. Most partners would be put off that their associate identifies them by smell."

"I am not most partners, and I think it's fascinating. You and I are going to make a great team, Liz, I can just feel it." She gave me a dazzling smile, full of warmth and camaraderie.

"To us," she said, raising her glass.

"To us," I replied, and drank mine to the bottom.

CHAPTER 5

The third year of law school started before I knew it. I had a broad mix of classes, some chosen because they would be tested on the bar exam and some, like estate planning, because I actually enjoyed them. I also had my work at *Quarterly*. Despite the glamour of the title, a notes editor does nothing more than check and recheck the citations for articles that will appear in the *Quarterly*'s next issue.

Citation in law school means the dreaded *Blue Book*. This epistle is published annually to torture law students with a blow-by-blow account of how to note every piece of source material known to man. Well, almost every piece. Despite the thoroughness of this tome, the authors I worked on invariably tried to cite something so strange and obscure that even the *Blue Book* held no answer. It was up to me, after a suitably long and tedious discussion with the other editors, to chart a new path in citation.

I sat, hunched over the worktable in the *Quarterly* offices, trying to come up with the appropriate citation for selected sections of the Code of Hammurabi – condensed and translated. I wanted to be outside or in class or anywhere but in the *Quarterly* offices. We'd had some really beautiful fall weather lately. Maybe I'd take a walk when I got home. My cell phone rang. I didn't recognize the number, but did notice the time. I was really late for my next class.

Stupid Hammurabi. I scooped up the cell phone, figuring I'd surreptitiously look at it in class and see if it was anything worth calling back about. My life was never exciting enough to warrant the immediate return of a phone call.

As it was, I didn't actually check my messages until two classes later, when I finally had a free moment. It was undoubtedly someone trying to sell me something. Instead, I heard the following:

"Hello, this is Detective James Paperelli. I'm calling to see if I can arrange a time to meet with you. I have a few more questions related to John Harding's death. Please call me back as soon as possible. I can certainly come to you if that is easier. No need for you to come downtown. Anyway, my number is 314-006-8666. Give me a ring. Ah, and thanks, of course."

His announcer-smooth voice sounded oddly nervous or maybe distracted. John Harding's murder had received significant press. I'd been following it, and I knew that there was a lot of political pressure on the police department to solve it quickly. The *Post-Dispatch* portrayed it as a robbery gone wrong and blamed the police and the lax security at the building. The door at the second floor landing of the garage stairs had been propped open with a chunk of cement. A door from the garage to the outside on the north side was unlocked as usual.

I looked for Detective Paperelli's name in the news reports, but only saw it once, in an article that mentioned he was the first homicide detective on the scene. I'd wondered if they'd taken him off the case. Apparently not.

I walked out to the courtyard and sat on the edge of a concrete container under the shade of a leafless and scraggly tree. My hands shook in anticipation and my pulse raced. Pathetic. The phone rang three times, which seemed like an eternity.

Then, "Hello, James Paperelli here."

"Hi, Detective Paperelli?" Stupid, he'd already said that.

"Yes?"

"It's Liz. Liz Howe. I'm ringing you back." Ugh. He knew this.

"Ms. Howe, thanks for calling me back so quickly." He seemed pleased.

I felt my heart beat a little faster, but managed to control my voice. "No problem at all. You said you wanted to meet with me?" I winced. Too personal. "You wanted to speak with me about John Harding?"

"Yes. Where would it be convenient to meet?"

I hesitated, trying to think.

"We could meet for coffee," he said.

"You're allowed to do that?" In all of the police dramas I'd ever seen on television, the witnesses were never invited for coffee.

"No one is going to have my head for it, so why not?"

"Okay." I continued to search my brain for a good location. Somewhere close but not too close to campus. I didn't want my classmates to force me to introduce them to a police detective. I'd had enough trouble when people found out that I'd found John Harding's body. No need to start the gossip up again.

"Maybe Clayton?" I said.

"What about Pomme Café?"

"Is that the place down the street from BARcelona?"

BARcelona was a tapas-style restaurant that had an amazingly active bar on Friday and Saturday nights. I'd been there a couple of times with a summer associate happy hour. I noticed Pomme, which seemed like an elegant little restaurant, and Pomme Café, its more relaxed sibling, as I stood on the sidewalk nursing a Diet Coke and listening to summer associate chatter. I added them to a growing list of restaurants that I would visit when I wasn't taking on an ever-increasing debt load. At least now I could try the coffee.

"Yes."

"Would 4:30 be okay?" I had to give myself enough time to do some more work on Hammurabi and then drive over and find a parking spot in Clayton. Not an easy task.

"Great! 4:30 it is." He sounded very boyish. I smiled to myself as we said goodbye.

I ditched Hammurabi early so that I could fix myself up in the bathroom mirror. I had a lucky break. I don't usually wear any make-up, but I'd bought some smooth powder foundation at the drugstore on a whim that morning. I still had it in my purse. Thank goodness, I thought, as I surveyed myself critically. It was that time of the month when my normally good skin suddenly decided to go splotchy. I dug around some more, and found a tube of lip gloss. Jackpot.

The traffic wasn't bad. It only took me three drive-bys and an illegal u-turn before I found a place to park. The space was narrow. I don't excel at parallel parking. Several minutes passed while I moved the car back and forth. It was also a 90-minute meter, but I only had enough change for 45. I'd brave the ticket.

I was breathless after the three-block walk to Pomme Café. Clayton has some hills, but really. I needed to look for a gym, and soon. I arrived ten minutes late with the parking and the walking.

Detective Paperelli must have come ahead of me. He wasn't sitting at one of the wrought iron tables on the sidewalk, so I opened the door. I wondered how long it would take me to find him. I hoped not too long. That was the worst part, standing stupidly in the door, while I scanned the crowd looking for any sign of identity.

But I knew him in an instant. It was the way he sat in the booth. Straight-backed yet relaxed. He was looking down. I could see how his hair curled over the right ear. He held a BlackBerry. His thumbs picked at the keys, back and forth. His hands moved delicately, in an unmistakable rhythm. He still wasn't wearing a wedding ring.

He looked up, saw me and smiled broadly. His teeth were as straight and white as I'd remembered. I smiled back. I had to concentrate on putting one foot in front of the other. I focused on the details. He wore a well-fitting sport coat, made of heathery brown fabric. It had to be fine lightweight wool by the way it hung. As I got closer, I noticed the precise cut. A narrow English style with three, maybe four buttons. He was sitting down so I couldn't tell. A Burberry for sure. His shirt was white with a fine blue-green stripe. The shirt points were narrow and sharp and not meant for a tie. It had a sophisticated edge. I guessed Kenneth Cole.

"Thanks for coming to meet me," he said, gesturing to the unoccupied side of the booth and tucking his BlackBerry into the inside pocket of his jacket.

My knees wobbled as I slid in, but I kept my voice calm. "I don't want to be accused of obstructing justice."

"True." He gave me a wry look. "But I appreciate you taking the time, just the same. Law students tend to be very busy."

"We are also notoriously poor and burdened with debt, so I couldn't ignore free coffee."

He chuckled and his eyes lit up. They were so very blue.

"I need to come up with the coffee then." He motioned to someone standing behind me and a waitress walked up to the table.

She was casually dressed in black, with layered dark hair and tattoos peeking out from underneath her tee shirt sleeves. She wore heavyweight cotton pants and Dansko clogs on her feet. She appeared to be in her early twenties and her demeanor was friendly but professional.

"What can I get for you both today?"

"Two coffees to start," Detective Paperelli replied.

"Espresso, latte, cappuccino? We are serving a lovely dark roast from Rwanda right now that I highly recommend."

Detective Paperelli turned to me.

"A latte sounds wonderful," I said.

He nodded. "Two please."

"Can I suggest some of our delicious apple walnut tart to go with the coffee? It has the most amazing nutty buttery crust and the tart apples are locally grown and organic. It comes with our own homemade vanilla ice cream on the side."

Detective Paperelli said, "How could we resist such a description? Two of those as well, please." He paused, turning to me. "Unless you would like something else?"

"No, it sounds fantastic. Law students don't turn down food either."

"Good," he said. The waitress didn't have to write our orders down, but instead excused herself to attend to another table. I watched her walk away, and when I turned back, I found Detective Paperelli looking at me with a speculative glance.

"Now tell me everything you know about her that I have missed."

"Who?" He'd caught me completely off guard.

"The waitress. Given our prior conversation, I'm sure you've now analyzed a number of details that have completely escaped me. I'm very curious. What do you know that I don't?"

"It isn't so much what I know, but rather what inferences I can draw from the details." I had a weird sense of déjà vu. At least this time I wasn't going to admit my defects. Janice Harrington was one thing, but a police detective I didn't really know – an attractive maybe single police detective – was another.

"A series of educated guesses then?"

"Yes. I'm positive that our waitress is training to be a chef or wants to train to be a chef."

"And you know this because —"

"She is in her early twenties and yet happy to be waiting tables here. This strikes me as unusual."

"Why?"

"Most people in their early twenties are waiting tables to pay the bills while they figure out what they want to do with their lives or pursue some career in the arts. Even if they are pleasant, there is a detachment in the way they carry themselves. Their hearts aren't in it."

"And she doesn't."

"Her attitude says this is where she wants to be. She views it as a stepping-stone to something else. When she described the tart I was sure. You can't fake that kind of enthusiasm. She's a foodie." I paused. "And she wears Dansko clogs."

"What does that mean?"

"She's worked in restaurants for a while. People working in food service stand on their feet a lot. Those shoes are essential. And she didn't write our order down, so that shows she is used to memorizing orders and keeping them straight in her head."

"Anything else?"

"She has tattoos on her shoulders, which is an unusual location for a woman to get them. I think she was a wild teenager. She now knows what she wants to do, so she dresses neatly. She also may be helping out in the kitchen every now and then. She has cut marks on her hands that look like inexperienced knife work."

Detective Paperelli looked at me in that way that might have been admiration and might have been something else. "What have you deduced about me, I wonder?"

The waitress appeared with the coffee. "Here you go, two lattes. Your tarts will be out shortly. Is there anything else I can get you?"

"No thank you," he replied with an ingratiating smile, "but I do have a question. You aren't in training to be a chef, are you?"

She seemed surprised and pleased by the question. "Soon," she said. "I just got accepted by L' Ecole Culinaire here in town. I'm starting next semester. How did you know?"

"Your enthusiasm for the food," I said.

"We just knew you had the makings of a chef," Detective Paperelli continued smoothly.

"The chef here has been letting me do some prep already. I'm very excited."

"Congratulations." Detective Paperelli took a sip of coffee and smiled at her to let her know it was good.

The waitress saw someone signaling her at another table, so she said, "Again, let me know if you need anything. I'll bring your tarts out shortly." She hurried away.

I looked at him and he looked at me. I hesitated a moment and then asked him a question he clearly did not expect. "So what is your story? I think I've deduced some of it, but I'd like confirmation."

He took another sip of coffee before saying, "What do you mean?"

"I don't mean to be insulting, but you don't really add up." I put the coffee cup to my lips and hastily lowered it before I burned my tongue.

"How so?"

"Are you wearing your Ferragamo loafers? I can't tell from here."

He eyed me suspiciously and slid one foot out so I could see.

"I thought so," I said.

"This conversation has taken a bizarre turn."

"You wanted to know what I've noticed. Maybe you can explain to me why a St. Louis City homicide detective wears Ferragamo loafers and a Burberry sport coat." I looked down at his hand. "And a Baume and Mercier watch." I met his eyes. "Is your shirt Kenneth Cole? I wasn't totally sure about that."

He nodded. "I like to look nice."

I shook my head. "But clothes aren't everything. You are very adept at your BlackBerry, which is a new model. I would imagine that it's not the first one you've had."

"My third."

"Then there is the name. It took me some time after I met you to put two and two together. You must own part of the family business, so you don't need to live on your salary."

Paperelli's Pizza was a local chain of restaurants. They had a frozen food division as well. I'd seen the pizzas and pasta sauces in the freezers at the local Schnucks supermarket.

"Very good," he said. "But that's something you could learn from back issues of the *Business Journal*. And the clothes, well, you clearly are a student of *Vogue*."

I felt indignation at the patronizing tone. I shot him a warning look.

"It's not that I'm not impressed," he amended. "I'm just curious to see how far your deductive reasoning goes."

"I'm not a parlor trick," I said tartly. I took a large gulp of coffee. It burned down my throat, but I didn't react. I stared at him over the rim of my cup.

He smiled. "I'm not saying you are – although I haven't heard that phrase since English Lit in college, so maybe I don't remember what it means. I'm fascinated by how your mind works. I'd just like to know the parameters."

"So you want me to prove myself with something only your friends and family know about you?"

"If you can," he said mischievously.

"I want something in return."

"That depends on what you want."

"A very lawyerly response." I took another sip of coffee. "I want you to answer one question."

"I can live with that."

The waitress reappeared with our tarts. She set them proudly on the table in front of us and then hurried back to the kitchen. I took a bite of the tart. It was heavenly. I chewed slowly. Detective Paperelli took a bite as well, and we watched each other across the table.

"This is better than chocolate," I said, impressed.

"You like chocolate?"

"Who doesn't?"

"Have you been to Bailey's Chocolate Bar?"

"Not yet, but it's on my list of places to go. Chocolate is a weakness."

"They also have a very good beer selection."

"Another weakness." I continued to watch him.

"Well?" he said.

I took a sip of coffee and swallowed. It had finally cooled. "You play the piano. I imagine you find it relaxing after a long day at work."

"Wow. How did you know that?"

"I watched you working on your BlackBerry. It's the way you move your hands."

He smiled broadly. "I haven't underestimated you. And, you're right about when I play. Sometimes it's the only thing that keeps me sane."

"That brings me to my prize," I said.

"Ask away."

"Why did you become a police detective?"

"You cut to the heart of the matter, don't you?"

"Well, it is an odd choice for someone who doesn't have to work."

"You make it sound like any job would be an odd choice. Money doesn't equal happiness."

"But why this profession in particular?"

"I love the work. I could do without the paperwork, of course. No one likes the paperwork."

"But the crime scenes?" I thought about John Harding lying in the stairwell.

"You have to think analytically and turn off your emotions. It's hard, I admit. But you have an obligation to the victims to keep your head as clear as possible."

"Hmm." I thought about this. I wanted to ask more questions, but hesitated. I took another bite of tart, trying to assess the taste. Cinnamon, certainly, but maybe something more subtle. Allspice, perhaps?

Detective Paperelli watched me as he sipped his coffee. Finally he said, "All out of questions?"

"I didn't think I got more than one."

"I'll give you another."

"So generous." I picked a question that was sure to get a response. "Where did you go to high school?"

He grinned and his eyes crinkled up in the corners. That is the question St. Louisans always ask someone they don't know. The answer tells something about the geographic, socioeconomic, religious, and ethnic background of a person – or at least, that seems to be the point of asking the question.

"SLUH," he said. Saint Louis University High School. A well respected private Jesuit high school. "What about you? Are you from St. Louis?"

"No, Wisconsin. I went to Marshfield High School."

"That tells me nothing. Leave it to you to know the secret St. Louis question."

"If St. Louisans had a secret handshake, I'd probably know that, too."

"You don't know the secret handshake?"

I laughed.

"Maybe I should stop testing your powers of deduction and actually explain why I wanted to meet with you," he said.

"I thought you wanted to see the parlor trick in action."

"Are you going to help me or not?"

"I don't think I've actually been asked to do anything."

"I'm not going to get the best of you, am I?"

"Don't take on a law student in a verbal joust."

"I have been duly warned." He leaned in. "Let me explain myself and maybe we can get somewhere."

I nodded in agreement, feeling the excitement seep into my veins. I took bite of tart as a distraction. Really, it was divine.

"I'm going to be honest with you about certain aspects of the investigation. I assume that you can keep this confidential."

I rolled my eyes, my mouth still full of tart.

"That's right, I'm talking to a proto lawyer. Anyway, I want you to understand where I am going."

I nodded again. My mouth was full with another piece. The apples were perfectly tart with just a hint of sugar to take the edge off and the ice cream to smooth it all out.

"We have almost entirely discounted the theory of a random killer motivated by robbery."

I swallowed. He waited for me to say something.

"I didn't entertain that theory for long," I said. "John Harding couldn't have had much money on him because his things were in his office. That, and the body hadn't been turned over. Wouldn't a robber have turned the body or moved it to get the wallet out of the back pocket? He looked like he lay exactly where he fell. That's bothered me."

I paused, not sure how much I should ask. "Did you find the wallet? Was it in his briefcase? I know some men can't stand to carry something that cumbersome in the back pocket. It's uncomfortable when they sit down."

"You're right. It wasn't in the briefcase. We haven't found it, at least not all of it. I'd like to hear your theories, since we've drawn the same conclusions."

"I think he must have known his attacker, or at least conversed with him."

"Why?"

"The way he was laying, with his feet towards the stairs to the fourth floor. Either he was facing someone coming down towards him or he was facing someone who stood on the landing. A robber would have lain in wait below the landing, because he couldn't be seen the way the stairs curve down. So John Harding had to either go there to meet someone or someone caught up with him."

"Have you thought about teaching at the police academy?" he said, teasing.

"Flatterer."

"Only a little. I'm very impressed so far."

"One more thing has bothered me. I think the attacker must have been crouched down, but I can't think of a scenario where that makes sense."

"Why do you think that?"

"John Harding's face was so torn up. I doubt the killer toted a shotgun into that narrow space, but wouldn't bullets from a handgun enter more cleanly than that?"

"It depends on the size of the bullet and other factors."

"Like distance and angle?"

He nodded, urging me on.

"I think the gun was fired close to his head and at an angle up under his chin. When the bullet exited, it took off part of the jawbone and most of the nose. That's the only way I can imagine destroying most of the face with one, maybe two shots."

"You don't think more were fired?"

"No. Any more and the shooter might attract attention. That stairwell is not entirely soundproof – close – but the killer wouldn't want to risk being caught. Unless the gun had a silencer – I hadn't considered that. But John Harding was probably dead from the first or second shot, so what would be the point of firing more? What do you think?"

"I know that there were exactly two shots fired, both at close range. One, as you inferred, at a weird angle, and one straight down, presumably while standing over the body."

"If you know what happened, why ask me to speculate?"

"As I said, I am fascinated to see how your mind works —"

Just as I feared. A rubbernecker. "This is way beyond the parlor trick. I'm not a circus act," I said coldly.

"I was trying to be complimentary."

"By making me feel like the trick pony instead?"

"I also wanted to see how much of an explanation I would have to give for what I'm going to ask."

I gave him no encouragement this time. He had some nerve asking me for anything.

"You've come to the conclusion I have – although probably more quickly – that this murder was an inside job." He waited for me to say something.

I took another slow sip of coffee, letting him sweat. Finally, I said, "Someone who knew John Harding killed him."

"Right."

"Someone with enough pull to lure him into the stairwell, or with enough knowledge of his habits to follow him down or wait for him on the landing."

"Right."

"You need me to be your inside source at the firm."

"Bingo."

He gave me his most engaging smile, complete with dimple, and I could feel the anger oozing away through my fingertips. I flexed my hands in my lap. What was I getting myself into?

"Attorneys are particularly tight-lipped when it comes to talking to the police. They are so afraid of incriminating themselves that they rarely give us anything useful. I need someone to be my eyes and ears."

"But I'm not even an associate yet."

"You are already working part-time." How did he find that out? "That will be all of the access I need." He paused a moment. "Frankly, I don't know that I can trust anyone else."

"How do you know you can trust me?"

"You have been completely ruled out as a suspect."

"That's a comfort."

"I hope you're willing to help the investigation," he said in his most sincere voice.

I caught myself staring into those deep blue eyes and then snapped back to attention. "I don't think I have a choice." If he weren't so attractive it would be a lot easier to think clearly.

"I've said you're not a suspect. I can't compel you."

"Just friendly persuasion?"

He looked me straight in the eyes. "No. This is a request, plain and simple. I'm asking you to do this because you have an amazing ability to synthesize details and because you have access to all of the right people. You are integral to solving this case." He lowered his voice and leaned in. "A man you knew was brutally murdered. I think he deserves a little justice, don't you?"

His gaze was so mesmerizing that I couldn't blink. His eyes pierced me through. I felt giddy all over again. I tried desperately to focus.

"So will you help me?" His voice was tender, pleading. I felt my stomach drop out from under me. I clutched my hands together to keep them from shaking. How could I refuse him anything – ever?

"Yes," I said. "What do you want me to do?"

He beamed at me with his whole face. "I knew I could count on you."

I nodded, too overwhelmed for once to speak.

"I just want you to pay attention and let me know about anything unusual or interesting. Frankly, even a general assessment of the state of the firm would be helpful. And I may have specific questions. I'll leave it up to your own ingenuity to find the answers."

"So we'll keep in touch?"

"Let's plan to talk at least once a week by phone, and we can meet if we need to."

"I'm not sure I'll be that helpful."

"You will, don't worry."

We both ate in silence. I felt the weight of responsibility settle over me like a blanket. I'd never used my abilities for anything but my own survival. How could I turn them into something more? It seemed like too much to ask my poor limited brain. I sat mulling over the irony. Detective Paperelli seemed to think I had extraordinary powers. In fact, I was permanently and irrevocably flawed.

"I wouldn't have asked you if I hadn't hit a wall in the investigation," Detective Paperelli said softly. I realized that he had been watching me.

"I don't know much about John Harding or the firm."

"I've gathered that as the managing partner his word was law."

"Funny," I said.

"No pun intended."

"Yes, the management committee could advise, but he had the final say. He was a self-made man. I'm told that he came from nothing."

"I know he grew up in Poplar Bluff," Detective Paperelli said. "What else do you know?"

"He was a player. Wait, can you use that term with a senior citizen?"

"I don't know, but I get the picture. He'd been married a couple of times."

"That's because of the affairs." I briefly outlined what Janice had told me. At one point, he brought out a little note pad and jotted some things down.

"This certainly expands my knowledge of the victim," he said.

"It's not unusual. I could tell you some stories."

"I never knew law firms were such a hotbed of sex and intrigue." I looked at him.

"What?" he said.

"A hot bed."

He laughed. "See, valuable information already."

"About the sex lives of lawyers? I don't think it's an insight that will get you anywhere."

As soon as I said it – without thinking of course – I started to blush. This was not a safe subject. I looked down again for something to do. I ate the last piece of tart on the plate. The coffee was gone.

He cleared his throat, aware of my confusion. "Would you like another coffee?"

"No thank you." Silence settled over us again.

Then he leaned closer and asked in a quiet voice, "How do you know so much about everything? It's more than perception or deductive reasoning. This is second nature to you – a completely seamless process." He placed his hands together, fingertip to fingertip. My breath quickened as I waited for him to say something more. "I'm sorry. I don't have a right to ask personal questions, but I have to know."

I took a deep breath and thought about what it would mean to tell him. The look of shock and horror that would cross his face. The look of revulsion – of pity.

Janice had taken it well, that was true, but Janice was unique. I couldn't count on being lucky twice. And what did I know about Detective Paperelli? I knew what kind of shirt he wore, but not the caliber of his soul. I couldn't take the risk. But I couldn't lie to him either. He was too perceptive.

"Some things are better left alone."

"You can trust me."

"I'm sure I can, but —"

"I'm ready to listen whenever you're ready to tell me." He reached across the table as if to squeeze my hand, but thought better of it. "You have my contact info, right? Call me if you need to, but I'll check in with you in a week."

"Thanks for the coffee and the tart." I got out from behind the booth.

"I'll make it dinner next time if you like," he said, throwing money on the table.

"Dinner?"

"Law students never refuse dinner, right?"

"No. Free food is always acceptable."

He walked with me out of the door. I turned the corner to begin the trek to my car. He followed without a word.

After half a block, I said, "You don't need to walk me to my car. This is Clayton and its not even dark."

"Crime happens everywhere. I want to make sure you get home safely."

I felt my stomach do a little flip inside my rib cage. I needed to get back under control. Even if he was single, he was out of my league in so many ways. First, there was the model aspect. Okay, he wasn't a Calvin Klein model — all muscled and sullen — but maybe Ralph Lauren, with some English castle backdrop. You would never see me with the polo ponies. Then, there was the family money bit. Better not to even touch that. Then, there was the fact that I was now an informant. Could you date your own informant? I didn't think so.

Of course, the real issue was obvious. Who would want to be with someone who couldn't even pick him out of a crowd? I had dated as much as your average-looking geeky law student, but that wasn't saying much. I'd never had a serious boyfriend. I wasn't going to count Nick Lee. He and I had been on and off during high school. The relationship was so fraught with conflict that I think we were both relieved when it finally ended senior year.

Then again, I'd recently gotten an email from him. It sat there in my inbox waiting for a reply. I'd never actually told Nick about my issues. His father was my neurologist, so I figured he knew. That's what happens when your small town is home to a giant medical clinic — you date the son of your neurologist.

"You seem lost in thought."

His words startled me. I said the first thing that leaped into my brain. "I was wondering how the murderer got in and out." Explaining that I was mulling over my never-ending spinsterhood didn't seem like a good idea.

"You mean how did he escape?"

"Sort of. If it were a common robbery, I would assume the murderer got into the garage on foot and left the same way, taking the gun with him. Have you found it, by the way?"

"Not yet." We reached my car and he leaned his hand against the roof.

"But, if it is someone at the firm, would they have entered and exited by foot? Not likely. They would have had to arrive by car. Unless they left and came back, of course. That implies premeditation. Even then, they would have had to enter the garage like normal and park somewhere – it's tough to find a spot unless you've got one of those reserved partner spaces on the second floor. And then somehow get the car out without looking suspicious. Of course, the gate opens automatically, so the exit wouldn't necessarily be recorded. Does this mean that they hid out in the building until everyone left? That's risky. If they didn't have a car, what did they do, hail a cab? Going anywhere with blood all over your clothes would seem like a bad idea."

"Unless the murderer lives in the city and can walk back and forth to work."

"I'm sure some of the younger attorneys do." St. Louis was in the middle of a revitalization boom where industrial warehouses became beautiful loft apartments. "So I would start by matching the key card summaries with the people who were there when the police arrived. Then, I would see which employees live within walking distance, or maybe close to the metro." The MetroLink system ran to certain parts of the city and county. "Undoubtedly, someone has already done this."

"Yes, but we were working on the random robbery theory. I think it's worth a review."

"If you can, I'd like to know what happens with the analysis. Oh, and Vince took me home, so my car stayed there all night."

"Vince."

"Vince Lopez. I'm sure you have his interview in the file. A friend of mine drove me back to get my car the next morning. You have that in the file as well. We had to do a lot of talking to get into the garage to get it."

I pulled my car door open. "I would also check out the IT staff – there are some strange people working for the firm."

"Will do," he said. "Ms. Howe, it has been a pleasure." He extended his hand and I put mine in his. I felt a strange electricity wick its way up my arm. He gave my hand more of a squeeze than a shake and let go. I got in my car and resolutely shut the door. As I drove away, I watched him in my rearview mirror. He stood very still, watching me.

CHAPTER 6

I decided to join a gym. When I got home from my meeting with Detective Paperelli, I sat down and took a good hard look at my existence. I was twenty-five and living alone. I had some friends, a few of them even close enough to know about my prosopagnosia. But despite going to school every day with intelligent men, I had no dating life to speak of. My career seemed to be taking off – at least after that meeting with Janice – but that was a positive and a negative. I had only to look at Janice to see the toll that long hours took on a relationship. This left dating someone who was also an attorney. Given what I had seen of attorneys, this did not seem likely. I was not attracted to self-satisfied men.

Then I thought about Vince. We met every so often for coffee. There might be interest, but our conversation was usually so chummy, it was hard to tell. I certainly didn't feel that zing of electricity when I touched his hand.

I tried to analyze the situation logically, and realized that I was holding myself back. I couldn't help the prosopagnosia, but I could change everything else. I was an average looking woman. But what made me average? I'd never actually asked the question. When you grow up where I did, this is not surprising. Utility, not beauty, is the order of the day.

I wandered into the bathroom and looked at myself in the mirror. My features weren't perfectly symmetrical. My nose was too long and my mouth too wide. I had a very toothy smile. I wasn't going to have plastic surgery, so I had to work with what I'd been given. My skin was uneven at the moment, but usually pretty good. I always blamed it on the time of the month, but maybe washing my face on a regular basis would help. I could even moisturize. That, and cut back on the inordinate amount of chocolate I'd eaten lately. Chocolate always made me break out. I'd been willing to live with it. It was just so hard to resist.

I bared my teeth. I drank a lot of coffee and it showed. I'd never actually tried those over-the-counter whiteners. Again, I blamed my upbringing for my shameful ignorance of beauty products. I'd have to get some and see what they could do. If my smile had to be toothy, at least it could be white. Then I'd have to cut back on the coffee. That one would be harder than chocolate. Mitigation. That was the best I could hope for.

I stepped back, trying to get as much of myself in the bathroom mirror as possible. The body. I had to get rid of those fifteen pounds. I grimaced. It could be twenty by now. I'd never bought a scale, so I hadn't weighed myself in a long time. I needed a scale and a full-length mirror to really assess the damage. This wasn't going to be pretty. I'm not a good dieter, because I'm grouchy when I'm hungry. If I went to the gym on a regular basis, I wouldn't have to cut back so much. Plus, muscle tone couldn't be bad.

I decided to join the gym in Clayton because it seemed to be open all of the time and was very close to my apartment in Richmond Heights. My friend Holly agreed to go with me since she was already a member. She thought that she could get me a discount, or at the very least, talk them into giving me free time with a personal trainer. I was thrilled to have someone along who seemed to know what she was doing.

Holly and I met as undergraduates. We'd bonded as only two nerdy girls can. But for sheer, unadulterated, testosterone-fueled insanity, engineering students put law students to shame. I'm not sure how Holly survived the Ph.D. program, except that despite her petite frame, she was tough as nails.

Holly was a vegetarian and a health nut. In fact, had we not agreed to disagree about the meat issue, we might never have remained friends. As it was, we had so much else in common, that I ignored her sporadic attempts to preach to me about animal cruelty, and she ignored my comments about vitamin deficiencies. She'd tried several times to go vegan, but her strong disgust for tofu always drove her back to eggs. Just as well, I thought, since a girl like me from America's Dairyland couldn't imagine life without milk or cheese.

Holly was also an avid runner. She joined a gym because she felt she needed strength training, but refused to conform to the spandex uniform. She was still as granola as they come. I figured that if she was comfortable there, maybe I could stand it.

"This is wonderful, Liz. You just don't know how great you'll feel!" she said.

I thought about all of the sore muscles and nodded. "It will be good – eventually."

"I'm really proud of you. This could totally change your life."

"I'm still eating meat, so don't start."

Caught, she smiled innocently. "I wouldn't dream of it."

"I will promise to eat more vegetables, if that helps."

"You never know. It's one small step."

"I'll keep my options open."

"That's all I ask."

"What should I wear? Please don't tell me I have to get something fluorescent and clingy."

"Are you going to exercise or do you want to meet a guy?"

"Am I the type to meet someone at a gym? Really?"

"Good point. Your usual ratty tee shirts and stretched out shorts should be fine."

I smiled. "I guess I can invest in some new tee shirts and shorts. What else?"

"You'll need new shoes."

"I have running shoes."

"From when, high school?"

I nodded guiltily.

She looked at me like a naughty child. "They wear out you know."

"I never ran that much."

"I'm sure you didn't, but if you don't get new shoes, your feet won't have the right support and you will injure yourself. Trust me on this."

"I will leave myself in your hands."

And I did. Within two days, Holly had me all ready to go. A new outfit, new shoes, new socks – designed to breathe and thin enough to prevent rubbing – new water bottle and new gym bag. Who could ask for more? She then drove me over and marched me up to the membership desk. In less than twenty minutes, I had a one-year membership. I even had free sessions with a personal trainer courtesy of Holly's ability to sweet talk the young sales associate. Holly told me I could thank her later. I got assigned to Kendra. My first appointment was in two days.

"Mission accomplished," I said to Holly as we were walking out of the gym.

A woman walked by us on her way in. I turned as she passed and watched her. I was almost certain that she was Beth Jones from the firm. She had the same distinctive walk – small steps with a light tread. Like a child on tiptoes. I called out to her and waved. She didn't even turn her head. She just kept walking. I'd made a mistake.

"You don't look so good," Holly said.

"My radar's off." Holly knew what I meant.

"I confuse things all the time." She put her hand on my shoulder to comfort me.

"I usually don't."

"Well, that's because you are a walking computer."

"I'm not that good, apparently."

"You are the closest thing to a cyborg I know – and I'm in engineering. I would put you up against any of them, and you can't get more cyborgy than that."

"Is cyborgy a word?"

"It accurately describes most of my department."

"They're not that bad."

"You have no idea."

"Even Ben?"

"He's almost normal most of the time, but get him with his CS buddies and – they're another species."

"Like me? Telling me I'm not human really makes me feel close to you."

She laughed. "When I tell you you're a cyborg, I mean it as a compliment."

"Back-handed."

"Unlike the engineers, you use your vast intellect to be normal. They use theirs to be as weird as possible."

"And your vast intellect?"

"I use it to end hunger and promote world peace," she said in her best Miss America voice.

"World peace – hah! You're using it to learn Klingon like the rest of them."

"Only the verb conjugations."

"Well, to show you I still love you even if you know Klingon, we can go to that juice bar you always want to go to. I'll even order something with wheat grass."

"Done!"

I didn't tell Holly the real reason I was so anxious to join the gym. I couldn't even admit it. I didn't mention Detective Paperelli at all. I persuaded myself that it was the confidential nature of the investigation. It felt so adolescent to like someone unattainable. Holly was so sure of herself, and as a cute girl in engineering, she could take her pick. Who wouldn't want to date a girl who could speak Klingon? Her boyfriend, Ben, looked at her like he'd won the lottery.

I also didn't tell Holly about my appointment at the swank salon, "Blue," in the heart of Ladue. Ladue is a wealthy suburb where many families with old money live. Holly would never think twice about spending $200.00 on running gear, but she wouldn't think much of someone who spent that on her hair. Even if that someone was cursed with enough curl to frizz at the first drop of humidity. And the color was so blah. My mom called it dirty blond. Like I didn't try my hardest to shampoo it into beauty. Holly never had to do anything to her hair. It was flame-colored and hung in soft waves down her back. Even when she put it in a ponytail, it looked fantastic.

I arrived at the salon ten minutes early to get my bearings. The décor was modern, but not so modern that it would frighten away the Ladue ladies who formed the backbone of its clientele. Chic was the operative word, not edgy or hip. I had an appointment with Marcela, who turned out to be a thirty-something woman with a faint Spanish accent and the most amazing blue-black hair.

"What can I do for you today?" she asked as she turned me this way and that in the chair.

"Anything you want. I need help."

She smiled. "I'm glad we agree. Let's take this ponytail out and see what we have to work with." She ran her fingers through my hair, shaking it out. "Well." She drew a strand of hair through her fingers. "I think you need layers and something shorter. Maybe here." She indicated my collarbone.

I nodded.

"And more blond highlights, especially around your face. I'll make you look like a million bucks."

"I don't think that's possible."

"Just watch me." She walked to the back to get her supplies.

Ah, the transformational promise of a haircut. I sat contentedly looking at myself in the mirror and wondering what new person would appear. I couldn't recognize the person reflected back at me, so change was never a threat to my sense of self.

Marcela came back with a stack of foils and papers and three bowls of colored paste. My hair needed more help than just simple highlights. She proceeded to color every last inch with one of the three pastes, in an intricate pattern I tried to follow but couldn't. My head became a giant Chia pet of papers and foils.

"Now, we have to wait," she said, motioning to a section of chairs at the back. "Would you like a cup of coffee or tea? Water?"

I shook my Chia head and found a chair. I looked around for a magazine. There was a stack next to me on a little table. I flipped through a couple of old *People* magazines – not really reading, just looking at the pictures and wondering how much plastic surgery was required to produce those bodies. I dug down in the pile and found a *Redbook*. I scanned the recipes, looking for something useful. I dug some more and came up with a copy of the *Ladue News*.

The *Ladue News* is a periodical best known for its chatty write-ups of society functions, its pictures of pricey real estate, and its amazing domestic service want ads. I was always curious to read it because I didn't grow up in a world of private chefs, personal shoppers, and chauffeurs. I realized that it must be an old issue. There on page five, under the title "Lawyers for Cancer Cures" was a photo of John Harding, smiling, cocktail in hand, under an LFCC banner. Cheri Harding was in the picture too, also with cocktail. A third woman was listed as Lori Chandler, president of the St. Louis chapter of the LFCC.

Normally, photographs are impossible for me to decipher. They are too static to capture the gestures and context that my brain requires. However, the *Ladue News* had the happy custom of naming each individual under the photograph – left to right. The article spoke glowingly of John and Cheri Harding and their tireless efforts on behalf of the cause. I looked again at the photograph. There was something about how Cheri stood – how she held the glass in her hand – that seemed familiar. And then it was gone. A lone neuron firing in my synaptic wilderness.

I continued to read through the magazine, wondering at the lives that seemed so alien from my own. I turned the page and found I'd stumbled into the weddings and engagements section. I take a vicarious pleasure in reading about other people's happy endings. I read about Charles and Lucy Bateman (*nee* Hoffmeister) who were married at the St. Louis Cathedral and honeymooned in Puerto Vallarta. Then there was Kyle Kauffman, who popped the question to Nancy Kleinmueller on a hot air balloon ride over the city. A tasteful wedding for five hundred was to be celebrated at Shaare Emeth synagogue.

Also Darryl Smith, a 1995 graduate of MICDS, an exclusive private high school, married Mranali Chopra, a 1997 graduate of John Burroughs, another exclusive private high school, in a small ceremony at the Botanical Garden. The American wedding was followed by a lavish seven-day wedding in India. What were the Smith-Chopras doing now? Wouldn't life seem really dull after a seven-day wedding?

I got to the last announcement and my heart stopped. It read:

"Mr. and Mrs. Stan Zakarias and Dr. and Mrs. Gerald Piper are pleased to announce the engagement of their daughter, Angelica Rose, to James Antonio Paperelli, son of Mr. and Mrs. Antonio

Paperelli. Angelica is a 1991 graduate of Visitation Academy. She graduated from Webster University in 1996, with a degree in business, and is currently working for Zakarias Industries Ltd. James is a 1988 graduate of Saint Louis University High School. James graduated from Saint Louis University in 1992 *summa cum laude* with a Bachelor of Science degree in Biology. He is currently employed by the St. Louis Metropolitan Police Department. James proposed to Angelica on January 10, 2005, during an intimate dinner for two at Cardwell's in Clayton, where he went down on one knee in front of the delighted diners. He presented Angelica with a ring especially designed for her by Lane Jewelers of Ladue, incorporating a Paperelli family heirloom diamond. An October 2006 wedding is planned."

There was a picture of the happy couple neatly captioned Angelica Zakarias and James Paperelli. She was beautiful in a generic way, with very even features and chestnut brown hair. Her smile, so wide she appeared giddy, showed very straight white teeth. She stood slightly behind a seated Detective Paperelli – her hand, with the ring, resting confidently on his shoulder. He seemed subdued, his smile registering more contentment than joy. Perhaps in an attempt to appear dignified.

My first thought was – control yourself. My second – you're a fool to care. My third – keep moving forward. I was twenty-five with my whole life ahead of me. Why should I waste time on someone so clearly not meant for me? I repeated the last point over and over again until my stomach stopped pitching, and I could breathe without choking back the ridiculous tears that suddenly sprang to my eyes.

Marcela called me to the mirror and painstakingly removed every paper and piece of foil. Fortunately, she was so single-minded in her pursuit of my perfection that there was little room for conversation. I knew as I watched her that I was in the presence of true genius. She turned hair that was indifferent in color and difficult in texture into the softest, shiniest, most shampoo commercial hair I'd ever seen. Yes! Stephanie eat your heart out. I turned my head this way and that, marveling at the woman in the mirror. As usual, recognition eluded me.

"Amazing what a little cut and color can do, isn't it?" she said.

"It feels like different hair."

"The magic of product."

"Whatever it is, I have to have it."

"I thought you'd say that." She pulled out two bottles and a tube and told me what to do. "I'll put them at the front desk for you," she said. I followed her out to the reception area and thanked her profusely. Then, I made an appointment six weeks out. There was no going back now. When I went to pay for everything, I realized that I'd left my purse by her station. Feeling stupid, I walked back to get it. I saw the *Ladue News* I'd been reading out of the corner of my eye. On impulse, I grabbed it and stuffed it in my purse.

CHAPTER 7

The haircut raised my spirits in a way I couldn't have imagined. I told myself to move on, and I meant it this time. I decided to deal with Detective Paperelli in a businesslike way and to ignore any other feelings creeping up on me. I even looked forward to my meeting with Kendra.

She looked about my age and pretty in a natural way, with dark brown hair and light blue eyes that crinkled in the corners. She seemed sweet and a little vulnerable. She showed me around the machines and made me work muscle groups I didn't know existed. We chatted comfortably about this and that. She had relatives in central Wisconsin, and knew her way around a dairy farm. She'd spent summers there as a child.

She told me she was working on her associate's degree and hoped one day to go into sports medicine. The gym job paid the bills. She had a seven-year-old daughter to support. She got some help from her parents, but I gathered that the relationship was strained at times. The father didn't seem to be in the picture.

She talked to me about exercise and proper nutrition, and suggested I try to get exercise outside of my workouts. A walk at lunch, maybe.

"That's a little hard," I said. "Working in the city, you have to dodge traffic to get anywhere."

"Where do you work?"

"Ghebish and Long. We're in a building off of 4th street by Washington."

"Oh," she said sadly, "the murder was so senseless. He was such a good man."

"You knew John Harding?"

She hesitated. "Yes, but not well." Her eyes fluttered down. She was lying. "He was a member here," she added quickly. "I helped him with his workout a couple of times."

"Oh. Umm. He seemed very fit."

"He was," she said with too much confidence. I looked her in the eye and understood the truth.

John Harding came in with the money and the charm. Told her that she was special. Bought her things she could never afford. Took her places she could never go. And the little things – toys for her daughter, tuition, books. It was so easy. So easy to forget he was married, to forget he was older than her father. So easy to lose herself in a Cinderella dream.

"How many reps should I do?" I asked.

"Twenty-five." She looked away.

I got home from the gym to find a message on my answering machine from Janice. She had a project for me and wondered if I could stop by that afternoon. I showered – using a liberal dose of product as instructed – and dressed quickly. I went straight to Janice's office. She was on the phone. She waved me in and I sat down.

"Well, the problem with that approach is that you are going to have tax issues down the line – trust me on this." She nodded her head listening to the response. "Just put me in touch with Phil and I'll straighten him out." A shake of the head. "I don't care if he is an accountant, he's wrong on this one. Okay. Okay. I'll wait for his call. Sure. Yes. Fine. Say hello to Flora for me, won't you? Yes. You too. Goodbye."

She set the phone down with a clatter. "Humph," she said. "Clients!"

I smiled. "You can't live with them —"

"You can't live without them," she finished. "Exactly."

"So what do you need me to do?"

"Some research. We have this client in Florida who has an issue."

I picked up my legal pad to take notes. The problem involved a certain type of trust. There was a generation-skipping tax question and some otherwise very unusual circumstances. Just the kind of knotty problem I liked to dig into.

"When do you need an answer by?"

"They want an answer on Monday, but take your time. They always think their stuff is top priority. Right!"

I laughed.

"Liz, the first thing to learn about being a successful lawyer is managing client expectations." She paused. "Sometimes you have to tell them that they're crazy."

"And they're still your clients?"

"They respect you more if you give them boundaries. Kind of like big kids."

"You're terrible!"

She grinned. "I know. That's why I make the big bucks."

"I'll head up to the library to get started. How many hours should this take?"

"If you find yourself spending more than five or six hours, call me, and we'll see where we should go with it."

"Sounds good." I got up out of the chair.

"Hey Liz, I like the hair. I almost didn't recognize you."

"That makes two of us." I winked at her and walked out the door. Her laughter followed me down the hall.

The library was a large room in the center of the top floor. I usually started there because there were a couple of very good treatises that helped me to frame the issues. I found that if I framed the issues properly, I tended to spend less time in fruitless online searches on Westlaw or LexisNexis. So I stood in the stacks for about twenty minutes, pulling one volume and then another, trying to get a handle on the problem. I was about ready to give up and go to a computer when I heard some whispering behind me. My curiosity asserted itself. I stood very still.

"It's fucked up," one man whispered. "I don't know if we can dig out."

"Maybe the blowback won't hit this far," whispered another.

"Yeah sure," said the first voice.

"Steve thinks it will turn around."

"Steve always thinks that. We can't keep waiting. The line's almost tapped out."

"Shit. That's bad."

"That's what I'm saying."

"Cheri knows?"

"Yeah. She can't do anything yet – even if she wants to. She'll wiggle out though. They always do."

"So we just hang on?"

"What else? Steve said he's going to get the line extended again."

"Can he?"

"Somebody's willing to do it."

"And Tom?"

"He's got it covered for now. No one's asking questions."

"We haven't hit year end finan —"

I heard footsteps coming into the library.

"See you," the one voice said.

"Right," said the other.

I heard more different footsteps and the men were gone. I let out a long breath. They hadn't noticed me. Who were they? I didn't recognize the voices, and I couldn't see anything from where I was standing. They had to be lawyers. Any member of staff would have attracted attention hanging around the library. And the paralegals were all women.

I replayed the conversation in my head. A business deal gone bad, obviously. Real estate? It seemed everyone was buying land just then. I had three names to work with – Steve, Tom and Cheri. Cheri must be the wife of John Harding. She couldn't do anything, they said. Of course. Her affairs were probably still in a muddle because of the murder. So John Harding had been involved in something. Something that Cheri wanted out of.

That was certainly a juicy tidbit for Detective Paperelli. It was more than what I'd planned to tell him. Janice had given me a summary of the power struggle going on in the management committee between Thomas Green and Blane Ford. Tom. Hmm. Maybe that was the connection. As I walked out of the library, I passed Grant, the dime store Casanova, walking in. He seemed distracted and didn't respond to my "hello."

I went home. My apartment desperately needed cleaning, and mindless tasks helped me think. I lived in a small house in Richmond Heights, an older suburb of St. Louis. The house had once been a single-family bungalow, but was now upstairs and downstairs apartments.

The Hendersons, my elderly landlords, occupied the downstairs apartment. It was nice to have quiet neighbors who didn't play earsplitting music or pass out drunk on the lawn. As landlords, I couldn't complain either. They'd taken me in as one of their own. My rent hadn't gone up in years and their son, Joe, came by promptly every time something needed to be done. Actually, I saw a lot of Joe. He checked on them daily. Not that he needed to worry. I kept an eye on them myself and was available to run errands.

I closed the door behind me and looked around. This was going to take awhile. I changed out of my dress clothes into comfortable jeans and a sweatshirt. I pulled my hair back with a headband. Ashley told me that I looked like a white rat with my hair pulled back. Sisters. I stared at my reflection. She was probably right, but I had a job to do.

My apartment was small to begin with, and in a little over four years, I'd managed to cram it with more books and furniture than it could really hold. Not that the furniture was worth much. Many pieces had been donations from friends moving elsewhere. I needed to get organized. I cleaned all of the basics and then turned to the problem at hand.

I started with the books. I couldn't bring myself to get rid of books. It was like cutting off a body part. I scanned the titles. Some, like my undergrad textbooks, could certainly go into storage. Did I really need that book on astronomy? But the history books had to stay. Who knew when I might need information on the Austro-Hungarian Empire? Or the Moorish invasion of Spain? Or the diary of a runaway slave? And literature was always useful. I had novels of every description, from classics to trashy books I should have been ashamed to own. But really, what woman did not enjoy a good bodice ripper every now and then? They were an escape from Moby Dick, Metternich, or Torts.

I went down to get a box from the storage area under the stairs. I'd stored a few flattened boxes there when I moved in. I pulled one out and erupted in a fit of coughing. The dust went everywhere. The outer door opened.

"Liz!" I recognized the voice. It was Joe Henderson. Great. He stood there with two bags of groceries, one in each arm.

"Hi Joe," I said, wishing I wasn't totally covered with dust. Again, I have some pride. Joe was somewhere in his thirties and single. He and I had always been friendly. I thought he might be interested in me, but I didn't give him much encouragement. He was dull in that nice sort of way. It was hard to get enthusiastic about dull.

"Do you need some help there?" I said brightly. He clearly didn't have a hand free to knock on the door.

"Thanks."

I knocked three times very loudly – the secret knock. The Hendersons were a little deaf and afraid to open their door to strangers. I heard shuffling behind the door.

I called out, "It's Joe! He's got food!"

I heard a faint "Coming!" and more shuffles. I stepped aside to let Joe go forward. Mrs. Henderson undid the deadbolt and the chain.

"Joe," she said when she finally got the door open, "you didn't need to do this. We're just fine." She always the same thing. "Why don't you stay to dinner?" She looked past him to me. "You too, Liz."

I could sense a set-up. "Sorry, Mrs. Henderson. I promised to meet Holly for dinner tonight. Thanks so much for the offer, but I've got to get back to cleaning."

I grabbed one of the boxes and raced up the stairs before she could insist. I felt Joe's eyes on my back all the way up.

I closed my door with relief. Why couldn't I drum up any interest in Joe? He was sweet. He was kind. He was gainfully employed. He wasn't bad looking – a little balding at the back – but still okay. I loved his family. I could easily see myself as one of them. A sudden image of James Paperelli's blue, blue eyes flashed into my mind. I felt my pulse accelerate and cursed out loud. My life was perverse.

Holly called before I could feel too sorry for myself. She had a ton of work to catch up on. We agreed to skip dinner and meet for coffee at a little place close to her apartment in the Delmar Loop. The Loop is an area close to Washington University's main campus that had started out as a collection of artists' co-ops, vintage clothing stores, funky record shops, and odd ethnic restaurants, all populated with colorful characters. Like other areas of St. Louis, it had gentrified with alarming speed. You could now find chain stores and upscale marketing sprinkled into the arty mix.

Holly lived in a small apartment off The Loop on the university side. Her building had lost none of its down-at-the-heels appearance in the gentrification process. It had charm though – if you could get past the peeling paint. Holly and I had contemplated living together, but the thought of me cooking non-vegetarian food turned her off. Since she couldn't find anyone similarly insane (my word) or dedicated (her word), she decided to live alone. All in all, I was glad for it. Our friendship was stronger for not having to put up with each other on a day-to-day basis.

I finished boxing up books and sneaked them back to the storage space. I could hear noise in the Hendersons' apartment, so I assumed that the dinner had started. I tiptoed back up to my apartment and shut the door. Another escape. I got out a frozen dinner and heated it up in the microwave. The box said the meal was low in fat and calories. I figured it would be tasteless. I was right. I'd been on a diet for two weeks, but it seemed like forever.

I finished quickly. There was no reason to linger. I got out my notes and sat down to work on my outlines. The key to understanding law school is a good outline. Unlike every other teaching discipline, the law professor's job is to confuse the students so much that they are forced to meet in study groups to figure out what to study. By the time they are 3Ls, students have usually mastered this cat and mouse game. Then the professors change tactics and stop trying to hide the ball. About time, I thought. Most students have a hard enough life with school, law review and, most importantly, the search for a job. I had the job nailed down, but I was way behind with law review. The dreaded note. I switched gears.

In another week we had to turn in rough outlines of our notes. Notes are researched articles that are written by law students about some vibrant legal question. A published note is supposed to significantly enhance your résumé. The problem is that you can't write about a topic that someone has analyzed previously, unless you take a completely different tack. This leads to a search for the most esoteric subject imaginable. No one wants to be scooped. I picked an issue related to pour over trusts. It was a minor question – hardly worth writing about. I hoped it would be obscure enough for a decent note.

If only I could sit down long enough to flesh it out. Unfortunately, this wasn't the night. I didn't have the focus. My mind was in a thousand places – mostly back at the firm. I turned the whispered conversation over and over in my mind. What deal had gone sour? I decided to do some Internet searching.

I put John Harding's name in, but didn't get anything useful. Then I searched "John" with "Steve" and "Tom." A thousand hits. I added the words "St. Louis" and "real estate" and "development." After scanning about forty entries, I came across a blurb from the *St. Louis Business Journal*. It was a back issue that I couldn't access without a subscription:

"Steve King stated that … Thomas Green, a partner at Ghebish and Long, LLC … new development … titan of the Chesterfield real estate market …"

Interesting. Too bad I couldn't read the whole article. I thought a moment. As a student, I had access to LexisNexis online. The *Business Journal* just might be on there. I realized this was probably way outside the appropriate student access, but my curiosity was too great. I did a quick search and had the whole article in less than a minute. I sent it to myself as an email attachment, and then noticed the time. It would have to wait for later. If I didn't hurry, Holly would yell at me.

I found an outfit that, if it didn't make me look good, at least didn't highlight my defects. The green sweater brought out the green in my eyes. Their color tended to shift with the color I wore. The hair still looked amazing. That was some cut. I noticed for the first time that my jeans hung on me. I'd been too afraid to weigh myself because the last time I did, the scale sat stubbornly at the number I'd started with. Maybe something was finally happening.

I pulled out a pair of jeans I hadn't worn in a year. They were the tightest of my fat jeans. Would they or wouldn't they zip? I took off my other ones. To ensure success, I lay down on the bed and worked them up my legs. Then the final test. I slowly pulled the zipper up, making sure not to catch part of my stomach. It worked! The jeans actually fit me again! I bounded off the bed and beamed at my reflection in the new full-length mirror.

It was going to be a great evening. I could feel it.

CHAPTER 8

I found a place to park on a side street two blocks from the coffee house. I locked my car as best I could and started to walk. I drove a 1994 Chevrolet Corsica that was technically a loan from my parents. I doubted they would ever want it back. It had a number of issues that had never been fixed, no matter how many times I took it to the mechanic. The car stayed in shape long enough for inspection and then went right back to its bad old habits. One of the biggest problems was that the driver's side door didn't actually lock. It looked like it did, but one sharp pull was all it took to open it. Fortunately, no one had ever shown any desire to steal my car, even in the sketchy parts of town.

The air was crisp and I walked the two blocks in contented silence. I thought about what I'd say to Detective Paperelli. The conversation I'd overheard was important. I played the imaginary script in my head. He'd be amazed and pleased at what I'd discovered. His eyes would light up when I told him. But, no, he was engaged, I reminded myself. I gave my head a shake. I had to move forward.

Holly waited for me at one of the back tables. She waved, so I would know it was her. She knew how I hated to stand stupidly in the doorway.

"I love the haircut!" she said, bounding out of her chair.

"Thanks! I think it looks pretty good."

"Like a new woman. Your hair has a completely different texture." She reached over and touched it.

"That's the magic of product."

"What product?"

"Conditioner, infusion and a finisher."

"Not tested on animals, I hope?"

"No. I read the labels."

"Good. Then I really like it."

"I'm glad it meets with your approval."

"How's the gym going?"

"I met Kendra and she walked me through a number of exercises. I'm sore, but I promised her I'd stick with it. I liked her. She even knew where Marshfield was."

"Clearly a winner."

I smiled. The Wisconsin connection always helped.

"I think you are really going to like how exercise makes you feel. Maybe we can even go running together some time."

"Baby steps. It's going to be years before I can go running with you."

"Not if I go slowly."

"Even if you go slowly. Besides, you can't stand it when people don't keep up."

"Okay, so running might destroy our friendship, but at least it's something else we can talk about now. You've become one of us."

"As if we ever run out of things to talk about."

"I'm all about the backup plan."

"Since when?" Of the two of us, I was the responsible one. Holly wouldn't admit it, but she counted on me to bail her out. Her passionate nature led her to overextend.

"Let's get coffee," she said. She knew she couldn't argue.

At the counter, Holly ordered her usual, an organic fair trade roast, with soymilk and raw sugar. She could stomach the soy as long as it wasn't cubed and jiggly. I ordered a latte made with skim milk.

I tried to pay, but Holly shooed me away. "My treat."

I knew not to cross Holly when she'd put her foot down. We sat to wait for our coffees to come up.

"So what's new with you?" she said.

That wasn't the safest topic. "Nothing really. Just work and more work. I'm behind on my note. What about you?"

"In the engineering department?" she scoffed. "You've got to be kidding."

"And Ben?"

She looked down quickly. "I don't know." I knew something momentous was about to happen. She added very quietly, "He wants to move in together."

"What?" It came out louder than I wanted it to. The people at the next table looked over.

"Holly, your coffees are ready," the barista called from behind the counter.

We both jumped up, but I told her to sit and brought both coffees back to the table.

"Okay." I sat down. "When did this get serious?"

Holly stalled, taking a large sip of coffee and burning her tongue. "Ouch!" She pushed the cup away. "I don't know that it is that serious, but he worries about me living alone."

I thought of Ben, all lanky bones, and chuckled. "I don't know that he'd be much protection."

"I know, but —" Her gaze became unfocused. A tender smile crept to her lips. "He's really very sweet. We get along so well."

"When did he propose this idea?"

"Last night. He walked me back from the lab, and I asked him if he wanted to stay for a bite to eat. He actually said 'yes,' so I made him some fried eggplant." Ben was a carnivore, like most of us, but he was scrupulous about eating vegetarian in front of Holly. He just couldn't make himself like it – even to please her.

"So then what happened?"

"We were talking while I cooked and all of a sudden he said, 'Let's move in together.'"

"Just like that?"

"I left out the kissing part."

"Good. Too much information."

"I told him I would think about it."

"What about your lease?"

"I'd have to renew in December anyway," she said.

"And Ben? Doesn't he live with some friends?"

"No, that was short term. He found his own place. It's near you on the other side of campus."

"So what are you thinking?"

"I don't know. It seems like such a big step, but when I think about being with him —"

"It seems nice."

"Really, really nice. What do you think?" she said.

"I am the last person you should ask. My experience in these matters is pretty much nonexistent."

"But you know me. Will I drive him away?"

"Come on, he's crazy about you. You'd have to do something pretty serious to drive him away. Trust me. He looks at you like you're a goddess."

"Oh please, no one does that."

"I've watched him. When he thinks you won't notice, he just stares at you. Like he can't believe his luck."

She blushed. It was a revelation. She was falling hard for him, but didn't want to admit it to herself. In a flash, I could see them together on their wedding day: Holly with a wreath of flowers in her hair, Ben watching her possessively, unable to help from grinning. I felt tears well up. I blinked to stop them.

"Are you okay?" Holly said.

"Yes." I took a gulp of coffee. The warmth spread down my throat. I heard the door to the café open, but didn't look. I needed another moment to collect myself.

"Liz!" I heard a familiar voice. My head snapped up. It took me longer than normal to find him. I met his gaze unsteadily.

"James?" I forgot my professional demeanor. Holly's head whipped around. She kicked me under the table meaningfully.

Detective Paperelli stood in the doorway. I recognized the leather jacket from our first meeting. It hung open. Underneath, he wore a blue turtleneck that looked like cashmere. It clung to his chest in a way that left very little to the imagination. His jeans fit him like they were tailored to him. I had to force myself to look down for a moment and catch my breath.

There was another man behind him. He had similar dark wavy hair, but his build was different. Stockier and a couple of inches shorter. His clothes were very casual – a sloppy sweatshirt, frayed jeans, and tennis shoes. There was something familiar about his stance. A brother maybe? The other man looked at me critically.

Detective Paperelli strode over to our table. Holly and I stood up.

"Liz, let me introduce you to my brother, Mark. Mark, this is Liz Howe and —" He looked at me.

Holly jumped in. "Holly Schneider."

"James Paperelli," he replied.

We all shook hands. Holly gave me a look that said – you will tell me everything as soon as I can get you alone. I merely smiled.

"So how do you two know each other?" Mark said.

"Work." James and I said at once. Thank goodness we'd gotten our story straight. Mark and Holly exchanged skeptical glances. I suddenly remembered my manners.

"Would you like to join us? We have plenty of room."

"We don't want to interrupt you," Mark said. I could tell that he was just being polite.

"No interruption," Holly said cheerfully. "Mark, you look familiar. Are you in CS?"

Leave it to Holly to know all the computer science geeks. Mark hardly looked the part. He wasn't as attractive as his brother to my way of thinking, but he didn't look like he owned a pocket protector, either. Most women would have said he was handsome in a dark Italian way. He had beautiful eyes. Honey-colored.

Mark smiled and sat himself down next to her. "I'm working with Jim Wu. Are you in engineering?" Most men were surprised when they met Holly. She wasn't your typical engineer.

"Yes," she said, smiling. She'd clearly picked up on the tone in his voice. "I'm in double E, with Ed Otto. I'm doing a joint project with Claus Banner in Audiology. When do you defend?"

"By the end of this year if I can beat my committee into submission. How about you?"

"Not even close."

James and I stood watching this exchange, both of us unsure how to proceed.

"Maybe we should sit down," I said softly, so that only he could hear me.

"Let's get the coffee, then we can talk," he whispered back.

I nodded.

Mark looked up. I saw him give James a look, but I couldn't tell what it meant.

"What are you having Mark? Holly?" James asked.

"A quat espresso. I've got work to do tonight. Thanks." Mark turned back to Holly.

"Still working on mine," she said. "Thank you." She asked Mark a question that was too technical for me to understand. His response was even more incomprehensible.

James turned and I followed him. "Kindred spirits," I said lightly.

"If your friend understands half of what he is talking about, they were meant for each other."

We walked up to the line at the counter and were far enough from the table that Holly wouldn't hear me. "This is a surprise, running into you," I said.

"I hope not a bad one."

"Oh no, I just didn't think you lived around here."

"I don't, but Mark does. We decided to get together and catch up. With everything, we don't see each other much." He gave me a playful look. "And where do you think I live?"

"Lafayette Square," I replied without hesitation.

"I'm not going to ask how you know that."

I shrugged my shoulders and he laughed. Out of the corner of my eye, I saw Mark look over at us.

James leaned in closer so he wouldn't be heard. "I was going to call you tomorrow." Goosebumps of anticipation raced up my arms. "I won't bother you with work right now, if that's okay. I'd rather enjoy the evening."

"Murder gets in the way of the fun, doesn't it?"

"Almost always. Will you be home if I call at 4:00?"

"I have a class until 4:30. Can you make it 5:00?"

"Done."

The barista looked at us, waiting for our order. James ordered for his brother and himself and then turned to me. "And what would you like?"

"Another latte with skim milk, but I can get it."

"You're a poor law student, remember? It's always on me."

We moved to the side to wait for the orders to come up. I glanced at the table. Holly and Mark were deep in conversation.

"Once Holly gets going, I get lost," I said.

"I know the feeling."

"I have a question —"

"Shoot."

My brows went up.

He laughed. "That came out wrong, didn't it? Go ahead, have at it."

"Well, if you are a detective and your brother is a Ph.D. student, who is running the Paperelli empire?"

"It's hardly an empire. My father still does a lot."

"No heir apparent?"

"My sister Marie. She's the one with the head for business."

"Are there just three of you?"

"If you saw us together, you'd know that three is more than enough."

"I have trouble imagining that." It felt so comfortable to talk to him this way. I wondered if, in some alternate universe, we might become friends. That would be sufficient. Maybe.

"I have a question for you," he said.

"Shoot." I looked up with a smile.

He hesitated a moment and seemed oddly flustered. "Did you get a haircut?"

I don't know what I was expecting, but that wasn't it. "Yes," I said cautiously.

"No, I mean, I like it. That's all. It looks good."

"Like a new woman?" I couldn't help saying.

He regained some of his composure. "Not a new woman. It's still you."

"An enhancement, though."

"It's very nice, but you don't need enhancement." The moment he said it, he looked chagrined. I didn't know what to think.

Our coffees came up and he rushed over to get them. He handed mine to me without another word. We walked back to the table in uneasy silence. Holly and Mark made up for our lack of conversation. It seemed that they had a wealth of acquaintances in common. The anecdotes flowed freely without much intervention from either of us. I spent my time studying Mark, only occasionally permitting myself a glance in the other direction.

Mark was warm and engaging. He resembled his brother in the tone of his voice and his inflections. He even had the same small indentation in his lower lip. He had a good sense of humor too. He and Holly fell into easy banter. Mark seemed to grow more comfortable with me as the conversation wore on, even smiling encouragement when I asked what could have been a silly question about his dissertation. I saw him look over at his brother several times, but I couldn't tell what the looks meant.

I felt James watching me. I didn't know if I should look, but when I did he was smiling. I saw the elusive dimple. I smiled and my shoulders relaxed. We were back to friends again. I entered into the conversation with more enthusiasm. Soon we were all laughing. The engineering department contained some bizarre and colorful characters and Mark was an excellent mimic. Holly, who knew who he was talking about, almost fell out of her chair.

James looked down at his watch and then up with surprise. We'd been sitting there for over two hours. It was now past 11:00. "I'm going to have to go," he said. "Otherwise I won't be able to get up for work tomorrow."

Mark looked like he was about to argue, or to suggest we stay on and let James go. I caught James giving him a stern look. Mark fell in with good grace. "I have work tonight, too," he said.

We all got up. James reached over and pulled my chair out. I turned to thank him and our eyes met. There was something tender in his look. I felt my breath catch in my throat.

"Thank you," I finally managed.

"Good meeting you both," Mark said.

"It's been fun," Holly replied.

"Yes," I said.

"I hope to see you around campus," Mark said.

"Definitely," Holly replied. I merely nodded.

We walked out of the door together, but instead of parting ways, James insisted on walking Holly back to her apartment. Then, after seeing her safely in, he walked me to my car. I didn't trust myself in conversation. The ease of friendship was gone.

"I love these cold fall evenings," James said out of the blue. Our breath misted before us.

"So do I. It reminds me of home." A safe topic at least.

"It was great running into you tonight." Umm, not so safe.

"I hope we didn't intrude on brotherly bonding."

"There is such a thing as too much togetherness. I haven't had such a fun evening with Mark in a long time. He's in his element with an audience."

"I can see that."

"Do you have brothers and sisters?" he asked.

"One sister, Ashley. She's a freshman at UW Madison."

"Does she know what she'll major in?"

"No, she's pretty unsure about everything. I'm the responsible one in the family."

"Why doesn't that surprise me?"

"I've got that look."

"What look?"

"The responsible one – like I'm wearing orthopedic shoes or something. I look sensible."

He laughed. "Sensible is good. It's a good look. I like sensible."

He was clearly teasing me, but I blushed anyway. I didn't think he could tell in the dark. I said the first thing that came to mind. "Sometimes I would like to do the unexpected."

"Everything you do is unexpected." He glanced at me, but I couldn't read his expression in the half-light of the street.

We stopped at my car. I opened the door with one pull and got in. He leaned over the open door. "I'll call you at 5:00, then?" His voice was completely even.

"Yes."

"Goodbye Liz."

"Goodbye James." He moved back and I shut the door.

I drove slowly away, trying not to stare at the rearview mirror.

CHAPTER 9

The next morning I awoke earlier than expected, filled with a nervous energy I couldn't shake. I pulled up the email I'd sent myself the night before. The article was from 2003. It covered the groundbreaking of what the *St. Louis Business Journal* said was to be "the premiere golfing community" in the region, a place called "The Lodge."

Steve King was the developer and the article said he had large real estate holdings in Chesterfield. Thomas Green was quoted several times. He was a substantial investor in the project and planned to purchase the first house in the development. I didn't recognize the names of the other two people mentioned, Alan Klieg and Brian Havershein. John Harding was a bust. He was mentioned as "heading up Ghebish and Long," at the beginning of the article, but wasn't named in the rest of the piece.

The Lodge – that was a start. And John Harding had to be connected. The name Cheri was too much of a coincidence. I searched LexisNexis specifically and located a couple more articles. The *St. Louis Post-Dispatch* had also covered the groundbreaking ceremony. The Lodge was mentioned again in an article about the westward expansion of Chesterfield. Apparently The Lodge was even farther west than Chesterfield Commons at Boone's Crossing, a megalopolis of giant box stores.

Despite being submerged during the great flood of 1993, Chesterfield, a low-lying valley in the flood plain of the Missouri River, continued to grow. Chesterfield neighborhoods seemed to appear like magic out of the dust. Business was booming. Who wouldn't want a ten thousand square foot house on a quarter acre lot? The developer of The Lodge wanted to throw in golf and country club living to boot. What a deal.

I wondered how something like that could fail in this environment. Had we reached the limit of buyers for million dollar homes? It didn't seem so. The other articles didn't mention John Harding at all. But that didn't mean he wasn't a silent investor. How to prove the connection? Maybe this was old news to the police anyway. James was holding back all sorts of information.

James. Move on. Without thinking, I opened and stared at the message from Nick. "How are you?" was all it said. I should have responded before now, but couldn't think of what to say. My life didn't exactly give me bragging rights. And how had he gotten my email? And why? I thought distance was what Nick wanted.

I decided to focus on something else. I pulled up the rough outline I had for my note and sighed. Pathetic. I pulled out my "to do" list. I could at least do some of the research since I was already booted up. I spent the next hour reading cases and working them into my outline for the article. I was so focused that I didn't even hear the cell phone on the first ring. I'd left it in my room so I had to run for it. I picked up right before it forced the caller into voicemail.

"What took you so long?" Holly said.

"I was busy working on my note."

"Okay, spill the beans."

"What beans?"

"You know what beans I'm talking about. James Paperelli."

"What about him?"

"Why are you making this difficult?"

"I'm not."

"Yes, you are! Out with it! How did you meet him? Are you dating? What's going on?"

"Nothing. Nothing is going on. I know him from work."

"Is he a lawyer?"

"A police detective. I'm just helping him out with something."

It took Holly only a second. "Not that murder at your firm?"

"Yes, but I can't tell you any more. It's confidential."

"Mums the word, but it looked like you two were doing more than working. You couldn't keep your eyes off him."

Damn. I'd tried so hard to act normal. "He's engaged to be married, Holly. There is nothing going on."

"Oh." Holly got it. "Too bad."

"I know, but I'm just going to have to get over it."

"Maybe Ben knows somebody —"

"Don't. I'm not hurting for a boyfriend. Besides, whom could he possibly know that I'd have anything in common with? Excepting Ben, none of them have a sense of humor."

"Okay, but —"

"Can you see me dating someone with no sense of humor?"

"They'd just think you're mean."

"Right. I can't date anyone who'd take me seriously."

"That's not what I meant."

"I know," I said laughing. "I'm just proving the point. Irony doesn't get you anywhere with engineers."

"I'm still going to work on it."

"Go ahead. It won't be easy."

"You know you're not that bad."

"I refuse to comment since I can't imagine you mean to imply I'm not model beautiful. I'm hurt Holly, I truly am."

"Oh stop! I didn't mean it that way. I'm just saying you're picky."

"It takes one to know one."

"That's why you're going to be my special project," she said.

"Like a science experiment?"

"Only more fun!"

"We'll see how fun it is."

"I'm taking you to a party on Saturday."

"I was going to work on my note."

"Not anymore. Ben's friend is throwing a party and you're coming with me."

"I can be the awkward third wheel? Gee thanks."

"I promise not to ignore you or engage in any obvious PDA."

"Ben may object to the lack of obvious PDA," I said.

"He'll just have to lump it," she replied.

"Does this party involve Star Trek or any other science fiction?"

"Well, maybe Battlestar Galactica."

"Ugh!"

"I'm kidding. Talk about irony."

"Fine. Now let me go so I can get some work done."

"See you on Saturday!" She mercifully hung up the phone.

I did more work on the note and then went to class. After class, I wandered over to the law library. Washington University built a fabulous new law school in 1997. Aside from the wired classrooms and the real courtroom for mock trial practice, the library reading room was a work of art. The room was enormous, with skylights and a vaulted ceiling of exposed beams. The long tables and the dark wood paneling made it seem more like a college in Oxford than a law school in Missouri.

The only catch for all of this magnificence was the name of the building – Anheuser-Busch Hall. Named, of course, for the largest corporate benefactor. The joke was just too easy. After the first week, we'd all stopped noticing. In any case, the prior law school, aptly named Mudd Hall, was so horrific the students would have taken anything. It had been torn down so quickly that not a trace of it remained, although you still heard stories from older attorneys about the cinder block ambience and the leaky roof. According to legend, each classroom had at least one industrial sized bucket to catch the drips.

I sat down at one of the long tables to go over my note "to do" list once more. I pulled a couple of volumes and got to work. About half an hour later, I noticed a hand waving at me. It was Amelia, one of my few law school friends. I waved back and we both went on with our studies. Talking was not allowed in the reading room.

Compared to my fellow classmates, I was a loner. I wasn't unfriendly, I just wasn't interested in the law school scene. Law school is all about popularity. Those who didn't have it in high school or college looked to law school for their last shot at glory. And, given the type of person who goes to law school, anyone with half a personality can do all right. I had some friends from other worlds, like Holly, and that was enough. I'd grown up a misfit in a town full of academically inclined doctors' kids, but I didn't want the second chance. Popularity is highly overrated.

After another hour I got so bored I couldn't stand it, so I packed up and went to talk to another of my other world friends, the government documents librarian. I'd spent a full year post graduation in the strange and mysterious world of government documents. It was my year of living dangerously. I had come to understand that government documents are in a class of their own – both feared and hated by the other reference librarians.

The term "government documents" means anything published by the federal government. The Government Printing Office distributes these documents to designated libraries. The documents have their own classification system established by the Superintendent of Documents or SuDoc. Unlike the easily understood Dewey decimal system, the SuDoc number is a strange mix of letters, numbers, periods, dashes and slashes. The documents are organized by the agency of publication, not the content of the document. If this weren't enough, the periods, slashes and dashes all mean different things. Heaven forbid you put a dash where a slash should go or vice versa.

Given the nature of the beast, the law library had its very own government documents librarian, Katarina Steines. Kat for short. I'd worked with her frequently when I assisted the staff at the main campus. We'd become friends, and she helped me out with my legal research. I'd been looking for an obscure IRS publication for the past week.

Besides catching up, I decided to swallow my SuDocs pride and ask for help. The library offices were in the back behind the stacks on the main floor. The offices had large windows facing the hallway. I saw at a glance that she was in. I knocked and waved at her when she turned.

"Liz! I haven't seen you around lately. What's up?"

"I'm trapped in the *Quarterly* offices."

"Sounds like fun."

"Almost as much fun as figuring out a SuDoc number."

"Now, now."

"Some of the best months of my life."

"Let's not go that far."

We exchanged the latest gossip on the people we knew and reminisced a bit. Then she said, "So, what can I do for you?"

"It is actually a SuDoc problem of sorts. I can't find this IRS memo." I showed her the cite. "It's old, so that may be the issue."

"How old?"

"1986."

"And you don't have the SuDoc?"

"No." I grinned. "I would have found it by now if I did."

"So you've looked everywhere?"

"Everywhere I can think of – Westlaw, Lexis, the stacks."

"Write down what you have and I will see what I can do. I'll send you an email when I find it."

"You're very confident," I said.

She gave me a wry smile. "I'm very good. I'll find it."

"Thank you."

"There's nothing I wouldn't do for a fellow SuDocker. It's good seeing you. Come by even when you don't need help."

I raced over to the gym. I just had time for a run on the treadmill before the next class. I had another session with Kendra in a few days, and I wanted to show some improvement. As I ran, I let my mind wander. I thought about seeing Beth. I was sure it was her. Then again, it took me a while to recognize James in the door of the coffee shop. Neither was where I expected to find them. Context is a fundamental part of recognition for me. The party on Saturday was going to be a trial. There were so many variables, so many opportunities to get it wrong. I had to maintain laser-like focus.

That meant I couldn't drink. Holly was going to have a harder time than she knew. Either I could be the buzzed ditz who couldn't keep anyone straight, or I could be the teetotaling prude. Take your pick. And who was I to object to a mild science fiction obsession? That was much closer to normal.

I got home and ran for the shower. In less than fifteen minutes, I was showered and dressed. Impressive. I didn't have any make-up on and my hair was damp, but who cared? Fifteen minutes! I think it was a record. I grabbed my books and barreled down the stairs. I ran smack into Joe Henderson.

"Sorry!" I said. I was out the door without giving him a chance to respond. I didn't look back. If it had been James? I certainly would have stopped – maybe skipped class too. I sighed. I was a bad person. Bad and rude. I'd have to make it up to Joe in some obviously platonic way, but nothing came to mind.

My class was unusually dull. I doodled in the margin of my book. Although we were supposed to prepare a written synopsis or brief for each case, I had mastered the art of the margin brief. My system involved color coding the case with highlighters. Whenever I came to the issue, I would highlight it green. The fact patterns were pink. The holding was yellow. And so on. This system allowed me to look as if I'd memorized the case, when all I needed to do was find the right color to answer the question. Law school is all about looking smarter than you actually are.

When the class ended, I hadn't taken a single note. Pathetic. Instead, my brain had worked out an elaborate dialogue. I'd dazzle James with my brilliance and wit. Sure. The best I could hope for was that he'd be happy with the information I'd gathered. As it turned out, he was very happy.

He said he would follow up with some research into The Lodge's investors. I promised to email the articles I'd found. I also decided to mention the incident with Kendra. He didn't seem to be surprised about the affair. I wondered about John Harding's phone records or bank statements. The police must have reviewed them, although multiple mistresses likely meant multiple accounts. Maybe the police hadn't found everything.

Finally, I told him about the power struggle on the firm's management committee. Blane Ford and Thomas Green had thrown the firm into paralysis. Janice told me about one fight that almost came to blows.

"That's very interesting," he said.

"I think it's to be expected with two potential heirs."

"I wonder if there is something more. You said one of the articles mentioned Thomas Green was also an investor?"

"Yes. There easily might be a connection. I'll nose around some more. Maybe my eavesdropping will pay off again."

"It's not eavesdropping. You're involved in a police investigation."

"I wish you could tell me more about the information you have. I'm working in a vacuum."

"Some things I can't tell you."

"I get it. Super secret police information."

"I'd need the secret handshake."

"I'm all out of secret handshakes."

He laughed. "Good, or I'd have to kill you."

"Are you a spy or a policeman?"

"A spy sounds like a better job some days."

"Come on. This case isn't enough excitement for you?"

"It is if you think reams of paperwork and speaking to reluctant witnesses is exciting," he said sarcastically. And then, "Sorry, I'm just frustrated. We were working for too long with the wrong motive and the wrong suspects. The truth got tangled up."

"I'll do my best to untangle it."

"You're a born detective."

"Do you really see me as Hercule Poirot? You'll be disappointed."

"I'd put your little gray cells up against his any day."

"I'm more the Miss Marple type. And, St. Louis is like a small English village. You always run into the same people."

He laughed again. "Especially if they are addicted to coffee."

"We're an eternal brotherhood."

"Well then, goodbye brother. I'll call you next week."

"Same time? Same station?"

"Yes, Miss Marple. Take care of yourself."

"I will 007." I heard his laughter as I put down the receiver.

CHAPTER 10

Saturday arrived too soon. Holly came over in the afternoon. She said it was to help me get ready. I knew it was to ensure I actually went with her. She looked fabulous, as always. Despite Holly's granola principles, she cleaned up really well. You would never know that the black dress that clung so nicely to her tight curves was made of processed bamboo. Or that the makeup accenting her flawless skin consisted of plant extracts, with no animal by-products of any sort. Of course, it didn't hurt that she was beautiful.

I was a work in progress. The hair was good. The body was coming along. I'd finally bought an accurate scale. I was down five pounds. Plus, some of the jiggle had firmed up. Holly seemed pleased. She helped me pick out a flattering outfit. I even let her apply makeup to my face with abandon.

"Now," she said, "stand up and let me take a look at you."

I stood and did a slow turn. She scanned me critically. "You look great, Liz. You really do."

"Don't sound so surprised. You can feel surprised. That's normal. But it's not polite to let me know how surprised you really are."

"Oh, stop. I think you'll be a hit."

"Even if I don't speak Klingon?"

"I'm sure you'll find someone to translate – it's the language of love."

"Then I'll remain single."

But she was already handing me my coat. We got into her car and drove to pick up Ben. He was standing out front when we pulled up.

"Hi Liz," he said, as he wedged his long legs into the front seat.

"Hi, Ben. How are you?"

"Great." He looked at Holly. "Just great."

I surmised she'd said yes to moving in. Goodbye to the no PDA pledge. We pulled up to the house just as the party started. For most people it would be awkward to arrive that early, but it helped me. It meant I could meet the hosts without the confusion of the crowd. They were another strange couple – both in computer science. I wondered if they knew Mark Paperelli, but I couldn't get a word in edgewise to ask. The couple had fused into a single unit. Each finished the other's sentences. I thought of the Borg. A long night stretched ahead of me.

I stuck to soda and juice. Yet, even with my wits about me, I lost sight of Holly and Ben as the room filled. I didn't have an interest in finding them. I wasn't a voyeur. Instead, I stood by the wall talking to Craig, one of the men Holly had wanted me to meet.

He was a Ph.D. student in neuroscience, working on the genetic analysis of a family with a history of a familial neurodegenerative disease akin to Lou Gehrig's disease. He kept saying he was on the Ford Project, but I wasn't sure what he meant. Normally I am very interested in anything neurological, but Craig's conversation was so full of technical terms, I got lost. I listened with half a brain while the other half watched new arrivals at the door.

A couple walked in. The woman was petite, with dark hair cut in a pageboy style. The man was slight, but even I could tell he was unusually handsome – beautiful really. I turned to Craig, interrupting a long description of a PCR he'd just run.

"Who is the couple who just came in?"

Craig looked startled.

"I'm sorry," I said, giving him an encouraging smile. "I didn't mean to interrupt, but they seem very familiar."

"The guy's an engineering student at UMSL, I think. That's his girlfriend. I've seen them at parties for a couple of years now, but I don't really know them. So, as I was saying, the bands —"

I tuned him out and continued to follow the couple with my eyes. Then it hit me. The girl was Beth. I ran through my mental checklist just to be sure. She looked up and our eyes met. I could see the recognition on her face. She gave me a little nod and then turned away.

Craig continued to ramble. He was talking about funding. Apparently, the project had been privately funded through a local non-profit foundation started by the family, but now the principal investigator sought an R01. I wondered how I could possibly escape. I didn't want to be rude again, but if Craig went into any more detail about grant writing, I was going to scream. I needed a plan. Then, like a guardian angel in a bamboo dress, I saw Holly across the room. She came towards me. Craig droned on about percentages of the "must fund" category.

Holly wasn't above rudeness. She cut him off. "That's very interesting, Craig, but I promised to introduce Liz to other people this evening, if you don't mind." She grabbed my arm and started leading me away. I smiled back in apology.

When we were out of earshot I said, "You abandoned me!"

"I'm sorry. It's just —"

"Don't start. I prefer abandonment to PDA. Where are you taking me?"

"I told you, to meet people."

They were other friends of Ben. Unfortunately, none of them were marginally more interesting than Craig. I learned more than I wanted to know about online war games, particle physics, and C++. I kept wishing I could drink. Drunkenness had to be more fun than this. I thought about how drunk I'd have to be to find these guys exciting. No. I'd tough it out. I asked yet another guy about his avatar and nodded as he went on. And on.

When we finally left at 2:00 a.m., my legs were sore from standing in heels, and I had a splitting headache. Too much painful small talk. At least I wouldn't have a hangover tomorrow. Holly could sense my discouragement.

"We'll find someone for you," she said as she walked me up to the door. Ben waited for us in the car.

"No more matchmaking. I'll just wait for love to find me, okay?"

"Come on," she said. "No pain, no gain."

"You have no concept of the pain involved. And I was worried about Star Trek. Learning Klingon would be exciting compared to the conversations I've had this evening." I shook my head.

"Just get some sleep. Tomorrow is a new day."

"Fine, Pollyanna." I turned and opened the door. "And Holly," I turned back. "I'll help you move. Just let me know when."

"You're too much!" she said, and ran back to the warmth of the car.

I got the email I'd waited for on Monday afternoon. Kat told me that she'd located the IRS publication at SLU. She said SLU had old IRS documents going back at least to the 1960's. The document I wanted was located at the Pius XII Library on the main campus. They were giving her problems about inter-library loan, so it might be easier to go make a copy of it myself. I emailed my supreme gratitude and set out for SLU after class.

Saint Louis University has a lovely city campus that extends farther into the surrounding neighborhoods every year. Like many areas of St. Louis, there was a time when you took your life in your hands to go to parts of the SLU campus. That time was long past. SLU set about an aggressive campaign to stabilize its neighborhood and secure its borders. Its efforts had turned the entire area around.

The change was most noticeable on the campus itself, where courtyards and fountains sprouted up. Bronze statuary of every description appeared overnight – from astronauts to the beloved billiken mascot. A billiken looks like a rotund kewpie doll. I'd been told it was some sort of fairy creature, but the statues of them on campus were more sumo than fairy.

I found a metered space to park just off campus. I got out my backpack and crossed Grand Avenue with a large group of students. Pius XII Library was just inside the main campus, behind Frost Hall. Kat told me that the government documents were in the basement, so I headed down the stairs. It was eerie in the dank of the basement. You could get lost in the high stacks. I heard strange noises and peeped slowly around the last row. Ah, thank goodness. Only a Muslim student doing his daily prayers. Smart kid. He certainly wouldn't be disturbed down there. Government documents are an acquired taste.

I looked and looked until the dashes and slashes all ran together. Finally, I found what I was looking for. Now to find a copier. Photocopies were a legal form of highway robbery. I grumbled as I fed quarter after quarter into the machine. I could have eaten at a really nice restaurant for what I'd paid in copies that year.

My mood lightened as I emerged from the library into the late afternoon sunshine. I decided to take the long way back to my car. I was walking, lost in thought, when I heard someone call my name.

I turned, recognizing the voice. Vince walked towards me.

"Good to see you!" I said as he caught up.

"What are you doing at SLU?"

I explained my IRS publication search. He nodded knowingly. "I'm doing the same thing. I don't know how I'm going to pull my note together."

"What's your topic?"

"A circuit split on a minor ADA interpretation." Although my knowledge of the Americans with Disabilities Act could fit on the head of a pin, all law students knew the meaning of a circuit split. In the search for a note topic, circuit splits were like manna from heaven. If the federal circuit courts disagreed, the Supreme Court was bound to take the issue up at some point. This meant an issue worthy of a first class note. Of course, every other law student knew this as well, so it was a risky business. If someone beat you to publication, you were done.

"Sounds like a fun topic," I said.

"And yours?"

"You don't even want to know — trusts and certain tax code provisions."

He laughed. "You're right, I don't want to know." He paused, standing with his hands in his pockets. "Do you want to grab a coffee or something?"

I looked at my watch. "Sure, I've got time." We turned and started walking back to the law school.

"I've been meaning to call you," he said hesitantly. "I wanted to know if you were going back to G.L.?"

"Despite everything, I am."

"I thought you of all people —"

"I know. I surprised myself." I didn't want to admit that I suffered relatively few long lasting effects from my brush with murder. It made me seem heartless. But, aside from an aversion to the garage that I muscled through every time I went in, I'd settled back to normal. Only a week or so of nightmares and I was good to go. I realized Vince was waiting for more of an explanation.

"Janice Harrington made me an offer I couldn't refuse. Part-time during the year and then associate when I graduate. Working for her exclusively. Like Grant. He told me Tom Green couldn't stand to lose him."

"He would say that. Blane Ford made Beth the same offer."

"Interesting," I said slowly. "I haven't seen her at the office."

"She told me a couple of weeks ago, but I was in a hurry and didn't get a chance to ask more. I don't see her on campus much."

"It's a drive from Clayton."

We reached the cafeteria and Vince was nice enough to buy me a coffee. We found a table by the large windows and settled in. After some small talk about the weather and the need for coffee at this time of day, we ran out of steam. There was a long pause.

"What were you saying about Clayton?" he finally said.

It took me a moment to remember the previous conversation. "Oh, just that Beth lives there so maybe that's why she's not on campus."

"I'd forgotten she lived in Clayton. You've got a good memory."

"Not for anything really useful."

Vince smiled, and I noticed that his eyes crinkled up in the corners. He seemed very boyish.

"So what are your plans?" I said.

"I got an offer from Hart and Klein." Hart and Klein was a medium-size general practice firm downtown with an excellent reputation.

"Congratulations! They're very selective. I assume you will be in their employment group?"

"Thanks. And yes, I will be joining the employment group. I was surprised. One interview was all it took."

"I think every firm is trying to steal G.L.'s best summer associates."

He smiled at the compliment. "I'm surprised another firm hasn't snapped you up."

"You give me too much credit. I did get a couple of offers, but I want to work with Janice."

"Who else is staying at G.L.?"

"Other than Beth and Grant? I don't know. Kelsey hasn't said anything to me." She was the only other summer associate from Washington University. She had kept her distance since the murder. "Stephanie isn't."

"We'll have to have lunch sometime once we're both downtown."

"Sure, but I don't know if they let you out once you're an associate. We'll be like rats in a cage from here forward."

"More like hamsters on a wheel."

I nodded my head. "The honeymoon is officially over. How many billable hours does Hart require?"

"Two thousand a year baseline for bonus and then it ratchets up from there."

"Do they factor in write offs?" Partners would often write time off and not bill certain clients because they thought the number of hours was excessive or because they wanted to curry favor with the clients for other reasons. Sometimes those hours didn't count towards bonus.

"They go by what's listed, not what's actually billed."

"That's good. Janice told me not to worry about the billable hours."

"I can imagine that G.L. wants to hold on to everyone they have. A murder in the building isn't exactly a selling point."

"It isn't," I agreed.

"Doesn't it creep you out? I mean, even a little?"

"Will you say I'm weird if I say no?"

He laughed. "Not to your face."

I laughed with him. "Well, you can say it. I'm not sure how to explain my total lack of fear – even to myself." I looked down at my watch and realized I had an unfed meter.

"I have to go." I stood up. "I've probably already got a parking ticket. Thanks for the coffee."

"Sure. We should do this again sometime. Here, I'll walk you to your car."

"I'm parked over on Lindell," I said, walking briskly. It was a shame to walk so fast on a nice day. The sun hung low in the sky, spreading a golden warmth over everything and everyone. It felt like the kind of day to linger. Vince ambled beside me in companionable silence.

We reached my car with two minutes to spare. I yanked open the door and threw my bag on the front seat. Vince stood beside the car hesitantly. What made him so shy?

"Thanks again for the coffee," I said.

"It was great seeing you, Liz."

I nodded. "You too."

"Maybe we could hang out sometime, or —"

"Sure. That would be great. You have my email?"

"Yes. I'll send you an email."

"Okay."

He smiled.

I wasn't sure. Had he just asked me on a date?

"See you soon then," he said, stepping away from the car.

I got in and waved to him as I pulled away. My mind analyzed every nuance of the conversation. What if he had asked me out? I tried to think of him in that way. He was nice and smart. He got my sense of humor, which was essential. He was reasonably good looking. He had beautiful dark hair. His dark eyes were kind. Sure, I didn't feel that rush of adrenaline when he smiled. I couldn't expect that to happen every day. I'd wait and see.

When I got home, I had a voicemail from Janice. She had another project for me and wondered if I could stop by the office the following day. I called her back. She told me she was meeting friends for lunch as well, and would I like to come? I readily agreed. She mentioned a Maddie and a Susan. Could the Maddie be John Harding's ex-wife?

She was, but not what I expected. Maddie was slender with straight blue-black hair. Her eyes were dark brown with large black pupils. She had a sharp intelligence and a down to earth personality. She lacked the self-absorption of Cheri and the other partners' wives. Instead, she seemed dedicated to her children and her students. A born teacher.

Maddie showed a certain shy hesitation when Janice introduced us. Then I mentioned that my father was a middle school science teacher, and she opened up. Susan was involved in education, but from a different perspective. She was a lawyer who practiced at a medium-sized firm in Clayton specializing in education law. I'd never heard anything about this area of law, so I hoped at least some of my questions were intelligent. It turns out that school districts can get into all sorts of trouble. And Susan had great taste in shoes. Snakeskin stilettos I'd seen on clearance on the Macy's website last summer.

Susan and Maddie met when Maddie formed a foundation to help homeless students. Susan heard about it and volunteered to do some pro bono legal work. Maddie taught fifth grade now, but she still managed to run the foundation in her spare time. As if she had any. Today was an in-service day, so she and Susan planned to do foundation work after lunch. As I listened to Maddie, I wondered how John Harding could have picked Cheri over her. It was pathological.

The sandwich shop where we met was tucked in along Ladue Road. It had a bistro feel with white painted woodwork and a black and white tile floor. The quiche tasted fantastic. I was more than full after one slice, but still had a hard time resisting some delicious brownies. I ordered a cup of coffee instead. The lunch lingered on through two more cups with smart observations and female camaraderie. Janice was lucky to have such friends. I'd do whatever I could to get another invitation to join them.

CHAPTER 11

I dedicated the next two days to my schoolwork and nothing else. I wouldn't let James' blue eyes or even Nick's email intrude on my singular dedication. It was an epic struggle. I felt so exhausted by Thursday afternoon that I gave up and spent all of my European Union jurisprudence class daydreaming. The professor caught me up short once. Fortunately, color coding came to the rescue. I still didn't have anything by way of information for James. That meant that the phone conversation would be brief. I told myself that was a good thing.

I got a call from James on my cell towards the end of class. I'd set it to vibrate, so I hoped no one noticed. I checked the message as soon as I got out. He had new information and wanted to know if he could stop by my apartment that afternoon. It would be quick, he said. I called him back and got voicemail. I did my best impression of a steady voice. After my last class, I could make it home by 5:00.

I wanted to scream with panic. My apartment looked better than it had at the beginning of the semester, but organization was still a major issue. I bit the bullet and skipped my afternoon classes. I'd get the notes from Amelia. Two hours later, the apartment no longer looked like I'd added hoarding to my other neurological quirks. I hadn't shifted so much stuff around since I'd moved in. What would the Hendersons think of the strange noises? I'd apologize later.

I focused on my list. Apartment? Check. Next: self. Then some sort of food – just in case. I rushed to the shower. I tackled my hair with more product than justified given the cost of the bottles. I even unearthed the hair dryer. It was dusty. Holly hadn't been able to get me to use it, but here I was pulling it out for someone not even on the market. Perverse.

I dressed in a way that I hoped was nice, but not forced. That thin pair of fat jeans and a dark pink v-neck top. The color was good, at least. Then, a little subtle lip gloss. Me? Check. I went to the kitchen. I had some soda, and I cobbled together a plate of crackers and cheese, and added grapes and the bag of chips I'd put up on top of the refrigerator so I wouldn't eat too many. I placed the food on the table in a casual way – as if I always left food for random friends who dropped in.

I was so focused on the placement of the food that even though he was late, I jumped when I heard a knock at the door. As I went to get it, I realized that I hadn't gotten my shoes on. Thank goodness Holly had insisted I get a pedicure. My toenails were a neat shade of red. I unlocked the door slowly, taking deep breaths to calm myself.

He stood in the doorway with a manila envelope in his hands. I tried not to concentrate on how hard my heart beat in my chest. He looked tired. There were lines of stress around his eyes.

"Come in, come in," I said as I moved out of the way to let him pass. "Let me take your jacket." He wore the soft leather jacket I'd seen him in on the night of the murder and again at the coffee shop.

"Sure, thanks." He shrugged it off and handed it to me. He walked farther into the living room. I could see that he was taking in all of the details of the apartment. I wondered what he would have said had he seen it before.

"I'll just set your jacket on the bed," I said over my shoulder as I walked into the bedroom. I took a quick look at the label. Kenneth Cole again. He had stayed in the living room, so I couldn't help taking a quick sniff as I set it down. My pulse jumped in a staccato rhythm. I took another deep breath to clear my head. I'd need a paper bag soon.

"This is a great little apartment," he said when I returned.

"Thanks. Please make yourself at home. Do you want to sit in the living room or at the table?" I indicated the small table and chairs that formed my dining room.

He looked around. "Table is probably better. You certainly have a lot of books."

"I'm a reader. You can tell from my TV that I don't watch a lot." I had the oldest and smallest television imaginable. It had one of the first remotes ever made and could only get two channels on the rabbit ears.

"Very unusual for your generation. Aren't you supposed to be wired to the hilt?"

"You speak as if we were so far apart in age."

"Gen X versus Gen Y, I think."

"What's a decade between friends?"

"Nothing at all, except you won't understand my nostalgia for the Brady Bunch or the Dukes of Hazzard."

"Don't worry, I saw them in re-runs."

He laughed. "You always have an answer."

"You haven't spent much time with lawyers if you're surprised at that." I gestured at one of the chairs at the table. "Please have a seat. Can I get you something to drink?" I walked to the kitchen. "I have pop – sorry – soda, juice, milk, water and coffee, of course."

"A soda would be fine, thanks." He followed me.

I stuck my head in the refrigerator. "Coke, Diet Coke, Sprite or Fresca."

"What is Fresca?"

"A diet drink that tastes like grapefruit."

He made a face. "Diet Coke, please."

I grabbed a Diet Coke for him and a Fresca for me. "Can or glass with ice?"

"Can is fine." I handed it to him and we walked back to the table.

"You don't have to feed me, you know," he said, suddenly noticing the spread at his elbow.

"I thought snacks might be appropriate at this time of the day." We sat down.

"You sound like my mom."

"Thanks, I think." I popped open the can of soda.

"My mom just likes to be sure people don't go hungry. It's an Italian thing."

"Is your whole family Italian?"

"You mean both sides?"

I nodded.

"No, actually, my mom's side is Irish – but it's the same thing with food."

"And the Italian part is Northern Italy?"

He nodded, looking at me expectantly. I was momentarily caught by the intensity of his gaze.

"Well, I've been wondering —"

Then I saw him catch my meaning. "About why I have blue eyes?"

"Yes."

"I'm finally on to you. I was a biology major in college, so I do remember my Mendelian genetics. Your deduction is impeccable, as usual. Some of my aunts and uncles on my father's side are very fair."

"I pride myself on my skills."

"I know you do." He ripped open the manila envelope. "Let's see what you make of my deduction. I checked the corporate documents that The Lodge investors filed with the state. There was very little useful information. Then, I remembered that one of the *Post-Dispatch* articles you sent me covered The Lodge groundbreaking. The article didn't include a photo, as you know, but I wondered if maybe a staff photographer had taken some just in case."

He pulled a large photograph out of the envelope. "I thought that if we could identify who was at the groundbreaking, we would know who the initial investors were." I felt my insides churn uncomfortably and my breath stick in my throat. He continued to pull images out of the envelope. "So I went through the *Post-Dispatch's* file photos and found four. I had them blow them up. I thought you might recognize a few people."

I felt like I was on the high hill of a roller coaster, just a second before free fall. I didn't want to tell him this way. I didn't want to tell him any way. I took a deep breath and let myself go. "I can't help you," I said softly.

"What?" His tone was incredulous. It got my hackles up. I thought about all of the time I'd wasted hanging out at the firm, trying to gather information. Time I didn't have. I could feel my cheeks flush.

"I'm afraid I can't help you," I said. I didn't bother to hide my annoyance.

My tone must have pushed him over the edge. He looked at me with such anger and frustration, I had to look away. "What?" He said again with deadly clarity. His jaw clenched.

"I can't do it," I said, trying to stay calm, but failing miserably.

"You don't understand anything, do you?" His lip curled derisively. I'd unleashed something. He couldn't contain his agitation. He stood up and started pacing back and forth. "You have no idea, do you, how important this investigation is to me? To my career – to everything!" He was yelling now.

I sat there, bubbling over with anger and shock. I'd never seen him upset. I had to grab the table to keep myself from yelling back at him. My knuckles were white.

"You've no idea how hard it is for me, do you? What do you think? I'm the average police officer? You said it yourself, Liz. I don't fit. I've never fit. Some days it's like banging my head against a brick wall. Over and over again. But you don't understand that, do you? You sit there with your perfect logic, your perfect answers."

I opened my mouth to speak but nothing came out. I closed it and swallowed hard. I willed myself not to cry.

He didn't look over. "They're all watching me, waiting for me to screw up. Just waiting. I've got people everywhere telling me what to think, what to do. The Major Case Squad is still on it, for Chrissake!

And the three other detectives? They all think I can't hack it!" He paused and looked at me. "You know why I'm even on the case? You want to know why I got assigned to the biggest case of my career?"

I didn't say a word.

"Luck, Liz. Dumb luck! I happened to be down the street when the call came in. That's how I'll ever get promoted – fucking luck!"

He stopped pacing for a moment, and seemed to try to pull himself together. His voice was dead calm again. I felt goose bumps up and down my arms. "And the one piece of good luck I have – meeting you – having access to the information I need and what? You can't help me. Why?"

I swallowed again, "You don't understand, James —"

"I understand. You can't be bothered anymore."

"No!" I kicked the chair out from under me as I stood. I turned on him with the full force of my fury. "I can't help you because I can't recognize anyone in photos!"

"Can't?" He sneered. My hand itched to slap him.

"Damn you – I can't recognize my own face! How am I going to recognize anyone else's?" I took a deep breath. I was on the edge of hysteria.

"What?" He sounded shocked. Good. I felt like shocking him with the whole story. I was done. Done!

"It's called prosopagnosia. Go look it up if you think I'm lying."

"I don't understand —"

"There's a lot you don't understand and you never will. It's a neurological defect." I watched this sink in. "Yes, defect, James. De-fect! I had a brain tumor and this is what I live with, day in and day out." I felt my voice rising uncontrollably. "I can't recognize you – my parents – my sister – anyone. I see a stranger in the mirror every morning. A stranger, James – only the stranger is me!"

I looked in is eyes and burst into tears. I couldn't take the mixture of fear and pity I saw there. It was humiliating. I ran to my room and slammed the door. I crumpled on my bed and sobbed. This evening could not have gone worse. I hoped he would just leave and I'd never have to face him again. He could finish the investigation on his own. I was crying so hard, that I didn't hear the bedroom door open. In fact, I didn't notice anything until I felt a hand on my shoulder and the bed sink down as he sat beside me.

He pulled me to him and I was too worn out to resist. "I'm sorry, Liz. So, so sorry."

"I don't want your pity," I said between sobs. In all of the fantasies I'd had of James in my room with his arm around me, sobbing uncontrollably was not part of the picture. I would have laughed if I could only stop crying.

"It's not pity," he said. "It's awe."

"Sure." I was not in the mood for lies. I leaned over to the bedside table and grabbed a tissue. I could feel my nose running and my eyes puffing shut. Wonderful. I took a deep breath and tried to steady my racing heart. After several long minutes, I finally got the sobs to hiccups and then to sniffs.

James said nothing. He just waited, his arm round my shoulder and his eyes watching me intently. When I had managed to calm down, he said, "So this was the deep dark secret?" His voice was so tender and sweet that I could feel my heart breaking in two inside my rib cage. I silently cursed myself. Then I cursed him.

I nodded and sniffed into the tissue. He put his arm down. "You could have trusted me, you know."

"I don't usually announce I'm a freak over coffee."

"You are not a freak. That's the last thing I would have thought." He paused and then said, "You are the most amazing woman. You have no idea."

"Ha!" I said bitterly. "I can't do what every other human on the planet can do. Don't tell me I'm special." I sat up a little straighter. "Give me a moment."

I got up and walked into the bathroom. I washed my face and surveyed the damage. I didn't think I could look much worse. I decided not to worry. What did it matter anyway? I was a fool.

When I walked back into the bedroom, he was still sitting there, watching me. I looked him in the eye.

"Do you mind if we talk?" he said. He glanced around and realized that the only place to sit was on the bed. "We can sit in the living room if that would be more comfortable."

"I don't think my comfort matters anymore." I climbed up on the bed and sat facing him with my bare feet tucked up under me. He kicked off his shoes and did the same. We faced each other for what seemed like an eternity but may have been only a minute or two. I felt crushed and defeated. My shoulders slumped.

Finally he said, "I want to apologize again. I shouldn't have said —"

I put up my hand tiredly. "You didn't know."

"But I didn't let you tell me, either." I opened my mouth to speak, but he stopped me. "Let me finish. What I'm going to say needs to be said. You are not responsible for finding John Harding's killer. I am. I have to figure this out and you are free to help me or not. The choice is yours. I won't think less of you if you don't want to have anything to do with the investigation or me. Especially now. I've behaved really badly and I know it." He gave me a look that was so humble my heart would have broken again if it were not already in two pieces laying sadly at the bottom of my chest.

He took a deep breath. "Please forgive me."

I looked down. I couldn't resist him. I ran the litany of curses over again in my head. He waited patiently for an answer. "All right, I'll help you."

"Will you forgive me?"

I told him the sad truth. "I've already forgiven you."

"Thank you. I know I don't deserve it, but thank you."

I suddenly felt very shy. I didn't know what to say.

After a long pause, he said, "Can I ask you a question?"

"I have no secrets anymore."

"How does it work?"

"My brain?"

"How can you not recognize faces, but notice every other detail?"

"I capture all of the details, but my brain just can't fit the pieces together to form that instant recognition everyone else has."

"And photographs?"

"Most photos aren't detailed enough for me. They're static. I can't see facial ticks or recognize smells or how someone walks or how they stand. Context is missing, too. I have trouble if people show up where I don't expect them to be."

"Is that why you didn't recognize me at the coffee shop?"

"You caught that." I looked down. "I recognized your voice, but it took me a moment to figure out that you were at the door."

"What made you know it was me?"

I looked up and gazed into his deep blue eyes. "Your eyes," I said simply.

"That was it?"

"Then I recognized the leather jacket and the distinctive wave your hair has. You have a certain way of standing. Very straight in the back. You don't slouch like your brother does. You also unconsciously run your index finger over the ridges of your thumbnail. Do you want me to go on?"

"I get the picture. But I'm curious about one thing. You mentioned smell. What do you mean by that?"

"I can tell people apart by their smell."

"Your sense of smell." He nodded. "I knew it was good, but I didn't know it was that good."

"Everyone has their own distinctive smell even if they don't wear perfume or cologne. I never forget a smell, so it's easy to recognize someone once I get close enough."

"So you could tell someone apart from their brother or sister – even though they have similar chemistry?"

"Sure, I could tell you apart from your brother with my eyes closed. I could also tell that you were related. As you say, people in the same family tend to have similar chemistry."

"This is probably the strangest question I've ever asked, but I'm too curious not to know. What do I smell like?"

The evening had somehow gotten even more awkward. I decided to ignore it. What did I have to lose?

"Come over here." I motioned to the spot next to me. He scooted over so that we were side by side. I could smell him where he had been sitting before, but I needed a really close assessment to analyze it in detail. That's what I told myself.

"I've never tried to describe someone's smell before, so give me a minute." I leaned in so my head almost rested on his shoulder. I inhaled deeply, letting his fragrance fill my senses. I felt the telltale jump of my pulse and closed my eyes. If I had dared, I could have kissed him gently on the smooth soft skin behind his ear. I wondered what that would feel like. My mind raced in a thousand fruitless daydreams. I tried to tamp them down, but they wouldn't be smothered. So I concentrated on identifying the fragrance.

"Well?" he said slowly.

I pulled my head away. I didn't know how much longer I could remain bottled up. He smelled incredibly good. "Your smell is earthy and sweet," I said, "like cloves and sea salt."

"So far so good."

"There is also an overlay of Eternity cologne and a hint of Ivory soap."

"Very impressive."

I shifted my body so that I faced him again. Distance was a blessing.

"Why didn't I meet you years ago?" he said. "I've missed so much. It's like a new world."

I looked down at my hands. I'm sure he didn't mean that the way I wished he would. I needed to move this conversation away from the shoals or the undercurrent of longing was going to drown me. I decided that it was my turn for some answers.

"I have a couple of questions, if you don't mind."

"Anything you want."

"What is going on with this investigation? I've read every article there is on the subject and you're never mentioned. Why?"

"Two reasons. One is I'm low down in the pecking order. I shouldn't have been assigned to such a high profile case. I haven't been in homicide that long and most of my colleagues don't know what to make of me. They don't trust me. I only got involved because, as I told you when I was a ranting lunatic, I happened to be close by when the call came. I was on the Landing having dinner with a friend."

The Landing is the cobblestone street area down by the river. It's located behind the G.L. building and has various restaurants and bars.

"And the second reason?"

"My last name. The department is uncomfortable with publicity. They've told me that my family connections might make me a target. I don't know. Other officers think I've pulled connections to get where I am, but the truth is I have to work twice as hard as everyone else."

"You could try to be more inconspicuous," I said.

"How?"

"I don't know. Shop at Walmart maybe."

"I don't think it would help, and," he gave me a mischievous smile, "I would hate it."

"I've noticed you're a fashionista."

"Can that term even apply to a man?"

"Fashionisto?"

"Good try."

"So the other detectives are running the show?"

"Yes, and the Major Case Squad is still involved."

"And that's why you waited months to contact me?"

"Yes. I told you before. Everyone started with the theory that this was a random street crime. A robbery gone bad. No one took me seriously when I suggested it was someone at the firm. It was only when a guy from the Major Case Squad proposed the theory that anyone gave it a second thought. That was in September when we already had a robbery suspect. We'd picked him up on a parole violation and were holding him."

"How did he become a suspect?"

"He tried to use one of the victim's credit cards. He said he'd found it on the ground. We didn't find the wallet."

"Did he say where he found the credit card? Or is that confidential?"

"He's since been released, so I don't know that it matters. He claimed he found it on the floor of a metro station."

"The one by the firm?"

"Yes."

"So now they all think someone at the firm did it?"

"That's one theory. There are others, including that it was a contract hit."

"Mafia?"

"Maybe – or a business deal gone wrong."

"But you decided to call me."

"I'm convinced it was someone at the firm. It's the only thing that makes sense."

"Does anyone else know about my involvement?"

"I've been jealously guarding you as my secret informant. I keep hoping I can solve the case ahead of the others. I know, it's selfish, but it would make my career." He sighed. "I should be talking to you about justice and here I'm talking career advancement."

"Maybe the two aren't mutually exclusive."

"I hope not." He gave me that mischievous grin again.

"Look, I will help you as much as I can, but you are going to have to trust me, too."

"I do."

"Then I may need to get someone else involved."

"Who?"

"Janice Harrington. She's a partner on the management committee. She'll have access to information I can't get. And she is friends with Maddie Harding, John's ex-wife."

"You think she would help?"

"I know she would."

"Can we trust her?"

"I trusted her with my own secret."

"Oh."

"She didn't even bat an eye."

"Better than my reaction," he said ruefully.

"Yes, but I told you that I forgive you."

"I still feel terrible."

"Well, be my guest, but I won't mention it again."

"You're a good person, Liz."

"I try." I felt my stomach rumble and looked over at the clock. It said 7:03. "Are you hungry, by any chance?"

"I'll take you to dinner."

"Not the way I'm looking right now."

He started to argue, but I cut him off. "I know my eyes are so puffy I look like a boxer who has taken blows to the head, so don't tell me I look fine."

"Only a few blows."

"Let's order in," I said.

He nodded in agreement. "Chinese? Italian? I think there is even a Thai place that delivers."

"Would you be offended if I skipped Italian and went for Chinese?"

"There is no dishonor to the family name in ordering Chinese."

"Good. I'll get a menu." I clambered down off the bed and walked into the kitchen.

James followed behind me. I pulled a bunch of menus from a drawer until I found the one I wanted.

"There is a place down by the Amoco sign that delivers," I said.

He nodded. "I know that place."

There was a gas station nearby with a humungous Amoco sign on the roof. The sign seemed as big as the station itself. It looked so out of place and had been there so long that people in the neighborhood used it as a landmark. The sign remained even after BP bought Amoco, either out of nostalgia or because it was too big to move.

We sat down at the kitchen table and reviewed the menu. We came to easy agreement over an order of beef with broccoli, moo-shu pork, and chicken fried rice. James said he was really hungry, so we decided on an order of crab rangoon as well. He called in the order and insisted on paying. I didn't argue. Forgiveness is one thing, picking up the check is another.

We sat in companionable silence for several minutes, eating grapes and waiting for the food to come. He began to shift in his chair.

I said, "So what else do you want to know? I can tell you have some question on the tip of your tongue but are afraid to ask."

"Many actually."

"Try me."

"When did you realize you were different?"

I thought about that for a moment. "It was a slow process. I didn't know any better for a long time."

"What made you realize it?"

"I get confused in certain situations – you've seen that. As time went on, that happened more and more until I put the pieces together. Later, a doctor gave me a name for what I was experiencing."

"Prosop —"

"Prosopagnosia," I said.

"It's a tongue twister."

"A strange name for a strange condition."

"And this was in Marshfield?"

"The diagnosis?"

He nodded.

"Yes. I'm surprised you remembered the name – but wait, I'm forgetting – you should have a dossier with my whole life story in it, shouldn't you?"

"No."

"What kind of detective are you?"

"Not a very good one. You weren't under suspicion so there was no need to do an extensive background investigation."

"Logical, but disappointing. When you knew I was working part-time at the firm, I thought my life was an open book."

"That was an accident. I called the firm because I expected you to be there. I didn't double-check my notes and didn't remember you were still in law school. A secretary told me you worked part-time and were expected in later that afternoon."

"So you don't know everything about my childhood?"

"That's why I'm asking. Where is Marshfield?"

"Two hours outside of Madison in the center of the state. But tell me, haven't you heard of the famous Marshfield Clinic?"

"Should I have heard of it?"

"We'd like to think that everyone has heard of it, but if you don't live within a hundred mile radius, there is no reason you should. It is a giant medical system that reaches throughout central and northern Wisconsin. It's where I got all of my treatment. State of the art medicine in the middle of nowhere."

"What do your parents do in this town?"

"My mom's a nurse in oncology and my dad is a middle school science teacher in the Marshfield District."

"How big is Marshfield?"

"Under twenty thousand, but because of the Clinic you couldn't throw a stone without hitting a doctor or a nurse. It can be very strange to see some doctor with whom you've recently discussed the most intimate details of your life suddenly appear next to you at the high school football game in a sweatshirt and ratty tennis shoes."

"And I assume, like all small towns, everyone knows everyone else's business?"

"Of course."

"It sounds delightful," he said, half serious and half sarcastic.

"It's not bad. Most of my childhood was pretty happy – and the schools are first rate. Plus, there is something about a long winter. I think about the winters when it gets to be a hundred degrees and ninety-nine percent humidity in St. Louis. I like winter. People need each other when the cold could stop your heart in three minutes flat."

"Again, you make it sound so inviting."

"It's hard to explain."

"You mentioned your sister – do you see her often? She's in Madison, you said?"

"Yes. I see her as often as I can, or as often as we can stand each other."

"You don't get along?"

"It's not really that. She's over six years younger than me. And she's different. I told you, I am the responsible one. I don't understand her sometimes." I paused, considering the matter. "She's not very focused."

"I think that's the role of the second child."

"You, for example?"

"Definitely. I spent a year wandering around Europe with no future plans."

"You did?" He seemed the last person to strap on a backpack and go unwashed through the length and breadth of Europe.

There was a knock at the door. James jumped up. "That will be the Chinese food." He paid for the food and brought the cartons to the table. I got some more soda from the refrigerator and some napkins. I also grabbed silverware. I'd never learned how to use chopsticks.

He opened the cartons and put them in logical order – wrappers and hoisin sauce next to the moo-shu, plain rice next to the beef and broccoli, chicken fried rice and crab rangoon on their own. It was exactly how I would have placed them.

"Forgot the plates," I said. As I walked back with the plates in my hand, I saw that James was setting the table properly.

"Your mother taught you well," I remarked.

"We're a well mannered family." He gave me a sly look. "Most of the time."

I felt at ease with him again. There was something about his personality. Had I met him in any other circumstance, I would have said we were kindred spirits. As it was, maybe we could be friends. He couldn't help that he loved another woman. I should try to overlook it.

But then, what was he doing here with me? I understood the pity. He wanted to make nice. But wouldn't his fiancée wonder where he was? It was close to 8:00. Maybe she knew about me. She would think he was pursuing the investigation. Certainly nothing had happened that should make her worry. And nothing would happen. Anyway, there was no way to broach the subject politely. How do you ask a grown man if he is allowed to stay out this late?

"A penny for your thoughts?" he said.

"They're not worth that."

"Then let's eat. I'm starving."

We sat down and he picked up a packet of chopsticks and handed them to me. "No thank you. I never got the hang of those."

"Really? You seem to have mastered every other trick in the book."

"I'm a one trick pony."

"I'll show you." He pulled them out of the packet and broke them apart. "See, the key is to keep one fixed and grab the food with the other." He demonstrated the technique. "Here, you try it." He handed them to me.

I wasn't very successful. He showed me again by placing his fingers on mine. I got the usual jolt at his touch. He let go of my hand. I tried to work the sticks but finally resorted to a fork.

I wanted a subject I could trust myself with, so I asked about his year in Europe. What started out as a travelogue ended in a series of hilarious stories – each one better than the last. I had to time my bites so that I wouldn't choke on my food. He'd gone everywhere, including Andorra, and had seen most of the things I'd only read about.

He was just telling me about how he had nearly been picked up by the Italian police – the culmination of a long story involving the loss of all of his money, a fellow backpacker named Sven, and a case of mistaken identity – when he caught sight of his watch. The carriage suddenly turned into a pumpkin. "I should be going. I didn't realize it was so late."

I looked at my watch. It read 10:13 – not late for a law student, but late enough for someone who had work to get up for – and a fiancée.

"I'm sorry," I said. "I shouldn't have kept you. I didn't think that we'd been talking so long."

"What do you have to be sorry for? The evening has been wonderful."

I lifted my eyebrows.

"Well, the second part has been wonderful – and the first part was all my fault."

"I won't argue that point."

We stood up. I was stiff from sitting so long. He started to gather items from the table. "And I'm leaving you with a mess."

"Don't worry, I'll take care of it. You just run along to," I hesitated, "to wherever you need to go."

He insisted on helping me clear the table. When we were done, I walked with him to the door. At the last minute, we both remembered his jacket. I ran back to the bedroom to get it and held it to my nose for a second or two before I returned with it to the living room. I handed it to him at the door. He slid his arms in and zipped it up.

I said, "Have a pleasant evening."

"I already have. Take care of yourself, Liz. I'll call you soon."

I stood in the doorway, still in a fog, listening to him leave. I couldn't make myself move. I heard the rattle of the chain on the Henderson's door. Mrs. Henderson shuffled out. She called up, "Liz? Are you okay up there?"

"Fine, Mrs. Henderson."

"I thought I heard shouting earlier this evening, but Floyd said it was just the TV."

"I'm fine. No need to worry."

"Who was that nice young man who just came down the stairs?" Someone had looked through the keyhole.

"Just my friend James."

"I haven't seen him around before," she said suspiciously.

"He hasn't been here before, but I've known him for awhile. He's a policeman." That should calm any fears that I'd taken to inviting undesirable men over to my apartment.

"Oh, good."

"I'm going to go to sleep now. Good night, Mrs. Henderson."

"Good night, Liz." I heard the door shut and the latch move into place. I closed and locked my own door.

I walked slowly to my kitchen and put the food away. Then I went to my bedroom and lay down on the bed. I threw off my jeans, but didn't bother about the rest. I was physically exhausted. As I snuggled under the covers, I noticed that the smell of his presence still lingered in the room. I shut my eyes tight. I could see him sitting there beside me – feel my head on his shoulder – the soft skin of his neck just brushing my lips.

CHAPTER 12

I slept so long the next morning that I missed two classes. I'd forgotten to set my alarm the night before. I fought distraction as I showered and dressed. If I didn't stop daydreaming, I'd miss a third class. We were getting close to final exams. I didn't want to take a risk. Final exams in law school are always essay and they are always the entire grade for the semester. Thanksgiving was a week away and my exams all fell in the second week of December. This meant I got them over quickly, but it also meant that Thanksgiving was a wash.

Aside from the exams, our final note outline was due the first week of December. I'd made good progress the last couple of days – despite distractions – but the thing still needed work. I decided to dedicate myself to law school for the entire day. No detective work, no nothing. Even an email from Vince couldn't sway me. I wrote back that I was up to my eyeballs in work for the next few weeks. He wrote me that he was in the same boat and maybe we could meet after my finals. I agreed. I had a week to kill in St. Louis before I flew back to Marshfield for the Christmas break. There would be plenty of time to hang out with Vince and to get my head on straight about James. And Nick. I still hadn't answered his email.

I felt very virtuous as I attacked my class work and my note. If I could just keep it up for a couple of days I might be on top of something. Unfortunately, I decided to watch the Lehrer News Hour while I ate some reheated Chinese food. My TV only got NBC and PBS. I put my feet on the rickety coffee table, which is a terrible habit I only indulge in when there is no one there to see me. My foot brushed against something. James had left the envelope with the photographs on the table. I told myself to wait until after dinner to look at them, but I couldn't contain my curiosity. After finishing half the food, I opened it up.

I spread the photos out. They'd been blown up to 8 by 11 size. Group shots – a bunch of men in suits standing around a shovel with a bow on top. I stared at them, looking for any significant detail. The man holding the shovel had snakeskin boots that seemed vaguely familiar. I'd certainly seen them before.

I sat back and mulled it over. Someone at the firm owned those boots, but whom? I tried to call up the memory associated with them. Someone standing in John Harding's office – not Thomas Green, but someone who worked for him. And then I had it. A young partner named Shane David. Okay, so I had one name. But there was only one person who knew the firm inside and out and would be able to identify each and every attorney in those photographs – Janice Harrington.

James had given me permission and so there was no time like the present to consult her. I looked at my watch. If I called now, I might just catch her before she left work. I was in luck. She picked up the phone.

"Janice, it's Liz."

"Hello. What are you up to?"

"Do you have plans this evening?"

"Other than work and more work? No. Why?"

"Do you mind if I come by? This is sort of work related."

"Don't tell me you've had another offer?"

"No," I said quickly, "nothing like that. But I can't explain it over the phone. I wouldn't ask if it weren't important."

"Of course, I'll be in my office."

"And if anyone asks, would you mind saying that I'm just coming to get a new project?"

"This gets more interesting. I've got the story down. But hurry. Now I'm really curious."

I threw on a pair of dress slacks, a thin sweater, a pair of flats and a short jacket. I put my winter coat on over this ensemble and ran for the car. Joe Henderson stood in the doorway.

"Liz!"

"Joe, how are you?" I tried to sound pleasant rather than irritated.

"Oh fine. Are you okay? My mom said she heard you and your friend arguing yesterday."

"I'm fine, it was just a small disagreement. We worked it out in a couple of minutes. I appreciate the concern." I set my teeth in a smile.

He seemed about to speak, but I cut him off. "I'm afraid I don't have time to chat – I just got a call to go into work."

"Oh." He stepped aside to let me pass. "Just wanted to make sure you were okay."

"Thanks." I walked by him. "Take care, Joe."

I got to G.L. and parked my car in the garage. As usual, I took the elevator up to the offices. The receptionist was still packing up her things to go. She waved at me and I walked on to Janice's office.

Janice looked up from her desk and smiled. "What have you come in all this secrecy to tell me?"

I shut the door behind me.

"So it really is top secret?"

I nodded.

"Well, out with it – the suspense is killing me."

I sat in one of the client chairs that faced her desk and unbuttoned my coat.

"I have been recruited by the police to assist with the investigation of John Harding's murder." I looked at her face. She was so stunned she didn't have words. "I've been working with Detective Paperelli —"

"Wait." Janice stopped me. "I haven't gotten over the first part. You're a police informant?"

"No, not like that." I shook off my coat and stood up. "I can tell that you have had a long day. One that involved speaking with one, maybe two lottery winners. You haven't eaten yet and you didn't pick up the dry cleaning for at least two weeks, and —" I walked behind the desk. "Yes, your back has been killing you. All in all I can see why you might not be taking this well."

"How do you do that?"

"Simple. I know you've talked to lottery winners because you always chew your bottom lip – otherwise you'd scream at them over the phone. Your lip is swollen and a little red. You haven't eaten because I can hear your stomach growling. You haven't been to the dry cleaners because you're wearing that blue pantsuit you dislike but can't bring yourself to get rid of. You only wear it as a last resort.

Finally, your back hurts because you are wearing flats today. You always try that, but it doesn't usually do much good."

"So the point is?"

"Detective Paperelli thought my skills might be useful."

"Because —"

"Because he thinks the murder is connected to the firm somehow." I paused. "And frankly, so do I."

I returned to the chair and sat down. She looked at me cautiously. Finally she said, "I've thought the same thing. John made a lot of enemies."

"I need your help. You know this firm inside and out. I can't do this alone."

"You need my help?"

"Detective Paperelli gave me permission to come to you."

"That name is familiar. Is he connected with the pizza?"

"That's his family."

"And instead of hanging out with the family money he's working as a homicide detective?"

"Yes."

"He needs more help than I can give him."

I laughed. "He likes the work. It's like a puzzle."

"Except that this one has him stumped."

"Basically."

"Okay, what are the active theories so I know what to look for?"

"You mean you'll help me?" I said.

"Sure. It will be a change of pace. The law is a dull master sometimes."

"Don't tell me that."

"Oh no, you're right – ignore what I just said. The law is always fascinating."

"Well, one theory involves business dealings with other attorneys at the firm. Some attorneys, including maybe John Harding, invested in The Lodge development."

"Is that that sprawling thing beyond Boone's Crossing?"

"Yes." I repeated the conversation I had overheard in the library.

"That does sound fishy. What else have you got?"

I told her about the newspaper clippings and then pulled out the photographs. "Detective Paperelli thought I could help him identify any firm attorneys in the photos. But, as you know, I couldn't help him much." I pointed to the man with the shovel. "I know that is Shane David because I recognize the boots."

She laughed. "He looks like a complete idiot – but he wears them just the same."

"Can you recognize anyone else?"

"Sure. That's Tom Green, that's Mark Keegan, that's Joe Smiley, and right there is Terrance Moore." She picked up one of the group photographs and examined it closely. She put it down and pointed to a figure in the back. "And there is John Harding." I jotted the names down on the photo. Janice sat back and said, "I don't recognize anyone else, so they must be people from the development company."

"I wonder if someone isn't skimming firm funds to shore up The Lodge," I said.

"It would be hard to hide that from the management committee."

"Even if everyone is fighting for control of the firm? Or if members of the management committee are involved?"

Janice thought for a moment. "Every meeting is so contentious that we rarely get down to business. But wouldn't the accounting firm catch something like that?"

"What if the attorney managing the accounts is involved, or if the money is moved around so much that the accountant doesn't have the whole story? If the accountants only get certain information, they can only draw certain conclusions."

"True."

"My father used to say about computers – 'garbage in, garbage out.' If you start with bad information —"

"You will make bad decisions."

"Right."

"Let me think about this a moment."

I waited quietly in my chair.

"Do you have anywhere to be this evening?"

"No. I was planning to get some school work done. That's it."

She smiled. "Good. What would you say to a little breaking and entering?"

I opened my eyes wide. "Janice, whatever do you have in mind?"

"Nothing illegal – well – nothing really illegal. If there is something going on around here, I want to know about it."

"It's your duty as a member of the management committee."

"I like how you think."

"So what are we breaking into?"

"The file room next to John Harding's office," she said.

"Is anyone moving into Harding's office?"

"They are still fighting over it."

"Typical," I said.

"I know. Men are like dogs sometimes – they all have to mark their territory."

"So what is the plan?"

"First we have to get the keys. Tom Green and Blane Ford both have a set, but Blane is out today, so that leaves Tom."

"None of the other partners have a set of keys to the file room?" I said.

"Crazy, isn't it? This place drives me to drink sometimes."

"I'm not above picking Tom Green's pockets, but I don't think I can do it with any degree of skill."

"You have a good criminal mind, but we won't have to resort to that. It just involves a little cunning." She outlined the plan.

"Now that's style," I said with admiration.

"You don't get anywhere in this business without some chutzpah. Are you ready?"

I took off my jacket. "As ready as I'll ever be."

I headed down the stairs and got into position in the secretarial station just in front of Tom Green's office. He didn't see me as I crouched down. He was talking with Grant about a project. I noticed that Tom had taken his jacket off and it hung off the back of the chair. Good. He worked his finger around his shirt collar as he sat at the desk. By some quirk of the building code, the temperature controls for both the attorney offices and the secretarial stations were located on the wall behind the secretarial desks. I peered at the thermometer, which read 75 degrees. I turned it all the way up to 85. Grant left and I sent Janice a text message, "allclr."

Within a minute I heard her voice over the intercom, only it didn't sound like her at all. In fact, you couldn't even tell if it was male or female. "Paging Mr. Ghebish. I repeat, paging Mr. Ghebish." Paging the long deceased founder of the firm was a distress call. Whenever someone heard it they were supposed to come to the front desk to provide assistance.

Tom Green got up quickly and ran from his office down the hallway toward the stairway. I leapt out from the secretarial station as soon as I heard him start up the stairs. The hallway was clear. I dashed into his office and reached my hand into the inside pocket of his sport coat. I found the keys just as Janice said I would. My hand shook as I pulled them out and shoved them down into my pants pocket. I moved silently to the doorway. Someone was coming – one of the associate attorneys. I had an idea.

I got down on all fours, pretending to look for something in the pile of the carpet. He walked up. "What are you doing?"

"Wait," I held up my hand. He stopped where he was. "Don't move. I've lost a contact. I felt it fall out as I was running to the lobby." I felt around with both hands.

"Can I help?" He hitched up a pant leg as if he were about to crouch down. "No, no," I said. "They're disposable ones, so if I can't find it, I'll just get another one." I stood up. "No dice. Thanks."

"I'm going to see what's happening at reception. You coming?"

I nodded, holding my head as if my depth perception were off kilter. "Meet you there." As I hurried down the hall, I met Chester walking slowly in the opposite direction.

"Elizabeth!" I stopped. "How's that mouse working out for you?"

"Umm. Best mouse I've ever had. Hands down." I started walking again.

"Oh, okay. I'll let you go." His voice was strangely wistful. I felt a spasm of guilt. My parents had not brought me up to be rude. I turned at the end of the hall, ready to apologize, but Chester didn't see me. He was ducking furtively into Tom Green's office.

The reception area was filled with bewildered attorneys. I noticed Grant in a corner and went up to him. "What happened?"

"False alarm. Someone must be playing a joke."

"Some joke."

"I know," he said with irritation. "I was in the middle of something important." I caught myself before I did an eye roll. Grant sounded serious.

"Quiet everyone!" Tom Green shouted. The chatter died down to a low hum. "There is no emergency. Please go back to your work. And whoever did this," he eyed the group suspiciously, "it is not a joke. There will be serious consequences if this happens again."

The chatter resumed. I watched Grant worm his way through the crowd to speak to Tom. There wasn't a discreet way to eavesdrop, so I went to the ladies room to fix my supposed contact, and then wandered casually back to Janice's office. I shut the door behind me.

"So?" she said.

I removed the key ring and jingled it in front of her.

"Good girl! Now, I'm going to write down the address of a hardware store in Olivette."

Olivette is a suburb that was once part of the outer ring of the city before the massive expansion of the county even farther westward. The 1950's ranch homes there were giving way to the large homes on small lots so pervasive during the housing rush.

"Why a hardware store in Olivette?" I said.

"I went to high school with the manager. He can copy any key exactly and he won't ask questions. Just tell him I sent you. I've lost more keys over the years, and I'm always coming in for extras."

"Are we going to slip the real keys back in Tom Green's pocket?"

"That would be too obvious. We'll throw them under the desk so it looks like they fell out. He never leaves before 7:00, so you have time to get there and back, even with traffic. Did you turn up the heat?"

"As high as it would go."

"Good. He won't try to put his jacket back on."

"What if he goes out and turns the thermostat down?"

"The offices don't cool down that fast. He'll be nice and toasty until he goes home. Now scoot."

She pushed the paper with the address across the desk at me. I grabbed it and my coat and hurried out the door. I was in luck. The traffic was light and I reached the hardware store in twenty-five minutes. The door clanged as I walked in. It was small but very well stocked, like the stores back home where the salespeople actually used what they were selling. If only there were a section dedicated to deer hunting. I saw a sign at the back that said "Keys Made," so I went to that counter. I knocked at a small sliding glass partition. A fiftyish woman pulled the glass back and said, "Can I help you?"

"Yes." I dug the ring of keys from my purse. There were about twenty in all – each one a different shape and size. Many seemed like filing cabinet keys, but some were a mystery. "I need copies made, please. Janice Harrington told me to ask for Darryl."

"Thank goodness. That's too many for me to make." She leaned over to the intercom microphone. "Darryl, you're wanted in keys – ASAP."

Within a minute, a pleasant looking man ambled over to the counter. He seemed friendly and easygoing.

The woman said, "This young lady needs about twenty keys made." He looked at me in surprise.

"Janice Harrington sent me," I said quickly.

"Oh." His face lit up with a smile. "That makes sense. Give me the ring and let me see what I can do."

I handed him the ring and he flipped through the keys methodically one by one. "Okay, give me twenty minutes."

"That fast?"

"You can time me if you like." He had a twinkle in his eye. "I've been doing this since I was fifteen, so I should be good by now."

"Wow."

"Go have a look around. I'll call you when I have them bagged and ready."

I walked back through the potting supplies. There appeared to be no end to the gadgets needed to take care of houseplants. I had one spider plant that started life as a few sad leaves in a glass of water. It now overflowed the pot. It didn't seem to matter how much or how little I watered it. One had to admire that kind of resilience.

I walked to the end of the aisle and turned the corner into tools. Although I could recognize a hammer and a wrench, other things defied explanation. You really get a sense of your own uselessness standing in the tool aisle. I knew how to parse a phrase or research a point of law, but I didn't know how to do anything with such tools. In rural Wisconsin, knowing how to do things is a positive virtue. The cold forces dependence on others, but conversely, it forces hard-nosed self-reliance.

My ever-practical mom had drilled certain basic skills into me. I could prepare a meal that did not involve a can or a box. I could bake a birthday cake or a pie. I knew what rhubarb was and how to cook it. The important things. My friends here at school thought I was strange to begin with, so I never mentioned that I could sew, knit and crochet. That would have been too much.

I wandered around for exactly nineteen minutes before a voice on the intercom announced, "Would the customer who ordered duplicate keys please return to the key counter? Your keys are ready."

That guy was good. I hurried back to pick them up.

Darryl stood at the counter with a bag in one hand and the original key ring in the other. He shook the keys in the bag. "Here you go. The Janice Harrington special." The keys made a muffled clinking sound that was instantly recognizable. I stood there a moment, stunned.

"Are you okay?" Darryl asked. "You look like you've seen a ghost."

I swallowed hard and gave my head a little shake. "No, no. It's nothing." He handed me the bag and the key ring. "Thank you. How much do I owe you?"

"They're on me. And tell Janice I'm going to collect one of these days."

I grinned. "I will. Thanks again." I walked quickly down the aisle and out of the store. The trip back took even less time. My mind turned this new information over and over again. That rattle was the noise I'd heard in the stairwell, just before I found John Harding's body. The killer? I didn't know.

"Mission accomplished," I said, plunking both sets of keys on Janice's desk. "And Darryl says you owe him and he'll collect one of these days."

"I'm sure he will." A strange look came over her. There was a story there, but I didn't press for information.

"So what is the plan now?"

"I'm going to have an undeniable urge to argue some management committee issue with Tom Green and you are going to do your part."

"Can I say that I'm incredibly impressed with your cunning?"

"I'll take that as a compliment?"

"It's meant as one."

"Why do I like you so much? You're pure trouble," she said.

"It takes one to know one."

"You're like the exasperating daughter I never had. Now go hide yourself somewhere while I lure Tom to my office."

"Said the spider to the fly."

She laughed and shook her head at me. "Just go. I'll give you the signal."

I walked down the hall, making sure that the coast was clear. I stepped into a darkened office and stood behind the door. I pulled my cell phone out. I got the text "go" ten minutes later. I stepped out from behind the door and looked both ways down the hall. No one. I walked past Janice's closed door and down the stairs. My heart was going a mile a minute, but I managed to walk calmly. I tried to put on my impassive metro face. I only met one other person and he seemed to be in a hurry to leave the office so we just said "hi" as we passed. I didn't know who he was.

I got to Tom Green's office and walked in slowly as if looking for him. I was relieved to see that Chester was not still there. Tom's jacket remained on the back of the chair. I hoped he hadn't noticed anything. I placed the keys on the floor behind one of the desk supports and then sat back to examine the angle. Yes, that looked right. I started to get up. The office was like an oven. I could feel little drops of sweat roll down my back.

I heard footsteps approaching. I looked at my phone – no warning message from Janice. Could that be him? I listened more closely. No, that wasn't Tom Green. He walked with a shuffle on the outer edges of his feet like many heavy people whose ankles aren't really up to the task. The footsteps stopped and I saw a pair of snakeskin boots in the doorway. Damn. I held my breath. A bead of sweat rolled down my forehead and into my eye. I couldn't do anything but blink fiercely. The feet stayed in the doorway for the longest minute of my life.

Then I heard Shane David mumble, "I guess I'll just go home if he's not here." He hesitated again. I didn't know how much more I could take. He turned at last and walked back in the direction he'd come. I let out a long breath and wiped my forehead with the back of my hand. I looked at my phone. Another minute and the visitor would be too far away to hear me.

Finally, I got up and carefully made my way out of the office to the secretarial station across the way. I'd just ducked down when Grant came up to Tom's doorway and looked in. He shrugged and walked away. I texted "allclr" to Janice and wiped my face with a tissue I'd taken from the desk above me. I heard Tom Green shuffle back into his office. His chair creaked loudly as he sat down. I noticed he didn't shut the door. Smart man. I waited another five minutes until Tom turned to work on his computer. Then I made my way back to Janice's office. I felt wilted.

I closed the door behind me and leaned against it. "Whew. I nearly had a heart attack," I said.

"What happened? I was running out of things to say and he kept trying to leave on me."

"Shane David came looking for him."

"Oh." She eyed me seriously.

"I thought I was going to die of heat exhaustion behind that desk."

"You do look pink."

I put my hands up to my burning cheeks. "Admit it, I'm as red as a lobster."

"Just a little." She grinned.

"No one saw me on the way back, so I don't care."

"Now we just have to wait."

"I'll take doing nothing over the last couple of minutes any day." I grabbed another tissue from the box on Janice's desk.

"Spoil sport."

"You're enjoying yourself, aren't you?"

"I wish you'd gotten me involved earlier. This is more fun than I've had in a long time."

"If you're going to comment on how dull law is, please refrain. You should have mentioned it before I spent three years and over $100,000 training myself to do it."

"I wasn't, although, if I'd known you then —"

"So now we wait," I cut her off.

"Until everyone is gone. I ordered dinner by the way. I hope you like pizza?"

"Love it. What kind?"

"St. Louis style with pepperoni and olive." St. Louis style pizza had a cracker-thin crust, so that the toppings formed the main component of the taste.

"Paperelli's?" I said.

"They are the closest delivery. Ironic, no?"

"Very. What are we going to do about the cleaning crew? Or another attorney?"

"We'll have to take our chances that no one notices the light under the door."

"I wonder if we'll actually find anything."

"I have access to all of the online accounts as a member of the management committee. I'm thinking that if there is a record of anything, it should be in paper. But who knows? If there are records, they could be stored somewhere else."

I thought about Chester. Data could be changed by someone with access to the servers. The network was doing strange things on the night of the murder. Maybe there was a connection. "At least the experience has been memorable," I said.

"That's an understatement. I've never had to lie so much in one day."

"As an attorney, that says a lot."

"I know!" She laughed. "I should be better at it. I hope Tom doesn't suspect something."

"I'm sure your performance was Oscar-worthy."

"I babbled like an idiot. But he already doubts my intelligence, so I played true to type."

"He doubts your intelligence?"

"I hate to break it to you, but every male attorney doubts your intelligence."

"It can't be that bad."

"Don't fool yourself," she said.

"Many law schools graduate more women than men. What is everyone going to do when we are the majority at the firms?"

"Replace the golf outings with trips to the spa?"

"That would be good. I hate golf," I said.

"Me, too, but I've had to buckle down and learn to play. The move up the ladder is very slow."

The phone rang. Janice answered it. "Yes?" She nodded, and then said, "I'll send Liz right down." She hung up. "The pizza is ready. Would you mind running down to the lobby while I straighten my desk? I'd hate to smear my clients' important documents with pizza grease."

"Not very professional," I replied, walking to the door.

CHAPTER 13

I strolled to the elevator. One benefit of the gym was the complete lack of guilt I felt about using the elevator at work. The door closed. Someone in building services had turned the music up full blast. I heard a stirring but wordless rendition of "Jessie's Girl" by Rick Springfield, adapted for acoustic guitar. I'd liked the song from the first time I heard it on an all 80's radio station. It was the only pop song I'd ever heard use the word "moot," and use it correctly, too. I found myself humming and then singing along. Singing to myself was a single girl habit I'd acquired over the years. The doors opened just as I belted out "Jessie's girl, you know I wish that I had Jessie's girl!" I stopped, suddenly aware of where I was. I heard laughter in the distance. Louis was on duty.

I walked hesitantly to the reception desk.

"Nice pipes." Louis grinned.

"One of my few talents," I replied sheepishly.

Ever since that terrible night, I'd gone out of my way to get to know Louis. He had done the same for me. Although the murder shook him, Louis needed the job. His wife had multiple sclerosis, and he depended on the health insurance. He also had three little girls to support. He lived in the city, not far from where he grew up, but he worried about the schools and the crime. He wanted his girls to have the best of everything. He'd been toying with a move to the suburbs, but couldn't quite make his mind up to leave the old neighborhood behind.

"Can't fool me – you have many talents," he said.

"Thanks. How are you doing this evening?"

"I'm working."

"Enough said."

"Your pizza smells good. I would have sneaked a piece if it had been anybody but you."

"Here," I opened the lid of the box, "take a piece or two – however much you like."

He did. "Thank you. They don't feed us like they feed you folks."

"Anything to increase productivity."

"Lawyers think of everything."

I took the box from the counter. The firm had an account, so attorneys never had to mess with cash or tips. "How's Phyllis doing?" I said.

"Some days good, some bad. She's still working part time."

"And the girls?"

He lit up. "Good. Real good. Camille won first place at the school spelling bee." Camille was the oldest. From what I could tell, she was going to be the star of the family.

"She is such a smart girl," I said.

"Sometimes it's scary how much she gets. She'll be way above me soon."

"Not too soon. She gets her genes from somewhere."

"Phyllis says it's all her."

"She may be right."

"She usually is," he said ruefully.

"Give her my regards, won't you, and the girls? I should get back with the food. Janice is as hungry as I am."

"Sure. Give me a call when you leave and I'll get someone to walk you to the car."

"I'm going to be here pretty late."

"I'm on till eleven. Barry's on after, so I'll tell him if you're not down by then."

"Say, do you know if Grant Abrams or Tom Green have left yet?"

"Not sure. They didn't ask for anyone to walk them out."

I nodded. "Of course, they wouldn't. Thanks. Well, have a good evening if I don't see you."

"Will do." He gave me a cheery salute.

I pushed the "up" button while I tried to balance the pizza box in the other hand. It would be just like me to drop it. I managed to maneuver it safely into the elevator and then pushed the button for my floor. The box tilted precariously and I gripped it with both hands to make sure. The music was still loud. "The Long and Winding Road" on the steel drum. How original.

I looked down at the pizza box. "Paperelli's Pizza" was written out in blue letters across the top. The script was vaguely gothic with a heraldic crest underneath. But instead of crossed swords in the center panel, there was a knife and fork. The motto of the chain followed: "Five hundred years of tradition in every slice."

The TV commercials featured Antonio Paperelli, James' father, dressed in a white apron and chef's hat, with his sleeves rolled up, extolling the virtues of the family recipes in front of a brick oven. He was a large man, tall and round. He looked like he'd eaten a fair number of pizzas over the years, so you believed him when he said Paperelli's made the finest pizzas in the world.

It was strange to meet the sons when I'd seen the father on television for so many years. Did he look different in person? I'd once seen a local newscaster who looked normal on screen, but actually had a giant head and a short stumpy body. That desk hid a multitude of sins. If James were single – I shouldn't go there. But still. I might find out.

The Paperellis wouldn't think much of me, though. I wasn't Catholic, for one thing. I was nominally Methodist, although I could only boast of spotty church attendance. I went to a beautiful Methodist church close to campus when the mood struck me. But instead of listening to the sermon, I'd find myself staring at the Tiffany stained glass window of the risen Christ. It was sublime in its Art Nouveau splendor.

They'd think I was immature because of my age. Also, I didn't come from money. I thought about introducing James to my parents and realized that that would be problematic, too. My parents were wonderful people, but they were eminently practical Wisconsinites. I could imagine how they would appear to sophisticated, moneyed St. Louisans. James seemed down to earth, but there were limits. The elevator door snapped open, bringing my speculation to a merciful end.

The pizza was just as good as the advertisements promised. Janice and I sat together at her desk, both ravenous, chewing without conversation. All of this sleuthing was good exercise. After we'd finished eating, we got down to work not related to corporate espionage.

After several hours, she looked up and said, "You seem pensive."

"I'm just thinking how glad I am that you took me on."

"My pleasure. I'm still amazed you agreed to stay on."

"Where else would I go?"

"Anywhere. Listen, I've been thinking about this lately. The firm is shifting, and I don't know where it's going. There is so much tension you can cut it with a knife." She paused, pursing her lips. "If we find something, I don't want to be around to suffer the consequences."

"What are you thinking?"

"This is totally hypothetical, but if I were to open my own firm, would you come with me?"

"In a heartbeat."

"Now, wait a minute. It isn't a given that my clients would follow me. I couldn't offer you the big firm perks."

"I didn't stay here for the after-hours food. I'll go where you go."

"Thank you," she said sincerely.

I looked at my watch. "Do you think it would be safe now? It's ten o'clock."

"I think we should give it a try."

"Good. Otherwise I might fall asleep."

"Some detective you are. And I thought you were thirty years younger than me?"

"I'm twenty-five going on eighty-five. I can't pull an all-nighter like I used to."

"Clearly over the hill. Let's get moving."

We threw the pizza box away and prepared to leave the office. After an uneventful and unnoticed walk to the file room, we shut the door and got to work. Neither Janice nor I had any idea what we were looking for.

"When was The Lodge built?" Janice asked.

"The groundbreaking was in 2003."

"Okay, so we'll back it up a year and start with the files from 2002."

Three hours and one run-in with the cleaning crew later, we weren't closer to anything.

"Let's call it a night," Janice said. "I'm exhausted."

"Me too. Plus, I'm going to bleed to death from all of the paper cuts."

"Wimp."

I stuck my tongue out at her.

She laughed. "Now who's showing her age?"

"I'm eighty-five, remember."

"You're just punch-drunk from lack of sleep."

"There has got to be an easier way. I wish we knew what we're looking for."

Janice nodded. "It's either something or the absence of something."

"Maybe it's more simple than we think. If you wanted to embezzle money —"

"We don't know for certain that we are talking embezzlement at this point."

"It's the most logical. If The Lodge is going under, there must be a cash flow problem. What is the firm's biggest account?"

"The trust account. Then we have accounts for operating expenses and payroll. The thing is, we review all of those accounts at the management committee meetings."

"So you'd need to hide the fraud in plain sight if you didn't want to create a second set of books."

"I don't know." Janice seemed skeptical. "Maybe if we sleep on it, it will come to us."

"I'm all for that," I said.

And yet, when my head hit the pillow, all I could think of were Chester's unblinking eyes staring back at me.

The next morning I got up too late to get to my first class on time, so I went to the gym instead. I only had another two sessions with Kendra. Maybe I could impress her with some extra weight training. I ran into her on my way in. She was just coming out. She looked like a different person in her regular clothes, tight-fitting jeans and white tailored shirt, open at the collar. I noticed that she wore a very pretty pendant on a gold chain. It was a series of golden swirls around a calligraphy "K" picked out in diamonds.

"What a lovely necklace," I said. "It's very unusual."

"Thank you." She pulled it out and held it up to the light. "It was a gift from a friend." She gave me a look. I knew it must have been John Harding.

"Well, it's just beautiful. Are you off to class?"

"Yes. And you?"

"I'm skipping mine."

"That's why I've never seen you here at this time of day."

"I'm usually a better student, but I couldn't get up this morning."

"Late night?" Her tone implied something exciting.

"Nothing but work."

"Oh." She seemed disappointed.

"The life of a law student is full of thrills."

She laughed. "Don't let me keep you from your workout. Remember the tricep curls."

"Wouldn't miss them. See you Tuesday."

She waved and walked away. I went into the gym to apply myself. I sweated away for the next hour and a half. I could finally see a real change from the workouts and the diet. I was down a little over ten pounds and one dress size. My old jeans were finally and triumphantly unearthed from my closet. It wasn't a comfortable fit and I thought the top button might pop off at any minute, but I counted it as success nonetheless.

The next few weeks were a blur of frantic studying. I never felt as prepared as I wanted to be. I'd spent way too much time lost in fruitless daydreams and working on the John Harding murder. Janice and I spent two more nights going through the file room, looking for any clue about what was going on. So far we'd found nothing out of the ordinary. James called punctually at his appointed days and times. Our conversations were brief. I had no specific information to report, and he seemed tense and distracted on the other end. Some days it was a relief to get off the line. I felt depressed, so I redoubled my efforts to bring my studies up to speed.

I spent Thanksgiving with Holly and Ben and an odd collection of other Thanksgiving-less friends. Holly had invited as many single men as she could locate. None of them could carry on more than a monosyllabic conversation. It was a strange meal. It did not involve turkey or any of the usual side dishes. That is the problem with an uncoordinated potluck. There were many bags of chips, a few salads, an assortment of frozen entrees, and some foreign dishes that baffled me. I'd brought the only desserts – a pan of brownies and a pan of rhubarb bars.

It wasn't like home. I called my mom and dad when I got back to my apartment. My sister Ashley answered the phone. She was up from Madison for the break. She told me Mom went all out with the meal, despite the fact that she had to work in the morning. A nurse never sleeps.

"So we had the turkey and that good stuffing with celery and onions," Ashley said. It sounded like she was chewing.

"What are you eating now?"

I heard a swallow. "Nothing. Some pumpkin pie. Mom made it from scratch."

"Mmmm." I could just taste it.

"She made me help her with the pumpkin – ugh."

"It's the least you could do."

"I know, I know." I heard more chewing. "But the seeds are all stringy and slimy. It grosses me out."

"That last part was a little garbled, Ash. Why don't you put Mom on so you can go back to your pie?"

"Are you trying to get rid of me?"

"Is it working?"

"Here I am your poor sister, trying to talk to you —"

"Just put Mom on the phone."

"Okay, fine." I heard the sound of the phone being set on the counter and "Mom! Mo-o-o-m!" in the background.

My mom got on the phone. "Happy Thanksgiving!" I said.

"Happy Thanksgiving to you, too. How was the potluck?"

I described the cacophony of dishes. I could almost hear Mom wince over the phone.

"That sounds great, Liz," she said with a decided lack of enthusiasm.

"It was good," I replied, trying to convince myself.

"I'll make all the same food when you come at Christmas."

"It's not the food. I just miss being with everyone."

"We miss you too, honey. Ash had no one to fight with."

"Mom!"

She chuckled. "We can't wait to see you again." She paused. "Oh, and I was going to tell you last time but I forgot. Dr. Lee said Nick will be in town over Christmas. Maybe you two can get together."

My mom had never gotten over the fact that Nick and I had broken up. She always liked him. She thought he was smart, hardworking and a gentleman. She was right about the first two. I think she still secretly hoped Nick was "the one."

"Oh, maybe. Say Mom, did you give Nick my email address?"

"No, but I gave it to Dr. Lee. He said he wanted to follow up with you about something. I assumed it was medicine-related. Did Nick email you? Is there something you want to tell me?"

"I should probably get back to work."

Mom was smart enough not to press. "How is your work going?"

"I still have a lot of studying to do."

"Even on Thanksgiving?"

"Even then." I didn't want to go into the real reason I was so far behind.

"I won't keep you. Take good care of yourself and call me when you get a chance." The mother guilt trip, like a one-two punch.

"I'm sorry I haven't called. My life is really hectic right now," I said lamely.

"I understand." The one. "I just miss talking to you." The two. "I love you very much, Liz." A knock out.

"Love you too, Mom!" I hung up and sat dejectedly by the phone. I wanted to get into bed and pull the covers over my head. Instead, I fired up the computer and tried to cram in as much tax law as my brain could hold.

The day of my first final, I got up early and ate my usual final exam breakfast – a bowl of Grape Nuts cereal and a large mug of strong coffee. Final exam breakfasts needed to be calibrated precisely. Sufficient protein to sustain you during the exam, but not so heavy you end up with an indigestible lump in the pit of your stomach. I'd taken enough final exams to know. Grape Nuts had the highest protein of any cereal I'd encountered in my years of reading the back of the boxes in the supermarket aisle.

Two hours later, my No. 2 pencils were dull and my right hand hurt. I filled one entire blue book with my scribbling. God only knew if it would be enough for a good grade. I decided to run out and get something to eat before exam number two. It started at three o'clock. I just had time to cram down a little food and as much information as possible. The trick for me was to quickly forget everything I'd learned for the first exam and fill that neuronal space with the information needed for the next.

I drove over to the place where I'd had lunch with Janice and her friends. It seemed like a quiet place to study, and the food was first rate. I sat at a small round table in the corner. I was ahead of the lunch crowd, so the place was serenely quiet. I ate forkfuls of quiche while I reviewed my notes. A couple hours of study and I might actually be prepared.

"Liz!"

I jumped, so startled that I dropped my fork. I looked around. A dark-haired woman was waving at me from the sandwich counter. Maddie Harding. I could tell by the cut of her bangs.

"Maddie!" I waved back.

She walked over to me.

"What brings you here?" I said.

"In-service. I have been sent to get sandwiches. And you?"

I motioned to the pile of paper on the table. "Final exams. I thought I would eat and study at the same time."

"Don't let me stop you," she said with a smile.

I smiled back. "I won't keep you, either. Your fellow teachers would never forgive me."

"We should get together again. You liven up our little lunch group."

"I would love to." I glanced at the table piled high. "Maybe after finals?"

"We'll set it up. Good luck with your exams."

"Thanks. Good luck getting back before the ravenous hordes tear the school apart."

"Right. Got to go." She went back to the sandwich line.

On the way out of the sandwich shop, I noticed a sign for the store next door. It read "Lane Jewelers." My breath caught in my throat. That was where James had Angelica's engagement ring made. I looked at my watch. I didn't have time to stop. When finals were over, I'd come back to investigate. My curiosity could not be contained.

By the time my second exam was mercifully over, I didn't think I could move. I drove home in a stupor. When I got home, I grabbed a Fresca from the refrigerator and lay down on the couch. I felt like someone had hit me over the head – repeatedly. Two down and three more to go. I wasn't sure if I was going to make it. I drifted in and out of exhaustion-induced sleep. Dreaming surreal semi-conscious dreams, I didn't actually hear my phone ring until the answering machine started to pick up.

"Hi, Liz, it's Vince. I, uh, well, wanted to see how you were, uh, doing —"

I rolled off the couch and made a grab for the phone. "Hello?" My voice was unsteady. I wiped the drool off my chin with the back of my hand.

"Liz," he said. "Are you okay? You sound funny."

"I was half asleep on the couch."

"I didn't mean to wake you."

"I don't usually go to sleep at 5:30. It's just I had two finals today. I'm completely wiped out."

"Oh, sorry about that. Mine are next week. Look, if I called at a bad time, I can call back —"

"No, no. I have another one tomorrow, so now is as good as any time this week."

"I just thought that maybe we could get together like we talked about – go see a movie or something."

"This week is a little booked, but —"

"How about Saturday?"

It could just be a friendly invitation. In any case, spending time with Vince was never a bad thing.

"Sure," I said. "What do you suggest?"

"Want to meet at the mall? We could grab dinner and then see what's playing at the theater."

"Sounds like fun." Now I was totally confused.

"Or I could pick you up, if that's easier. You live close by Galleria, don't you?"

"Yes." My apartment was only a couple of miles from the Saint Louis Galleria mall. I gave Vince directions and we agreed on a time. "See you on Saturday," I said.

"See you then." His voice sounded buoyant. "Good luck with finals!"

We hung up and I crawled back onto the couch. As I lay there, I wondered if I should just go to bed. I would have to get up really early to study, but it would be better than trying to do it now. I dragged myself to the bedroom and changed into an old pair of flannel pajamas. Unattractive in the extreme, but soft as a second skin.

I fell asleep immediately, but it was not a restful sleep. I tossed and turned and then woke up with a start. I looked at the clock. 2:07 a.m. Wonderful. I lay back on the pillow and stared at the ceiling. I'd been dreaming about something. I couldn't remember what. My mind grasped at the wisps of dream still floating around my head. Keys. Something about keys. The sound of keys in the stairwell? No, something else. Some other keys. I tried to concentrate. Still nothing.

I got up and made myself a cup of coffee. I poured a bowl of cereal without milk. I went over my notes as I picked at the cereal with my fingers. Another bad habit. My mom would be horrified. I tried to study, but couldn't concentrate. I couldn't get the dream out of my mind. I finally closed my eyes and let my mind wander. My conscious brain floated along, stringing one random thought to the next. Unfortunately, most of these thoughts were about James or Nick, so it didn't help.

I decided to go back to bed. I cleared the dishes and walked back to the bedroom. I lay down, but sleep was not forthcoming. I sat up and turned on the light. What to do? On impulse, I reached over and opened the drawer of my bedside table. I pulled out the now dog-eared copy of the *Ladue News*. Totally pathetic. I flipped through the pages.

I knew the engagement announcement by heart – every word and even the most minute detail of the photograph. I could close my eyes and recreate it perfectly, down to the way Angelica's French manicured hand curled slightly as it rested on James' shoulder. His blue eyes were unfocused, the way eyes often are in photographs. What was he thinking at that moment? I would likely never know.

The wallowing had to stop. I forced myself away from the engagement announcement, flipping back through the magazine. I opened it to the photograph of John Harding. There was something about it that bothered me, but I could never tell what. Then, like a lightening strike, it hit. I'd been focusing on John, but it wasn't John, it was Cheri. The way she held her glass was familiar. Two fingers and a thumb around the glass, the ring finger and pinky slightly extended, the arm held away from the body just so. I'd seen the gesture before, but not with Cheri.

Where? My mind ran through a thousand possibilities. Nothing. I closed my eyes again. Come on. The answer was somewhere in there. Who did the gesture belong to? My sluggish neurons did not want to cooperate. Maybe if I slept on it. I turned off the light and lay down. It took me awhile, but I finally drifted off.

I heard the alarm clock shriek and looked over. It read 6:30. As I hit the button to turn it off, I knew the answer. Beth. Beth held her glass the same way. I'd seen it at summer associate happy hours and again at that party Holly had dragged me to. Once I made the connection, other vague resemblances aligned themselves. The lift of the eyebrows, the asymmetric smile, the walk. Now that I thought about it, the walk was exactly the same. So they must be related. Mother and daughter? The resemblance seemed too slight for that, but one never knew.

CHAPTER 14

However, I knew someone who knew more about Beth than I did. Vince. As I was going to see him on Saturday anyway, I decided to ask a few questions without drawing undue attention. Twenty questions about another girl on a date would be awkward on so many levels. This date, or whatever it was, promised to be awkward enough.

Vince picked me up in a Honda Civic that had seen better days. We drove over to the mall in fitful spurts of small talk. A mall seemed like a good place for a sort of date. If we couldn't make decent conversation, there was always window-shopping to pass the time. According to people I knew, the mall had once been small and average looking. At some point in the recent past, the owners had nearly doubled the square footage and revamped the ambiance. Gone was the colored tile and painted metal. The theme was now marble and polished hardwood. The transformation was so seamless that only a true St. Louisan could tell which was the old mall and which was the new. They seemed to forget this. If you asked for directions to some store, ten to one you'd get an answer like "third floor of the old Galleria." Helpful.

We parked in the middle section between the two anchor stores, Dillard's and Famous Barr, which was soon to become a Macy's. Vince got out and opened my door for me.

"So how did finals go?" he asked politely. He seemed unusually shy.

"I'm just glad they're over. I can't cram one more fact in my head without my brain exploding."

Vince laughed. The doors of the mall entrance slid open with a whoosh. We passed a giant wall sculpture of a clown. I'm not fond of clowns anyway, and this one had a demonic expression. Vince caught my look of disgust.

"Not a big fan of clowns?" he said.

"Certainly not those." I shivered. "They give me the willies."

He laughed again. "You must have been a strange kid. I thought everyone liked clowns."

"That's just one of the strange things about me," I said without thinking.

"Oh really?" he said with a mischievous smile. "Is there something else I should know?"

I felt stupid, but decided to brave it out. "Which quirk would you like to know about?"

"Are there that many to chose from?"

"Only a couple dozen or so."

"Give me one, and I won't pry anymore."

"You're a gentleman, Vince." I stalled for time. My brain tried furiously to come up with something that wouldn't seem too strange. My biggest quirk was out of the question.

"You're stalling."

"Yes," I said, "I am."

"Come on – I'll tell you one of mine."

"What an offer."

"You're not going to get a better one."

"Okay, okay. I have a very, very good sense of smell."

"How good?"

"Good enough to know someone at your house was making rice before you came. I could smell it on your shirt when you picked me up."

"Oh great." He rolled his eyes. "So I smell like cooked rice?"

"And Cool Water cologne."

"Perfect."

"Don't worry. I haven't met too many people who can smell what I smell."

"So the average person might not notice the rice?"

"I assume they would just smell the cologne."

"And the cologne smells —"

"Very nice. It smells good on you."

"Thanks."

I looked over at him. He walked with his hands stuffed in his pockets. "So are you prepared for finals?" I said.

"I never feel totally ready, but I can't study more. I'm just glad to be out with you."

"Me too," I said lightly. I felt him relax as he walked beside me. His pace slowed and took on the easy-going shuffle I recognized. Maybe this was a date after all. And maybe that was a good thing. My obsession with James had reached an unhealthy level. I could never have him. I had to get over it. Vince could help me do that, if he wanted to. And if I let him. I decided to relax my guard and see what happened.

Almost instantly, I felt his shyness start to slip away. We walked to the California Pizza Kitchen and talked about nothing in that familiar friendly way we always did. We sat across from each other at a small table that faced the mall. It was surprisingly fun to people watch. Vince had a wry sense of humor that matched my own. We got so involved in the commentary that we hadn't even bothered to look at the menu when the waiter came back the second time.

After ordering at random, we got back to business. Nothing was too large or too small to escape our notice. The food arrived before we knew it. As we tucked in, the topic changed to classes, professors, and all things law school. I saw my chance to see what Vince knew about Beth.

"I saw Beth at a party awhile ago," I said.

"Really?"

"Yes. It was strange. My friend in engineering invited me, so it was a big group of science and math people. I'm standing talking to someone about genetic research and Beth walks in. I guess she's dating a guy who's a friend of a friend of the people who had the party." I took a long sip of Diet Coke. "Anyway, I was surprised to see her."

"I don't know her that well," Vince said, "but I have heard her mention a boyfriend. I want to say his name is Brad."

"They've been dating a long time?"

"I think since she started law school."

"She's from the south somewhere, right?" Beth had an accent that I hadn't quite placed.

"Texas. She told me she's from Houston. Her father is a big time real estate developer."

"Beth talks to you?"

"She doesn't talk to you?" he said.

"Not since the murder. I've run into her a couple of times and she barely acknowledges my presence. Do you think she's just shy? Or just freaked out that I was the one who found the body? Some people at school acted like I was contagious."

"Could be. Let's hope murder isn't catching," he said with a smile.

I decided not to press my luck any further, and switched back to the people watching. A woman walked by with skin-tight neon orange polka dot capris.

"Some looks aren't good no matter who wears them," I said.

Vince looked over and grinned. We were off again.

When we finished dinner, we argued over who would pay the check. Vince firmly rejected my offers to pay and even snatched the receipt out of my hand.

"I've never had to fight a woman to pay for something," he said, shaking his head.

"You've obviously not been out with the right kind of woman."

We got up and wandered down to the theater. It's hard to know what to watch on something that may or may not be a first date. I agonized for several minutes. Should I suggest a romantic comedy? No, too many ideas there. Plus, not even a nice guy like Vince would really want to see a romantic comedy.

An action film? Vince would probably like that – and it wouldn't give anyone the wrong ideas. But then I'd be stuck – bored out of my skull or nauseous – depending on how jerky the camera work was. That left the vast middle ground of comedies, children's movies, and legal thrillers. I looked up at the board. There was one of each to pick from. I toyed with the children's movie – that had "feel good" written all over it. But could I convincingly tell Vince I wanted to see it for the computer animation? Probably not.

I suggested the legal thriller and Vince agreed. I wondered if he'd been doing his own mental calculations. He glared at me when I tried to pay again. Even though we'd just eaten, we got in line for popcorn. It smelled too good to resist. Vince started to tell me a very funny story about a cousin of his who, without any prior experience whatsoever, was embarking on a rehab of his house. He'd just gotten to the part where the poorly installed drywall collapsed, when I heard someone call my name behind me.

I turned around. It took me a moment, but I finally recognized Mark Paperelli at the back of the line. The hair. The laid back slouch of his shoulders.

"Mark! Hi!" I waved at him. He stood in line with several other people who all looked like graduate students. Each one had a different sweatshirt and a pair of jeans. Mark's read "Cornell" in big letters across the chest. He said something to one of them and then stepped out of line to come talk to me. It was only when he got closer that he noticed Vince.

"Liz," he said smiling. "Oh sorry, I didn't mean to interrupt."

I felt Vince tense up beside me. I smiled back anyway. "Let me introduce you. Vince Lopez, this is Mark Paperelli. Mark is doing a Ph.D. at Wash U. Mark, Vince is a law student at SLU. We were summer associates together."

Mark looked at me, and then quickly at Vince, sizing him up. He stuck out his hand. "Good to meet you, Vince." They shook hands solemnly. Then with a shrewd look he said, "Say hi to Holly for me when you see her." He glanced at Vince. "Again, sorry to interrupt. I'd better get back to my friends."

"Take care of yourself," I said as he turned to walk away.

"Will do. See you around." He gave me a jaunty wave and sauntered to the back of the line again.

"So how do you know him?" Vince tried to sound casual but failed. I felt a stirring of irritation, but I got it under control. "A friend of that engineering friend I was talking about – Holly," I replied coolly.

"Oh."

"So then what happened with your cousin?"

He started up where he'd left off. It wasn't quite the same though. Mark's sudden appearance had me thinking about James. I listened to Vince with half an ear and let him pay for my popcorn without argument. The movie was okay, but not stellar. It hinged on mistaken identity. Given my recognition issues, that was usually a spellbinding topic for me, but the screenwriting left a lot to be desired.

At some point, I felt Vince's arm sneak up around the seat. The old standby. I didn't flinch away, but I also didn't lean in. I wasn't sure what I wanted him to do. I couldn't get James out of my head. As we walked back by the demonic clown, Vince said, "So what would you like to do now?"

His question caught me off guard. My thoughts were where they shouldn't have been. "What?" I said.

He seemed annoyed. "What would you like to do now?"

"Sorry, I was just thinking about something."

"What?"

I scrambled. "You never did keep up your end of the bargain."

"What bargain?"

"Your secret quirk."

"Oh, I completely forgot. Well, don't tell anyone but —" his voice dropped conspiratorially, "I love hot foods."

"That's not a quirk," I scoffed.

"It is when you put Tabasco on everything."

"Everything?"

"I eat it on ice cream sometimes."

"Okay, okay. That is weird."

"I'd carry it around with me if I didn't think people would stare."

"Like a hip flask?"

"That's a really good idea."

I rolled my eyes.

"So where do you want to go?"

"You promise you won't embarrass me?"

"I'll try not to."

"Coffee?" I said.

"Do you know a good place? I don't know this area that well."

Was this a hint for me to suggest my apartment? I didn't take it. Instead, I ran through the likely places in my head. There was the place by Holly's apartment. No. Too many associations. I suggested another one on Clayton road. That one was more upscale and better lit.

We ordered our coffees and sat down at a small table towards the back. Vince was in a buoyant mood. I got him started again with family stories. He had a seemingly endless number of cousins, aunts, uncles, friends of the family and so forth who provided him with an easy flow of anecdotes. I could barely drink my coffee for laughing. It was no surprise that I didn't hear the door of the coffee shop clang open. I sat facing Vince in any case.

"Of all the —" Vince bit back what was surely the first curse I'd ever heard him say in my presence. My head whipped around. There stood Mark and one of the friends he'd been with at the movies. I recognized the Cornell sweatshirt. Our eyes met. He smiled at me sheepishly and then headed over to a table on the other side of the room.

"Popular place."

"Yes," Vince said. I thought I heard his teeth grind together.

What followed would have been hilarious if I wasn't living through it. Vince and I continued to talk, but Vince could barely make eye contact. He was watching Mark, who was watching us. I knew every time that Mark looked over our way because Vince would tense up and then throw himself with greater fervor into the conversation. I wished I had the courage to turn around. Or to tell them both to cut it out. Instead, I sat there making conversation while the unspoken conversation raged around me.

After half an hour of this nonsense, I'd had enough. "I may need to call it a night," I said. "I have to get up early tomorrow."

"Sunday?" he said.

"Yes." I thought quickly. "I promised to hang Christmas decorations at church." This item was in the bulletin, so it wasn't a complete lie. They always needed volunteers.

"I didn't know you went to church."

"Yes, frequently." I assume that lying about going to church is worse than lying about other things, so I said a silent prayer asking for forgiveness.

"Where do you go?"

"Grace United Methodist. It's the one on Waterman, by campus."

"Oh," was all he said. He got up from the table and I followed. I saw out of the corner of my eye that Mark watched us again. I waved goodbye when I didn't think Vince was looking. Vince opened the door for me to pass through. He didn't say anything as we walked to the car. In fact, he seemed lost in thought – struggling with some intractable problem.

As we neared my apartment, I reviewed the events of the evening. Maybe the whole mess was my fault. I was living in a fantasyland. Yet, I had a real flesh and blood person beside me. I needed to give him the opportunity he deserved. I decided to salvage what I could.

"I've had a lovely evening," I said, smiling over at him. "Thank you for everything."

He looked relieved. "It's been fun. I'd like to go out again some-time – maybe after my finals?"

"I'm going home at the end of next week, so it might have to be after break."

"Are you staying for New Years?"

"Yes. I fly back the first week of January."

He nodded. "So I'll call you then?"

"Sure. The next one's on me."

He laughed. "Now that wouldn't be right."

"I'm a modern woman," I insisted with a smile, "and that means picking up the check every now and again."

"We'll see." We pulled up in front of my building. He turned off the car. "Well —"

"Thanks again," I said. There was an extended pause. I could sense that he was still debating. He leaned in a little closer. Ah, the kiss. I decided to let him. Why not? Besides, it had been a long long time. I'd worry about the rest later. I moved towards him and our lips touched.

It was strange to be kissing him, but not in a bad way. I tried to push any thoughts out of my mind and just concentrate on the moment. That helped. His technique was good, I decided clinically, just a little timid for my taste. I took control of the situation, putting my arms around his neck and pulling him closer still. I could feel the heat rising between us and wondered when I should pull away. I wasn't ready to go that far on a first date.

He made the decision for me, slowly pulling back. I disengaged my arms. We stared at each other for a moment, centimeters apart.

"I should really go now," I said, still a little breathless.

"Yes," he said without moving.

I reached for the door handle, but he anticipated me. He got out and walked around to open my door. He gave me his hand to help me out, and might have taken me in his arms, if I hadn't moved to one side. We'd done enough for one evening. He merely held onto my hand and then let go.

"Good night, Vince," I said. I had my keys in my other hand so I turned and opened the outside door.

"Good night, Liz." He stayed frozen on the pavement.

"Good luck with finals."

He shook his head slightly and then walked back to the driver's side of the car. "Take care of yourself."

"You too," I said.

He nodded and got into the car. I hurried inside.

CHAPTER 15

I spent most of my week off sleeping in, hanging out with Holly – my only friend without her own finals – going to the gym, and cleaning my apartment. In that order. I also managed to finish two projects for Janice and discovered that someone had already published on my note topic.

After an in-depth discussion with the other members of the *Quarterly* editorial board, I got them to agree that I was too far along to start a new topic. They also agreed that even careful manipulation could not salvage my old topic. So, in return for additional editorial duties, they absolved me of all further note-related obligations. A small part of me was sad to think that the world would not get to experience my note-writing prowess. But that part was very small. I had enough on my plate.

Vince emailed me. He repeated that he'd had a great time. I composed an email that I hoped wasn't too committal – agreeing that it was fun to spend time with him and wishing him well on his finals. I hit the send key and my cell phone rang. I looked at the number, surprised. It was James. This wasn't our appointed time. My guardian angel had a very sick sense of humor.

"Hello," I said cautiously.

"Hi, Liz." I felt an instant rush of adrenaline. Damn. How could Vince ever hope to compete with such a powerful attraction?

"How are you?" I kept my voice very calm.

"Fine. Look, I was hoping that maybe you might be free to meet?" He seemed distracted and hesitant.

"Sure. Is there a new development with the case?"

"Something like that, yes." Again, the hesitation.

"Okay. Where and when?"

"Pomme Café, in maybe an hour?"

I agreed.

"See you soon." He hung up.

I shook my head, puzzling over his strange tone.

Then I got to work. I spent the next forty minutes racing around my apartment and ransacking my closet for just the right outfit. Not that anything in my closet was up to James' usual standards, but I had to at least make the effort. I finally settled on a new pair of jeans that were significantly tighter than my other pairs. I tried to turn in the mirror to see myself from the back. Holly told me that they looked good. Maybe she was right.

I pulled on a fitted shirt and dug in my closet till I found a pair of kitten-heeled pointy-toed shoes I hardly ever wore. I hoped that I could walk in them on the uneven sidewalks of Clayton. It would be just like me to seriously injure myself doing a face plant into the concrete in front of the café. And then, because this was St. Louis in December, I topped everything off with a heavy wool overcoat that was now at least a size too big. So attractive.

I got to Clayton in record time. I even found a parking place after only one trip around the block. I prayed my luck would hold. James was already there. He waved to me from a table next to the tall mirror-backed bar. He didn't need to signal. I had thoroughly memorized all of the little pieces that made him James. I took off my coat as soon as I could and hung it on the back of my chair.

"It's good to see you," he said.

"Likewise," I replied evenly, sitting down. I didn't want him to see how good.

"What would you like?" He reached across the table to hand me a menu. "Besides coffee, of course."

I took the menu and our fingers touched by accident. I felt a ripple of anticipation and looked down. I forced my mind to concentrate on the menu.

"They still have the apple tart," he said. "Or maybe you want something more substantial? Have you eaten lunch?" It was now 2:30.

"I haven't," I admitted, "but I might go straight for dessert anyway."

He smiled at me. "That sounds like an excellent plan."

"Especially if it's the tart. I don't know how they do it, but that tart was the best apple anything I've ever eaten."

"I think it's the pound of butter they put in the crust," he said with a wry look.

"Don't tell me that."

"Butter is the essential ingredient in all great food."

"Do you cook yourself? Aside from pizzas, I mean."

"But of course," he said. Then more seriously, "I do cook some. Dabbling mostly – and not just Italian."

"What?"

"French."

"*Mastering the Art of French Cooking?*"

"My bible."

"Really?"

"Julia Child is pure genius."

I shook my head.

"What?" he said.

"I just have a hard time squaring this. What do you do when your fellow detectives want to go to McDonalds? Or Dunkin Donuts, if you want to stereotype?"

"I go and I eat. I just prefer something else."

"So you are not a food snob?"

"Well, maybe a little."

"A food snob whose family business is food that can be ready in twenty minutes?"

He nodded.

"You are a walking contradiction."

"How about enigma? It sounds better – more mysterious."

"But it means something different. I'll stick with contradiction."

The waiter arrived just at that moment. I saw James bite back what he was about to say. We ordered the apple tart and coffee again.

"So maybe you should tell me what this is all about?" I said as soon as the waiter left.

He paused for a moment, gathering his thoughts. Then he folded his hands in front of him and looked at me directly. "I've been informed that my duties have been reassigned."

"They're taking you off the case?" I saw him flinch for a millisecond and then recover.

"I was told that I needed to focus on other open cases."

"So, you won't be needing my services anymore?" I tried for non-committal, but my voice quivered uncomfortably.

"Not officially," he said flatly.

"Oh." I looked down at my hands clenched together in my lap. I felt tears pricking at the back of my eyelids. Dear God, I prayed with all the ardor of the undeserving, please don't let me cry right now, right here. I blinked furiously several times. I could not be a blubbering idiot in front of him a second time.

I took a deep breath and forced myself to speak. I still couldn't look at him. "I know I haven't been much help so far." I sat up a little straighter and put my hands on the table to steady me. "But I do think I'm getting somewhere. I have a feeling about this case – call it intuition – that I have all the pieces. I just don't know how they fit together yet."

"You've done everything I've asked and more." He crossed his hands on the table. I looked up, watching him for a moment. His shoulders slouched. He seemed resigned.

His attitude irritated me. "So you are just going to drop the case?"

"Don't have much choice."

I couldn't let that stand. "But I do."

"What?" I'd clearly startled him.

The waiter reappeared with the coffees and the tarts. I ate a forkful of tart before I answered. It was just as delicious as I'd remembered.

James eyed me over the rim of his coffee cup. "You were saying?"

I took a sip of coffee to steady me. "I was saying that I do have a choice."

"And?"

"I'm going to continue the investigation on my own."

He drank his coffee in silence and then slowly ate a piece of tart. I could see the wheels spinning, but I didn't know where the car was going.

"Just don't get caught."

"What is that supposed to mean?"

"I was going to try to talk you out of it, but I can tell from the way you're looking at me that it's not going to work. There is no way I'm going to convince you that there is no need for you to stick your neck out – for me or for the investigation."

I nodded.

"So I can't stop you, but if someone catches you snooping around, I can't protect you either." He looked at me meaningfully.

"I understand."

"Liz." His gaze was so penetrating that I couldn't blink. "We are dealing with a murderer here. Please, please be careful."

I forced my eyes to break away. "You should have thought of that before you invited me into your investigation. I'm in too far to back out."

"Don't you think I don't know that? I should never have called you." He ran his hand distractedly through his hair, disturbing its perfect wave. "I was weak and desperate. I'm sorry."

"You're sorry you met me, or sorry you asked for my help?"

"I just don't want you to get hurt."

Too late. I was already hurt. I'd take my chances with the murderer.

"Promise me you'll be careful," he insisted.

"I will."

"And one other thing – call me if you need information. I may not be on the team, but I still have access to the files."

"Will do."

"Oh, and something else —"

"A third thing?"

"Is that a problem?"

"No, but only because you asked so nicely," I said.

"Well, this is more of a favor. Would you mind if we kept in touch?"

"About the case?"

"And anything else."

"Of course." How could I refuse?

"It's just that I would miss our weekly chats. You have such valuable insight." He smiled boyishly. I felt my heart pound a little harder in my chest. I reminded myself that he could only have meant that in the most platonic case-related sense. Friends. Maybe I could steel my heart to that if I had to.

"Murder is a fascinating subject. I wouldn't miss the opportunity to discuss it with you – and to let you keep tabs on me – which is what you want to do," I replied.

"I'm glad you feel that way." His eyes were warm. "You are nothing if not interesting."

I could feel the blush stealing up my cheeks. We were in dangerous territory, but I couldn't stay away.

"I believe the word 'amazing' has been used," I said pertly.

"Amazing is certainly applicable. And I would add intelligent, articulate, and funny." He rattled them off like he was reading a list.

"Now, see, you had me till you said 'funny.' No woman wants to be considered funny. It's the word you use when you can't think of anything better to say about her. It's only a minor step above 'nice.'"

He laughed good-naturedly. "You always have to take issue with something, don't you?"

"Usually."

"I think that's why I like you. You give me a run for my money."

"Please stop. I'll stick with intelligent and articulate. There is no way 'giving you a run for your money' can be in any way complimentary."

He gave me a sly smile. "I wouldn't be so sure."

I couldn't go on. My cheeks flushed red. I gripped my coffee cup and took a steaming gulp, burning my tongue and forcing my unruly body back into good order. I couldn't have a simple conversation with this man without becoming a mass of raging hormones. And I wanted to be friends? Some friend. And no benefits.

His eyes were inscrutable.

"So you are on to other murders then?" I said.

"Unfortunately. Most homicides are routine. You either solve them in a very short period of time or not. If not, they go unsolved for years, maybe forever."

"So they're easy or they're impossible?"

He nodded. "In most cases you have a good suspect within a couple of days."

"That quickly?"

"If they are unplanned, the murderer and the motive are usually obvious. If they are planned, they are frequently planned badly. The murderer leaves witnesses or evidence or both behind."

"That says something about the quality of the investigation as well. I'm sure other places aren't so fast."

"Most places don't have the murder rate St. Louis does. Of course, those statistics are arguable. Unlike any of the other contenders, the City of St. Louis is separate from all of its inner-ring suburbs. It skews the numbers high for St. Louis, or low for everyone else, depending on how you look at it."

"Why is the city set up like that?"

"Historical accident, I think. Like the fact that the police department is controlled by the Board of Police Commissioners and not the mayor or the city administration."

"I'm sure the city wishes it had the tax base," I said. St. Louis County was booming.

He nodded. "The politicians curse their predecessors on a daily basis."

"They always do. Today's brilliant decision is tomorrow's disaster."

"The future is an enigma," he said with a wink.

"I'm glad you have it right this time."

"So, speaking of the future, what are you up to this week?" His tone was smooth and casual. Just a friendly question.

"I'm done with finals, so I only have a few things on my list before I leave for Marshfield."

"When are you leaving?"

"I fly out Sunday morning."

"I was afraid you were going to try to drive."

"My dad wouldn't let me. He thinks my car wouldn't make it."

"I have to agree with him."

I gave him a look. My car wasn't great, but it was reliable. I'd never had it break down on me.

"Where do you fly to to get to Marshfield?" he said.

"Central Wisconsin Airport – in Mosinee. I can see from your face that means nothing to you."

"My Wisconsin geography is very poor."

"Mosinee is just outside of Wausau, and Marshfield is a forty-five minute drive from Wausau."

"Okay. I've at least heard of Wausau."

"Central Wisconsin is another world."

"As ignorant as I am, I'll have to take your word for it."

We sat for a moment, eating our tarts.

"So what else is on your social calendar?" he said, taking a sip of coffee.

"I'm going to lunch with Janice, her friend Susan, and Maddie Harding."

"That should be interesting."

"Especially since I am now on my own. I'll have to be extra careful how I interrogate Maddie."

"I'd like to see that," he said appreciatively.

"Interrogation over chicken salad?"

"Yes, although most conversation is an interrogation of sorts."

"It is with me. As you are well aware, I have to discover and memorize all sorts of information."

He was quiet a moment and then he said, "I still feel terrible."

"Let's not bring that up."

"But I want to make it up to you."

"The Chinese food and," I gestured at the crumbs on my plate, "is more than enough."

"I'll come up with something. Just give me time."

"It's not necessary."

"Something you can't refuse, then."

I shrugged my shoulders. "Poor law students can't refuse charity."

"It's never charity," he said seriously. "What are you up to Saturday night?"

"I have the firm Christmas party."

That inscrutable look crossed his face again. I felt like I'd just missed some vital point. I opened my mouth to ask, but he moved on too quickly.

"So what is the Christmas party like? Most are pretty dull."

"I don't think that's the case here. I've heard some stories."

"What stories?" He leaned in in anticipation.

How to summarize everything I'd heard? Most of it was not fit for normal conversation.

"Well, only the staff and attorneys are invited to this party. No spouses. Ever." I gave him a significant look.

"Things get pretty wild?"

"This is my first one so —"

"Be careful, Liz." He looked at me directly. His eyes were very hard.

"I'm only going because Janice asked me to go with her. She told me that the party is totally normal for at least two hours and then all of a sudden, boom! We won't be staying post boom."

"Still." He seemed uneasy.

"Besides, I never drink at parties."

"Why?"

I touched my forehead with my index finger. "It dulls my precious faculties."

"Ah, that would be problematic."

"To say the least." I thought about it for a moment. "Plus, I hate feeling out of control."

He nodded. "Sometimes that's a bad thing."

"Only sometimes?"

"Sometimes it's better to be swept away." He gave me a long look that I couldn't interpret.

I glanced down and noticed my watch for the first time. Holly was waiting for me at the mall. She wanted me to help her find a gift for her mom. Her mom was notoriously hard to please.

"Do you have to go?"

"Yes," I said with an apologetic look. "I promised to meet Holly and I'm late." I stood up and he followed. He threw enough money on the table to cover our order twice over and helped me into my coat. His mother had trained him well.

"Let me walk you to your car," he said in a tone that prevented argument.

We walked in silence. He seemed lost in thought, and I wasn't sure how to restart our conversation. We got to my car.

"Well," I said, to say something. He looked at me for a moment and then put his hands on my shoulders. He leaned in. I looked up at him. I couldn't speak.

"Have a safe trip," he said quietly. "I'll call you when you get back."

I merely nodded, my brain sluggishly trying to process. Then he let me go. It couldn't have lasted more than ten seconds. He stepped back. It took me a long moment before I realized that he was waiting for me to get into my car. My limbs felt heavy and slow as I pulled open the car door and slid into the seat. He closed the door after me.

I turned the key in the ignition and pulled out. I watched him in the rearview mirror until I was too far away to see. He just stood on the pavement, running his hand distractedly through his hair.

CHAPTER 16

I wasn't very good company for Holly. I tried to concentrate on the task at hand, but my mind wouldn't listen. I played the conversation with James over and over again. I couldn't make sense of anything. Holly finally gave up and found a gift without my assistance. I apologized for being so distracted.

"You're probably just tired from finals," she said. "I forgive you."

"Thanks."

"Now that I've found the gift."

"And before that?"

"Don't ask."

"You're a good friend, Holly."

"The best," she said confidently. "Even though I can tell that you're still holding out on me. But I won't force your secrets – yet."

I couldn't bring myself to talk about James although she'd continued to press for more details. We crossed into the parking garage. I tried to come up with a plausible alternative.

"I'm just thinking about going home. My mom told me that Nick will be in town. I don't know if I should arrange to meet him or not."

"It's going to be hard to avoid. Your hometown is like the size of a postage stamp, right?"

Holly was from the vast urban metropolis of Lancaster, Pennsylvania. According to Holly, aside from being super-conservative and clannish, Lancaster had the distinction of being home to a large group of the even more super-conservative and clannish Amish. I often wondered if Holly's granola tendencies were merely a reaction to her childhood. It was like she'd been given to the wrong family at birth. There was some nice, liberal San Franciscan family missing their real daughter, horrified that the one they got adored Rush Limbaugh.

"That's true," I said. "And he sent me an email some months back, so the question is really – do I seek him out like he wants me to or do I avoid him and we meet awkwardly on the street?"

"From what you told me, he's bad news. I vote for the awkward meeting. At least it'll be short."

"But public," I said.

"A dilemma," she agreed.

"Speaking of – have you worked out your own?"

"Which?"

"Ben."

"No, not yet. I'm hoping my parents won't ask too many questions."

"Good luck with that," I said sarcastically. Holly had officially moved in with Ben. However, she'd never told her parents about him or even mentioned that she was dating anyone.

"I know," she groaned. "I'm only going home for a couple of days. I think I can avoid any conversation about my love life. They're usually too hung up that I'm still a vegetarian to ask about anything else." She smiled. "That and politics. If it get's sticky, I'll just tell them I campaigned for Howard Dean."

"The Scooby Doo strategy?"

"They think Howard Dean's a monster anyway."

I laughed. "Let me know how that works." We walked to our respective cars. She'd parked her Geo a couple cars away from mine. "I will. Let me know about the ex," she called back, and then added, "and whatever else you're holding back from me!"

I waved at her and got into the driver's seat. A very near miss. I started the drive back to my apartment, but soon lost myself in thought. I only woke up when I stopped at a light and realized that I'd gone the opposite direction from where I needed to go. I turned onto Ladue road. At least I didn't have anywhere I really needed to be.

As I drove past the enclaves of boutique stores, I caught sight of the sandwich shop where I'd gone during finals. Lane Jewelers was just behind it. Without giving my rational brain a chance to object, I turned the car into the parking lot. What sort of fool wants to see where a man purchased a ring for another woman? Me. James' choice of engagement rings had gotten such a write up in the *Ladue News*.

The door opened with a whoosh and a clang of little bells. The interior was hushed. The brilliant lights made everything sparkle. My heels sank into the velvety carpet. There were three long glass cases laid out in a "U" shape, with a smaller fourth case, back against the opposite wall. A neatly dressed woman in her sixties with small reading glasses perched on the end of her nose stood behind the central counter. Her name tag said "Cindy." She smiled warmly at me. "Can I help you?"

"I'm just looking at the moment."

"Anything in particular?" Her smile put me at ease. Clearly an expert saleswoman.

"Something for my mother." I lied.

"For the holidays?"

"Yes. She's hard to please, so I'll know it when I see it." At least that part was true, although my mother's taste ran to knick-knacks rather than jewelry. I hadn't seen her wear more than her wedding ring and a pair of gold stud earrings in my entire life.

"I understand perfectly. Mothers can be difficult to buy for. Look around as much as you like. If anything interests you, just let me know and I'll get it out of the case."

"Thank you." I moved to the nearest one. The engagement rings stared back at me. Row upon row of them. And further beyond, mountings of every description. Which one had James picked for Angelica? I tried to think about the picture but my brain resisted. Why was I torturing myself? I was suddenly overcome with a longing so fierce that my chest hurt.

I rushed to the next case, looking without seeing, while my body slowly recovered its equilibrium. Then I noticed a pendant at the end of the case. I recognized it instantly. Kendra's necklace. Except that this one had an "A" instead of a "K." Other than that, the design was identical. I stood staring at it until Cindy approached me discreetly.

"Would you like to see something?"

"I'd like to see that pendant if I could."

"Of course." She walked behind the case and unlocked the back panel. "This is an original design. We have a local artist we work with who designs pieces that we then have made. We made several for a special client and have now decided to offer it to the public." She carefully took the pendant out and set it on a black velvet pad. The diamonds glittered furiously.

I picked it up and held it in the palm of my hand. So delicate and so exquisite. This was how he did it, his calculated seduction. Who wouldn't feel beautiful with this around her throat?

"We can do any letter, of course."

"It is lovely," I said, handing it back to her. "But not what I'm looking for."

She put it back in the case. "Please keep looking. We have a lot of beautiful pieces."

"You certainly do."

I moved to another case and then another. There were some very unusual necklaces made of twisted silver wire in the last case. I lingered to look at them more closely.

"Those are made by the artist who does our other designs. Very original, don't you think?"

I nodded. "I've never seen anything like them." I'd already dallied enough for credibility. "Thank you very much. I'll keep these in mind."

I walked out the door. The evening was crisp against my cheeks. My breath came out in wisps. I stood for a moment filling my lungs with oxygen. I thought about the engagement rings and my chest burned. I breathed very slowly, in and out. Soon I would be home. I could forget about the murder, about James. Home would make it all better.

On Saturday, the weather changed abruptly. It got warm. So warm that I didn't bother to bring a jacket when I met Janice and her friends for lunch. Like a true St. Louisan, the schizophrenic weather did not faze me. We decided to sit at one of the tables out on the sidewalk in front of the restaurant in the Central West End. This area had been on the rebound longer than The Loop and so now was an established neighborhood of turn of the last century homes, trendy boutiques and good restaurants.

The area also boasted the 1930's era Chase Park Plaza hotel, which had recently reopened after an extensive renovation. If you closed your eyes, you could imagine yourself in a gorgeous cocktail frock, hurrying across the marble floor to meet the likes of Fred Astaire or Cary Grant in one of the elegant bars.

The four of us sat in the sun, enjoying the fine weather and people watching. Conversing with intelligent women is a genuine pleasure, so I regretted my true intention. Before lunch, I'd taken Janice aside and told her what was happening with the investigation. Janice agreed that we couldn't give up now, but left it up to me to turn the conversation in the right direction. She didn't want to put Maddie in an awkward position. Fortunately for me, Susan got the ball rolling down the hill. She mentioned her sister, who, I gathered from the context, was going through a nasty divorce. Maddie asked how the sister was holding up.

"She's hanging in," Susan said. "But she told me she's never getting married again."

"Has she found something else?" Janice asked.

"She hired a P.I. and he tracked down two more women."

"No —" Maddie said in disbelief. "He sounds just like John."

"I don't know how he found the time," Janice said.

Maddie sighed. "They always find the time. It's usually disguised as work."

"Well it is work," Susan said dryly.

Janice leaned in. "How are the kids taking it?"

"That's the worst part," Susan said. "She's done everything she possibly can, but she had to tell the kids that he'd moved out permanently. She didn't tell them about the baby."

"Wait, I missed that. What baby?" Janice said.

Susan lowered her voice to a confidential level. "Come to find out he got this woman pregnant. He called my sister up to brag to her about it. Had set the woman up in an apartment and everything."

"Wow," Janice said.

"I'm sure it's a stupid question," I ventured, "but how could he hide the expense?"

Maddie laughed at my naiveté. "You'd be amazed at what they can hide. John had secrets all over the place. Separate bank accounts, an apartment, you name it. He probably had children all over St. Louis. Who knows? If I'd been less trusting, I would have hired a P.I. early on. By the time we divorced, John had covered his tracks so completely, it was impossible to figure it all out. That's why I got so little in the settlement."

Susan patted her on the shoulder. "You got the kids – that's the important thing."

"I know." Maddie smiled. "I'm not bitter, trust me." She sighed again. "John was a terrible husband, but he was a decent father. His death has been a real blow to all of us." She paused and wiped her eyes with a napkin. "I miss him. I know I shouldn't, but I do. He was such a force of nature – it's hard to think he's gone." She took a deep breath and pulled herself together. "I will say this much, he provided well for the kids, at least in death." She chuckled wickedly. "You should have seen the look on Cheri's face when she realized how much the kids were getting. It was priceless. I understood then, like

I never had before, how much she counted on getting the money. I don't know if she ever really loved him. He was a means to her end."

"You don't think she killed him, do you?" Janice said in a hushed voice.

Maddie looked her in the eye. "I don't know, but I wouldn't put anything past her."

"I wonder if the case will ever be solved?" Susan said.

Maddie shook her head. "The police seem to have mangled the investigation."

Janice gave me a look across the table, but said nothing.

"How did we end up on such a sad subject?" Susan said. I watched my chance at interrogation slip away. Some detective I'd turned out to be.

"This is too nice a day to worry about the investigation," Maddie agreed.

"Does anyone want to do some shopping?" Janice asked. "I still have Christmas presents to buy."

"Yes!" Susan, Maddie and I said at once. We all looked at each other – the lunch broke up with laughter.

That night, Janice met me at the double door entrance to the hotel ballroom. The Christmas party appeared to be in full swing.

"You look great!" she said. I wore a little black dress I'd bought just for the occasion. Through the diet and exercise, I had finally gotten to the point where I didn't cringe at my reflection in the dressing room mirror. It was strangely liberating to like the way my clothes fit.

"So do you." Janice was very elegant in a severely cut silver gray dress. A modern Jackie O.

"You're in luck," she said, dragging me by the elbow to the group of estate and tax attorneys clustered around the bar. "The party is still deadly dull. No dancing on tables just yet."

"Thank goodness."

But after an hour of polite conversation, I wasn't so sure. I could have used a table. The party was so dull that I began to doubt Janice. There was no way this group of people could even produce a spark, let alone a boom. I wondered when I might be able to sneak out and go home.

Then someone unexpected walked through the door. I analyzed the walk. Beth. I suddenly remembered that she worked part-time for Blane Ford. That explained the invitation, but I'd never seen her at the office. Coincidence? Or was she still avoiding me? She didn't seem to notice me in the crowd. Then again, little black dresses are good for blending in. Every party has flocks of women in black, circling the room like so many ravens, waiting for the feast.

I followed Beth with my eyes. First she went to the bar and ordered a drink that came with a lime. She took a sip, plucked the lime off the side of the glass, took a small bite of it, and plopped it into her drink. For the next half an hour, she sipped her drink, chatted with other attorneys, and moved across the room. I could tell she was making her way over to Blane Ford.

He smiled when she came over. Their conversation seemed easy, but I was too far away to hear. I maneuvered closer. I'd done what I could to investigate Blane, but he was elusive. He didn't talk about himself like the other lawyers. Even Sally, using her network of secretarial spies, couldn't tell me more than what I'd already learned from Janice. He was truly an enigma.

Beth finished her drink and abandoned the glass on a small round table set against the wall. They were talking shop. Some breach of contract issue. I edged away. Nothing of interest in that. A couple of minutes passed. I scanned the ballroom for Janice. Maybe I should finally escape. I saw Grant talking to one of the pretty dumb secretaries. His sleeves were rolled up, and he was showing her his tattoos. She giggled and put her hand on his arm. Please.

Then I noticed movement towards the wall. Blane Ford slipped out a side door with something he held carefully with two fingers. Odd. I walked out the same door and followed him at a distance. Because of his long strides, I had to hurry to keep up. He looked back once and nearly caught me, but I ducked into an open doorway. It gave me a chance to realize how stupid I was being. He could be the murderer. What was I thinking?

But I couldn't conquer my curiosity. When I got up the nerve to peek out, he was still in sight. I followed after him, ignoring the little voice in my head telling me to turn around. He seemed to be going towards the parking garage, which was on the same level. My luck held. When I made it through two sets of doors and into the garage itself, I noticed him at the far end. I saw him approach his BMW. He looked over and I ducked down behind a car. My heart raced.

I counted to twenty and then raised myself up. His back was to me, but as he opened the passenger door, the light revealed the object he still clutched gingerly. It was a clear cup with something green at the bottom. He rummaged around in the car, pulled out a plastic sandwich bag, dropped the cup into it, and sealed it shut. He threw the bag back into the car and closed the passenger door.

I heard the beep of an alarm lock, and squatted down even further as he walked past me back into the hotel. I stayed crouched behind the car long enough that my knees began to hurt. When I was absolutely sure he wasn't coming back, I walked over to his car and peered in. There it was on the passenger seat – a cup with a mangled piece of lime at the bottom.

I mulled this over as I walked back to the party. I looked down at my watch. I hoped Janice would finally let me go home. I had a lot to think over and a flight to catch the next morning.

And then I heard them. Soft footsteps behind me. I stopped and they stopped. How to handle this? I started walking again, listening for the footsteps, evaluating their rhythm. Pitter patter. Pitter patter. Like a child. A child on tiptoes. It must be Beth or Cheri. Since spouses weren't allowed, it had to be Beth. Why was she following me?

But as I got closer to the ballroom, the footsteps were drowned out by the thump, thump of the bass. Someone had turned the music way up. Oh no. The boom.

I walked through the doorway into a party I did not recognize. Previously well-dressed people had taken off jackets, ties and maybe other things – I didn't really want to know. I spotted Janice over in a corner. She was trying to break up a fight between two attorneys who looked like they could barely stand up. They were throwing unsteady punches. One of them wore snakeskin boots. Forget about Beth, I had to save Janice. I ran over to help.

"My God!" I said, when I reached her.

"I warned you," she replied. She held the arm of one of the combatants. "Now you sit down!" He blinked with surprise and then did as he was told. She turned with fury on the other. "And you, you should be ashamed of yourself. Go!" She pointed to a chair on the other side.

I grabbed his arm since he didn't look like he could actually make it on his own. Dragging a stumbling grown man is hard work. Particularly one who wants to kick you with the pointed toe of his boot. Despite my workouts, I was winded when I finally pushed Shane David into a chair.

Janice came up behind me. "Let's get out of here before they trash the place."

I nodded and turned towards the door. Another movement caught my eye. "That's not —"

"Yes," Janice said grimly.

"Okay." I turned away from one of the management committee members who was alternately dancing and spanking that secretary Grant had been flirting with. She had her dress up, and I caught sight of a pair of black thong underwear. Unfortunately, some images stay with you forever.

CHAPTER 17

The flight to Marshfield was so uneventful that it gave me time to recover from the night before. I even had enough space between flights to walk, not run, through the multicolored tunnel at the Minneapolis airport. As I sat on the puddle jumper into CWA, I put my head in my hands, trying to make sense of everything. My head throbbed. Too many problems to work out. That, and I couldn't get the thonged secretary out of my brain. At least she was wearing underwear – who knows what happened after I left? I shuddered. Don't go there.

My dad met me at the lone baggage carousel. CWA didn't need more than one. He was the typical absent-minded professor, and one of the kindest people you will ever meet. He was the sort of teacher who continued to see his students years after graduation, who took collect calls from distraught relatives, and who managed to keep Ashley and me in line through the beneficence of his expectations. Disappointing Dad was like kicking a puppy. Dad would forgive you, but you couldn't forgive yourself.

He waved at me so I wouldn't be startled – as if I could ever forget the way he stood or the horrible pea green coat he refused to get rid of.

"Liz! It's so good to have you home." He gave me a big bear hug.

"It's good to be home." I hugged him back. I took a deep breath, feeling better already. He let me go and we stood chatting while the baggage came off the plane. He wanted to know about my finals. I told him and explained that my note was officially kaput. He asked about my friends, particularly Holly, for whom he always had a soft spot. He asked about Janice. I filled him in with as much detail as I thought I could. Strangely, neither Vince nor James was mentioned.

We got my bag and walked out the glass doors to the parking lot. Snow lay on the ground in drifts, but the parking lot was clear. If there is anything Wisconsinites do well, it's snow removal. The wind whipped around us, swirling delicate flurries this way and that. I shivered in my winter coat. To think I'd been in shirt sleeves the day before.

"Cold – eh?" said my dad with a grin.

I nodded.

"Wait till you see this."

We got closer to the car. He pulled a jumble of keys from his pocket and said, "You are about to see the best Christmas present ever."

"What?"

He pressed a remote and the car suddenly sprang to life – the lights turned on and the engine started.

"An electric starter!" I said. Living anywhere but the wintry north, one cannot truly appreciate the value of such a gift.

"Yep. Your mom got it installed last week. I didn't know any-thing about it until she gave me the remote with a bow on top."

"Leave it to Mom to plan it all out."

He grinned like a kid in a candy store. "Your mom's a wonder."

My mother was the most capable woman I knew. She managed her job, the house, my dad and everything in between with an energy that took your breath away. No job was too great or too small – you just had to get in there and do it. I am convinced that this attitude is what made her such a good nurse, beloved by patients and staff alike. When you are facing cancer, a healthy dose of Midwestern stick-to-itiveness can be just the thing.

Her practical love helped me immensely with my own diagnosis. She knew I could deal with a brain tumor, so I knew I could. When I'd come home from school depressed and tired of the stares and the teasing, she could always coax me out of it. When Mom told you that middle school wasn't real life, you actually believed her. Later, when I finally had a name for my recognition issues, she refused to let me off the hook. I just had to adapt and get over it. So I did the best I could.

That is not to say that my parents are perfect. Far from it. Within a day, I found all of the old irritations bubbling to the surface. But I knew that they loved and supported me. The same could be said of my sister Ashley. She drove me crazy on purpose. But we loved each other. Most of the time.

I contemplated all of this family togetherness as my father drove me to Marshfield in his super-heated car. The road spread out before us, over and down the rolling hills. Stark farmhouses stood in a sea of snow. The sun hung low and pale on the horizon, with a faint shimmer dancing in the frigid air. I caught my breath. It was incredibly and desolately beautiful. St. Louis was nothing to it.

We pulled into Stratford and turned left. I could feel my anticipation rising the closer we got to town. As we approached, I saw the

Clinic for a moment in the distance, rising above the city. We turned right on McMillan and then up the long hill to our neighborhood. We pulled in. I marveled at how little had changed. In St. Louis, it was unusual to see a neighborhood of ranch homes still standing. The "flipping" bug hadn't hit Marshfield in the same way. There was really no need. If you wanted to build big, you just had to move across Lincoln road and you were officially out of town.

My dad pulled into the driveway and turned off the engine. "Your mom's done at 5:00 today, so I have you all to myself for an hour."

"Where's Ash?"

"She went to visit Marisa. She told me to tell your mom not to wait dinner for her."

"Good luck with that." Even though Marisa was one of Ashley's best friends and they hadn't seen each other in months, Mom would still have Ashley back in time for dinner. Marisa was at Yale and seemed to be doing well. If the concentration of highly educated professionals had done nothing else, it had produced a great school system. Students from Marshfield routinely went to the Ivy Leagues, and anywhere else they wanted to go.

We walked in the door. I smelled the pot roast in the crock-pot. My favorite. It was so tender that you could cut it with a fork. My dad made some tea. We sat down at the kitchen table as if I'd never been away. That was another good thing about my dad – he listened well.

And he knew how to get you started on a subject and keep the conversation going. There was no breaking away once he got his conversational teeth into you. He asked about school and St. Louis, lulling me into a false sense of security. Then he asked about the firm. He knew about the murder, but I'd seriously downplayed my role in the affair.

"So how is the investigation going?" he said.

"I don't know," I replied as nonchalantly as I could. "I think the police got on the wrong track at first, but are exploring other leads now. Why do you ask?"

"I'm still concerned about you working there, and you haven't mentioned it in a while." Of course I hadn't mentioned it since I got involved with James.

"I guess it's gone off my radar screen," I said.

"You're not hiding something from me are you?"

"No —" I said unsteadily. That was a mistake. My dad's vast teaching experience made him an expert lie detector.

"Liz." He gave me his best teacher stare. "What's going on?"

"Well." I looked down. "I can't talk about it."

"Why not?"

"I'm helping out a little."

"In what?"

"In the investigation. You know, just assisting the police every now and then. But it's confidential."

He looked puzzled. "That's not what I was expecting to hear. How can you help the police?"

"I'm observant about details and James thought —" I stopped. I could have kicked myself. Stupid. Stupid. Stupid.

My father jumped on it. "James? Who is James?"

"Detective Paperelli. He's the officer who originally interviewed me. He thought I might have access to information at the firm."

"How much information could you possibly have?" My dad looked skeptical.

"I asked Detective Paperelli the same thing, but I notice things other people don't so – so I told him I'd give it a try."

"How old is this detective?"

How quickly fathers cut to the chase. "Dad. He's engaged to someone. It's not like that at all."

I'm a bad liar. He knew something was up. "Liz, honey, don't get in over your head just because —"

"I'm not," I insisted. "Anyway, I haven't uncovered anything. And I'm working with Janice. She knows all about it, and she would tell me if it's something dangerous. But we've found nothing so far, nothing at all."

"And what if you find something? Someone has killed once."

"I know. I know. Detective Paperelli is on top of it. Don't worry, I'll be fine." No need to mention that I could no longer count on his protection.

"Well —"

"Dad, I don't think they're ever going to find the murderer at this rate – with or without my help."

"You know you can always come home."

I patted my dad's hand. "I've got everything under control." How I wished that were actually true.

"Okay." He was still skeptical but realized that he wasn't going to get any more out of me. He changed tactics. "I saw Dr. Lee at Fleet the other day."

Mills Fleet Farm was the place to get everything for the sports that make living in central Wisconsin tolerable. They also carried a wide variety of agricultural products and camouflage clothing for every member of the family. This time of year they had toys stacked to the ceiling. Perfect for the Santa who also needed udder balm and ammunition. Fleet was called the "man's mall" because men of every type could be found wandering the aisles in search or something, or nothing at all. I think most men went there to get out of the house and meet their friends.

I knew my dad was headed right for a conversation about Nick. I tried desperately to steer it away. "So how did Dr. Lee do this year?" I asked.

Anyone who lived in Marshfield knew that the men were obsessed with deer hunting. My father understood exactly what I was talking about. "Pretty well. He got at least one buck."

"How many points?"

"I don't know."

"Must not have been many then."

My dad chuckled. "We didn't talk about that."

"Oh?" My diversion hadn't worked.

"We talked about you and Nick."

"Mom told me."

"Nick wants to see you when he's here."

"How did he know I was coming home for Christmas?"

"I mentioned it."

"In the same conversation, or a previous one you didn't tell me about?"

"Awhile ago," Dad admitted. "Dr. Lee was buying ammo for that new high powered rifle he got this year."

My dad was strange. He did not hunt and did not own a gun. That didn't mean he couldn't talk shop with the best of them. This was something that I had a hard time explaining to my St. Louis friends. Rural Wisconsin, like the south and west, has a gun culture that is integral to the fabric of society. Everyone has shot a firearm at some point. At a minimum, you know someone who has a range set up for target practice.

I'd practiced with rifles and even a handgun or two over at Nick's house out in the country. I had nothing better to do, and Nick told me I couldn't hurt anything. The recoil took some getting used to, but I knew girls younger than me who were expert shots. I wasn't that good, but I wasn't terrible, either.

Nick. I decided to bite the bullet. "Nick wants to see me?"

"Yep."

"So what's he doing these days?"

"He's at that hedge fund in New York."

"Still working crazy hours and making six figures?"

"Dr. Lee says he just got a promotion."

"Well, well."

"You'll have to ask him about it when you see him."

"If I see him."

"Come on, how bad can it be?"

"You seem very interested in this. Why?" I said.

"I've always liked Nick. You know that."

"But —"

"I don't know, maybe I hoped that with some maturity, you two might get along better."

"So you want to play matchmaker?"

He smiled. "I just want you to be happy."

"Okay, if he calls, I'll agree to see him. No promises, though."

"No promises."

"Good. That's settled. Tell me what else has been going on around here."

The choice was made. Just one very awkward pre-arranged meeting to get through. Fortunately, I was the one who picked up the phone when Nick called. Ashley would have said something obnoxious.

"Liz?" he said. His voice sounded just as I remembered. I felt a lump I wasn't expecting in my throat.

"Yes Nick, it's me."

"It's good to hear your voice – the last time we talked was —"

"Don't go there," I said gently. "If you remember, I was screaming at you."

"Maybe this time we can just talk."

"Let's hope. When are you coming in?"

"Really late on the 23rd. Are you free on the 24th?"

"Mom is making me go to church in the evening, but I'm free during the day."

"We could grab some lunch?"

"Sure. Call me then and we'll work out when and where."

"Sounds good," he said.

"You're flying out on the 26th?"

"How did you know?"

"High-powered jobs don't leave much room for vacation."

"You always know everything, don't you?"

"Annoying, isn't it?" My voice was light, teasing.

"Not really annoying."

"Water under the bridge, Nick. I'll be on my best behavior. It's only a day, after all."

I could hear the smile in his voice. "You better be or I won't forgive you for not emailing me back."

"I didn't know what to say."

"Come up with something before I get there. See you very soon, Liz."

He hung up the phone. I held the receiver for a moment, thinking about us. Nick clearly wanted to make amends. I wasn't sure why, but maybe it didn't matter. Our arguments had always been silly. He had a way of saying something that was so patronizing, I couldn't control myself. It didn't help that we were neck and neck in school. Two similarly competitive people shouldn't date. It wasn't healthy.

But high school was long gone. I didn't feel the surge of envy and wounded pride when I thought of him now. Somewhere along the line it had been replaced with tenderness and a certain nostalgia. I decided to put him out of my mind until I saw him face to face. After all, a lot depended on what he wanted from me. And there was the other problem, the one whose blue eyes were suddenly and intensely clear in my memory. I shoved the receiver into the cradle.

CHAPTER 18

The next morning, I agreed to go with my mother to Wausau to do some last minute shopping. She had the day off, and typical for Mom, had gotten up early to do Christmas cookies and a pie for Christmas day. I'd dragged myself out of bed to help. Some things never changed. Ashley was still asleep when the desserts were done.

Mom also had to drop off a gift for a co-worker at the Clinic. I agreed to go with her and then drive on from there. I parked the truck and went in to wait while she carried out her Santa duties. The Clinic is like a maze if you don't know your way around. It's also physically connected to Saint Joseph's Hospital, which is owned by another organization, so there is an added level of complexity. The place felt like a second home, but I still followed closely behind Mom. You never knew when building services might have added something new.

I took a seat in the waiting area. Mom wanted me to go in with her, but I didn't feel like facing all of the questions about my life in St. Louis. I'd catch up later. The waiting rooms at the Clinic are like any waiting room in St. Louis, except for the selection of magazines. St. Louis boasts *Sports Illustrated* and *Marie Claire*. The Clinic boasts *Field and Stream* and *Country Home*. I sat in the stiff chair, reviewing my options. The usual. But wait, I pulled something from the bottom. The *Wisconsin Bar Journal.* Someone must have left it there by mistake.

Law students in Wisconsin don't know how good they have it. Wisconsin doesn't require its graduates to take the bar exam. This is a serious perk. I thought long and hard about returning to Wisconsin for law school. I applied and was accepted at both U.W. and Marquette. In the end, though, I really liked St. Louis and wanted to stay if I could. Of course, I paid for it every summer with 100 degree heat – and the bar exam.

I flipped through the *Bar Journal,* thinking about what might have been. I got about two thirds of the way in and found the section on the recent bar sanctions. Unlike other states, sanctions by the Wisconsin bar carry with them a write up in the *Bar Journal* detailing the misdeeds and the punishment imposed. I read each one with a frightened fascination. There but for the grace of God. One attorney had alcohol problems, another missed his deadlines, a third lied to clients, and so on. One entry caught my eye:

Disciplinary proceedings against Thomas A. Stevens

On March 7, 2005 the Supreme Court suspended the law license of Thomas A. Stevens, Green Bay, for 180 days effective March 15, 2005, and ordered Stevens to pay the full $41,237.08 cost of the disciplinary proceedings. Disciplinary Proceedings Against Stevens, 2005 WI 35. Stevens stipulated to eight counts of misconduct concerning his client trust account. Stevens deposited client funds into an account that was not designated as a trust account and was not in an interest-bearing account with interest being paid to the Wisconsin Trust Account Foundation, Inc.; failed to create and maintain complete records of client funds regarding settlements;

had shortfalls in the account used for client funds such that the balance in the account was less than the total amount he was supposed to be holding for clients; failed to pay or give credit to three clients whose funds were on deposit in the account for an extensive period of time; and inaccurately certified on his state bar dues statements that he had complied with the trust account record-keeping requirements. This conduct is in violation of ...

The last paragraph cited all of the rules he had violated by his actions.

I stared at the text as if in a dream. I crumpled the *Bar Journal* in my excitement. I knew how they'd done it, how The Lodge investors had taken the money. The theft was in plain sight all along. I had to call Janice. I fished around my purse until I found the cell phone. I looked at it. Cell phone reception inside the Clinic was notoriously spotty. I didn't know how much longer Mom would be. Maybe I would just step outside for a moment.

I got up to leave and my mother appeared as if on cue. She waved to someone in the doorway that I couldn't see. "Ready?" she said.

I nodded. "Do you mind? I have to call Janice."

"Sure. I'll wait if you want."

"No," I said, holding the cell phone up to see if it made a difference. "Let's keep walking. This isn't working very well."

When we got outside, I finally had some signal. I called Janice, but got her secretary instead. She put me into voicemail after asking me how my visit was going.

"Janice, this is Liz," I said. "I figured out how The Lodge investors took the money. Call me as soon as you can. Keep trying if you can't get me. Cell reception is bad. I'll try you again when I get to Wausau. Take care!"

"What was that about?" Mom asked suspiciously.

"Part of the investigation," I said. Dad had filled my mom in on my extracurricular activities. "I think I just figured out another piece of the puzzle."

"Be careful, honey."

"I am, I am. Don't worry, Mom."

"I'm not worrying just yet."

We got to the truck and she unlocked the doors. Most Marshfield families have at least one four-wheel drive vehicle or truck to handle really deep snow. Ours was an old F150 that drank gasoline like water, but could start at minus 20 Fahrenheit. Mom usually drove it, since she had to be at work no matter what. Plus, as one of the few short women in town, she liked the feeling of riding high on the road. She told me she wanted to drive, so I moved over. She turned the key and the engine chugged along beautifully. You can't argue with that kind of performance.

I was quiet on the drive to Wausau. I kept checking my phone, but there were many roads with no cell coverage. True Wisconsinites always travel with a shovel, blankets and other emergency gear, because you never know what could happen. Help might not be a phone call away. Mom took my silence as an opportunity to bring me up to speed on the people in her department. That was one thing about the Clinic. Turnover was low enough that most of my mother's department had watched me grow up.

As we neared the mall, I tried Janice again. Her secretary told me that she was in a meeting. We pulled into the mall parking garage.

"What exactly are we looking for?" I asked. Mom had been uncharacteristically vague about the purpose of the trip.

"Nothing specific. You know I do most of my shopping early on." I wouldn't have expected anything less. My mother had most gifts purchased by August.

"Then why are we here?"

"Mother-daughter bonding. Let's see what they have."

We went to one of the department stores and looked at clothes. She urged me to try on a suit, but I wasn't in the mood. I needed to talk to Janice. Finally, after the third try, my mom was exasperated.

"Liz, in case you haven't figured it out, I want to buy you clothes for Christmas. Please, please try something on. Now!"

I looked at her and laughed. Sometimes the simplest things were over my head. I reached over and gave her a hug.

"I'm sorry, Mom. Tell me what I should try on."

She laughed too. "You are clueless. A suit, honey, a suit. You've said 'no' to every one I suggested."

"Okay." I flipped through the rack with renewed purpose. A black suit would be the most useful. I picked out four and threw them over my shoulder. We marched off to find a dressing room.

"Do you need help carrying those?"

"I'm fine," I called back. Finally, I saw the reason for all of the free weights. We found a dressing room.

"You can come in if you want. You've seen it all before," I said.

"Many, many times. You were a cute baby."

"And there are lots of photos of me in the tub to prove it."

We squeezed into the dressing room. I hung the suits on a peg on the wall. The first one I tried had a close-fitting jacket and a straight skirt. Straight skirts didn't terrify me the way they did in the past. Maybe it was that I could put one on without strange misshapen fat lumps appearing from out of nowhere. I turned and examined my backside. No fat lumps there either, at least not the ones I wasn't supposed to have. The jacket might even look good with a pair of jeans and those kitten heels.

"What do you think?" I asked. Daughters know that this is a delicate question, requiring a truthful but tactful answer. With two daughters, my mom was an old pro.

"I think it fits you just right. Lift your arms up." This was the true test. "Not too tight. That's good. It's well made." She pulled down on the jacket. "Double stitched."

"So, it's a possibility?"

"Yep."

I took the jacket and the skirt off. I turned to hang them up and my mother said, "You need new underwear, Liz."

"I know. I just haven't gotten around to it."

"Let's get you some."

"Another day. I'm not in the mood. I'd have to look at bras too, and you know how I hate that."

Mom nodded. She knew not to push me on that subject. I was just barely down to a "D" cup. Thank goodness. While I might be able to find something that didn't look industrial, even D's had underwire. I defy any woman of a similar size to find an underwire bra that is actually comfortable. The wire eventually works free and pokes you under the arm. It never fails. But if you don't have the wire, all the weight pulls on your shoulders. This makes the straps dig in, causing painful red stripe marks. You're damned either way.

If Dante had been a woman, he would have designed a circle of hell for bras bigger than a "C."

I pulled the next suit down. This one had pants and a longer jacket. I put one leg into the pants and my cell phone went off. I almost fell over trying to get it out of my purse. I saw the number.

"Janice?"

"Liz, what's going on? I've been in a client meeting all morning."

"I know how they did it! How they took the money —"

Her voiced lowered, "Hold on a minute, I'm just getting up to shut my door." I heard a shuffling and then a door close. "Okay, go ahead."

"They took it out of the trust account."

"How? The accountants would have caught any unusual withdrawals. And I've looked at those records."

"Not if the payments were small, over several years, and designated as settlement proceeds."

"But we track where the checks go. That kind of fraud would be easy to spot."

"Not if the clients are fake, too. Think about this. You get a settlement from a third party and deposit it in the account. Then you send part to the client and you retain part for fees. But what if the amount you put in doesn't equal the amount you pay out?"

"So, you put in $100 and send the client $120?"

"Yes. And what if the clients and the third party companies making the settlements are both entirely fictitious, and you do this over and over again with small discrepancies each time."

"But eventually the money in the account will be exhausted."

"Right, but, like all Ponzi schemes, the thing is kept afloat with new infusions of cash – namely legitimate client funds that are continually being deposited. Plus, I think they thought that when The Lodge turned around, they could put the money back by doing the same thing in reverse."

"But that would require a huge amount of coordination."

"That's why John Harding had to know about it. He may even have been the mastermind."

There was silence on the other end of the line.

"Janice?"

"People have been murdered for less," she said quietly.

"I know. We have to be careful how we do this."

Another long pause. "I think we should look into this ourselves. No use going to the police until we are sure."

"We're on our own anyway."

"I'm going to start by looking back through the accounts."

"I think you'll find certain people have had an influx of clients in the last couple of years."

"When are you getting back?"

"Right after New Year's."

"Okay, we'll be in touch. I'll let you know if I find anything. When you get back, you and I can plot strategy."

"Sure thing. And Janice —"

"Yes?"

"Thanks for taking me seriously."

"Now, I'm not completely sold on this idea, mind you, but I definitely think it's worth a look."

"Merry Christmas!"

"It won't be merry if you're right. You're still coming with me if this gets messy?"

"We're in this together."

"Good. I'll hold you to that. Merry Christmas to you. Take care of yourself."

She hung up. My mother gave me that hard-edged stare that meant I would have some explaining to do. I smiled weakly and pulled up the pants. This wasn't going anywhere good.

"Janice is looking into it," I said. "Please hand me that jacket." My mother frowned, but handed it over.

"I'll explain it all on the drive home," I promised.

"Yes," was all she said.

After much back and forth, and at least ten other suits my mom forced me to try on, we decided on the first suit.

"Merry Christmas," Mom said as she paid for it. This being my mom, she produced a twenty percent off coupon just for the occasion.

The drive back wasn't as painful as anticipated. My mother had even more skepticism than Janice about my theory. She didn't think we'd find anything. This was a relief and an annoyance. I knew I was right.

The rest of the week passed quickly. I did nothing but sleep in, eat Mom's food, and help with assorted Christmas tasks. I also walked the trail that ran through town for exercise and to take the edge off when my family drove me crazy. That happened at least twice a day. There is nothing more calming than tromping along with only the sound of your boots crunching in the snow.

Before I knew it, Christmas Eve arrived. I slept in late because I'd drunk way too much of my dad's super potent eggnog the night before. I was still slumped over a cup of coffee at the kitchen table when Nick called.

"Hello?"

"Liz!" His voice seemed too chipper. "You sound groggy. I thought I was the one sleeping in."

"Eggnog," was all I could get out.

I heard him laughing on the other end. "Your dad still makes that stuff?"

"Yes."

"And you still drink it?"

"This is Marshfield. There isn't much else to do." I took a sip of coffee. "And I was feeling nostalgic."

"For a hangover?"

"I'd forgotten about that part."

"Well, take some aspirin so I can come pick you up. Where do you want to eat?"

Lunch didn't exactly sound good at that moment, but I did not want to be rude. My thoughts were like molasses. I settled on the known and hoped he wouldn't take it as a sign. "Our place?" I said.

"You remembered."

"I'll probably die a premature death from all the food I ate there with you." Who was I kidding? The food was delicious. Our place was a family-style restaurant on Central. It served the best fried food imaginable. Nick and I spent many evenings there catching dinner before we walked to the movie theater down the street.

"Looking forward to it," he said chuckling. "See you in an hour?"

"See you then."

I struggled up from my chair. As usual, pride compelled me to put some effort into my appearance. I put on the same jeans I'd worn to meet James. They were the only ones that really fit. I didn't want to look droopy. This was Marshfield, so I had to skip the heels and the fitted top. I opted instead for snow boots and a sweater. The overcoat was the same. Still too big. I set it on the back of a chair and waited.

CHAPTER 19

Nick pulled up to the house in a Cadillac SUV. I watched him get out of the car from where I stood behind a curtain. He looked even more handsome than when I'd seen him last. Nick's father was from a second-generation Chinese-American family. His mother was a leggy blond Wisconsin woman. Nick was tall and lanky, with thick dark hair and chocolate brown eyes. When he moved into town sophomore year, I thought he looked exotic. The math teacher assigned him to an empty seat next to me. I spent the whole hour staring at him when I thought he wasn't looking. He told me later that he had been looking. He thought I was odd.

But I was fascinated by the smoothness of his skin and the angles of his cheekbones. He had the kind of face that becomes beautiful the more you study it. The kind of face you don't forget. Unless you're me. My recognition hinged on so many other things that I lost count. As we sat together in math class, and later, when the teacher put us together on projects, I studied every gesture with an obsessive concentration. I couldn't get enough.

Of course, his personality fueled my obsession. He was very smart and had a playful sense of humor. I can forgive a lot if someone makes me laugh. And despite the fact that his father had become my neurologist, Nick talked to me as if I were a normal person. I spent too much time on our work together just so I could prolong every minute, every second. At the end of three months, I'd fallen hope-lessly in love with him. He may or may not have known about the depth of my feelings when he asked me if I wanted to see a movie. Looking back, I think he must have meant it as a casual invitation. He'd decided I wasn't that odd after all.

I remember the date like it was yesterday. Our parents dropped us off in front of the theater. Neither one of us could drive. We stood there awkwardly, saying nothing and looking at the ground, before we went in to get our tickets. The plan was to see an early movie and then get something to eat. We had a deadline of 10:30, when our parents would pick us up in the parking lot behind the theater. It was very proper.

We spent the first fifteen minutes in tentative conversation about school. We got sodas and some popcorn. I paid for the sodas. He paid for the popcorn. Then he said something that made me laugh. I felt the constraint fall away. The next fifteen minutes we spent in our seats, talking about everything and nothing at all. The lights dimmed and we got comfortable. We sat in the back, third row from the wall.

I have no explanation for what happened next, except that there is something about a darkened theater. It does strange things. The movie started. He asked me if I wanted some popcorn from the giant tub we'd bought. His face was unexpectedly close to mine. I looked him in the eyes. He turned his head ever so slightly. I doubted only a second before I leaned in and kissed him on the lips.

It was my first kiss. I am amazed that I could have been that bold at fifteen. Nick must have been impressed. After a moment of sur-prise, he started to kiss me back, hesitantly at first, and then with a desire that matched my own adolescent longings. No one ever forgets the first kiss. I certainly don't remember anything about the movie. After that, we were an official couple. We saw each other as much as was humanly possible, becoming so close that we might have finished each other's sentences if we wanted to. Unfortunately, the honeymoon couldn't survive our own competitive tendencies. The same activities that drove us together drove us apart. After three years of yo-yo dating, we'd finally had enough. Still, Nick was my first everything. I hadn't found anyone since who even came close. Until James, but he was taken.

I stood there at the window and felt that old sense of anticipation bubbling up within me. Maybe this was a new beginning for us. I stepped from behind the curtain and waved at him. He waved back and grinned. I'd forgotten how his smile lit up his whole face.

I opened the door. He was inside in two great strides. "Liz!" he said, wrapping me in a big bear hug. I put my arms around him and hugged him back. His smell was so familiar that I felt transported back in time. Memories flooded my head. His smile, his laugh, his arm around my shoulder, his hand in mine. And other memories that were – I wasn't safe with those. It had been a long time.

I thought about the night his car broke down. We walked hand in hand through the snow to a farmhouse a mile up the road. We talked about our future. College and then graduate school. Someplace close to each other. Then we'd get married. We'd have two, maybe three, children and live happily ever after. Walking along, snow crunching underfoot and the stars above us, it seemed so very simple. We would be together forever.

I pulled away first. "It's good to see you again. You look great."

He grinned. "So do you. You've done something with your hair." He reached over and gently pulled a curl. "It looks good."

"Thanks. My dad's here. He'd love to see you." Nick hesitated. "Don't worry, Dad won't start with one of his stories. I've warned him," I said.

"Then okay."

He took off his jacket and laid it carefully over the back of the sofa. A Burberry. I must have a thing for men who wear that brand. Nick had moved up in the world. He slipped off his boots and ambled over to the kitchen in his stocking feet. You can't take the Wisconsin out of the boy. Removing the boots was still a matter of course.

"Hey Dad," I called back to the bedrooms, "Nick's here!"

My dad appeared at once. "Nick!" They shook hands. "So you're keeping busy?"

"Yeah. My job's pretty demanding. But it's good."

I heard his cell phone buzz. He had it clipped to his belt. He looked down and pulled it out of the holster. It was small and very thin.

"Excuse me a moment," he said. He moved to the opposite corner of the kitchen.

"Yes? I've got the BlackBerry in the car – no. Tell Jeff I'll email him this afternoon." Then he mumbled a series of instructions. "Okay, okay," he finally said. "Talk to you later." He hung up and put the phone back on his belt. "Sorry about that. Liz, maybe we should —"

"Sure. Dad, I'll be back in time for church, okay?"

"Good. Have fun kids." He shook hands with Nick again. "Good to see you Nick."

"Good to see you. Tell Mrs. Howe I said hello."

"Sure."

As we left, Nick turned to me. He had that look that reminded me of the boy I'd first kissed. "Still have to ask permission to leave?"

"Old habits die hard. I'm sure your mom does the same thing."

"I barely got out of the house."

"I love your mom."

He rolled his eyes. "There is a reason I live so far away."

"You love it. You can't tell me otherwise." Nick was a cherished only child.

"You know me too well."

We bundled up and walked to the car. "Nice ride," I said. He was clearly in a car rental class way above my own.

"Corporate discount." He shrugged his shoulders. "No big deal."

"Do you still remember how to drive around here?"

"You don't trust me to get you to Central?" Central Avenue was so close the car could barely warm up.

"I don't know," I said teasing him, "you look out of practice to me. And there is snow on the ground."

He gave me a playful push towards the passenger side. "Chicken," he said.

We got in and he started the car up.

"That's one thing you forgot," I said as I fastened my seat belt.

"What?"

"Always leave the car running for short stops."

"But I didn't know about your dad. I could have been there for hours."

"I wasn't considering the dad factor."

"Liz." He turned to face me. "It's really good to see you again. I've missed talking to you."

I held his gaze for a moment. "I missed you too. I didn't like how we ended."

"Me neither. I can't even remember what the fight was about." He backed the car out of the driveway.

"Calculus," I said.

"Calculus? Really?"

"Last week of school, practically last homework assignment. I told you I had trouble with a problem, and you told me that I was solving the problem wrong. I took exception to your tone."

"But that's ridiculous!"

"Agreed. Competition was always our biggest problem."

"When did you figure this out?"

"I've had years to ponder the demise of our relationship."

He didn't reply.

After several minutes, we pulled onto Central. He parked the car and we walked in the cold to the restaurant. I felt it more than I used to. St. Louis had thinned my blood.

"I wonder if they still have liver and onions?" he said, opening the door for me to pass through.

"I bet they do."

"I don't know how you could eat that stuff."

"I won't order it if it makes you uncomfortable."

"No," he said, "go right ahead. It wouldn't seem like this was really happening if you didn't."

"I don't think I have the stomach for it today."

We sat at a booth by the window and scanned our laminated menus. Liver and onions was indeed still there. The waitress appeared and asked about drinks. I had been spoiled by good artisanal coffee, so I ordered a Diet Coke instead. They couldn't make a bad one of those. Nick ordered a regular Coke and told the waitress we needed more time.

I smiled and shook my head.

"What?" he said.

"I suddenly remembered that you hate Diet Coke. Every time I ordered one, you told me that laboratory rats died from saccharine overdoses."

"I was an ass."

"Yes, I thought so at the time."

"And now?" He seemed strangely anxious for the answer. I saw the pucker between his brows. I hadn't lost my touch. Reading him was like riding a bicycle.

"Not so much. What are you going to order?"

He scanned the menu quickly. "I remember the hamburgers were good. You?"

"Maybe the BLT. I can always take the bacon off if I can't handle it."

He smiled. "I wouldn't want you to get sick. Your parents won't forgive me a second time."

"At least we're over 21."

"I couldn't drink peppermint Schnapps again, could you?"

"I couldn't drink any alcohol for quite some time after that," I said. "What were we thinking? The three of us drank that whole bottle!"

"I blame Jake. It was his idea and his mom's Schnapps," Nick said.

"But he was right. It tasted pretty good with the hot chocolate."

"Do you know what happened to Jake?" he said.

"I haven't heard from him in years." I looked at Nick. "I remember you had to carry me to the car. And I think you dropped me once or twice. It's all a little fuzzy."

"What I remember is that I had to pull over a couple of times so you could throw up. I was so afraid you'd ruin my car."

"So much compassion. So young."

"I'm not proud of it."

"Well, we were idiots."

He smiled at me and I felt as if time stood still between us, as if we were as close as we had ever been. Then his cell phone rang. He pulled it off his belt to read the number.

"Oh, I have to take this one. Do you mind?"

"No, go ahead."

"Hello. Yes, you're breaking up. Hold on." He slid out of the booth and walked to the door in search of better reception. I watched him as he stood in the doorframe. Then he opened the door and stepped outside. I heard the door clang shut behind him.

I watched him from the window. He paced back and forth on the street, without a coat, gesturing to no one. Despite everything, I was still attracted to him. That tall lanky frame and dark hair. It hit me all of a sudden that I had a type. Nick and James were definitely it. And Vince. If only Vince were a little taller. Then Nick was down the street and out of sight. My type. And what about John

Harding? What if? Another piece slid into place. I was either bril-liant or crazy.

The waitress reappeared with our drinks. She looked at me and then at Nick's empty coat in the booth. She gave me a sympathetic smile and asked if I wanted to order for myself. I decided to order for both of us. She was about to leave when I noticed her name tag. It read "Dawn Faust." I asked her if she was related to Don Faust who was two years ahead of me in high school. She was his third cousin from the Spencer side of the family. It was good to be back in Marshfield. I sipped my Diet Coke as an idea slowly crept up on me. Maybe the firm was more like Marshfield than anyone suspected.

Dawn brought me another Diet Coke five minutes later. I think she felt sorry for me. Nick was still AWOL. I did start to wonder if he had bailed on me. I looked in my purse. I had enough money to cover the meal, but I'd have to walk home. I started to get annoyed. Really annoyed. This was typical Nick. Just when I'd decided to leave as soon as I'd eaten, he reappeared.

He smiled sheepishly. I noticed he now had his BlackBerry and his phone. "Sorry that took so long. My boss wanted me to get an email out and well —"

"I understand," I said quietly. "All of that takes time."

"My job is very complicated. If I'm not there —" he said defensively.

I cut him off. This wasn't going anywhere good. "No need to explain. I work with lawyers."

"Right." He clearly wanted to move on. "Where is the waitress? I didn't remember that the service was so slow."

"It isn't. I ordered for both of us. I hope you don't mind."

"Not unless you ordered me liver and onions."

"The thought did cross my mind. You shouldn't leave me alone like that. You don't know what I might do."

"Won't happen again," he said sincerely.

"So why do you have a BlackBerry and a phone? I thought the BlackBerry was the phone."

"Yeah, but it's big and heavy, so I can't really hang it on my belt."

"Plus having two makes you look really important."

He grinned. "Is it working?"

"The people in this restaurant are impressed."

"Really?" He tried not to sound pleased, but I knew him too well. "How do you know?"

"I notice things."

"You always did, didn't you?" There was an edge of sadness in his voice.

"Are you happy, Nick?"

"Yes. And you?"

"I've got a handle on my life, at least. And your job? And New York?"

"I like the excitement." I couldn't tell if it was the job or the city. "I don't miss Marshfield, if that's what you're asking."

"I imagine work doesn't leave you much time to go out."

"No, but I'm not complaining. When we go out, we always have a good time. You should visit. I guarantee you'll have the time of your life."

"You know me. The life of the party."

"Don't sell yourself short, Liz."

Then he smiled at me in a way I remembered so well. It was a slow secret smile that lit up his eyes with mischief. I remembered how that smile made me feel. The force of it hit me in a wave of butterflies and longing. How I had loved him! And here I was, sitting across the table from him again, watching that perfect smile spread across his face.

Dawn arrived with the food, breaking the spell. I thanked her for her timing. I was on thin ice. It was too easy to trade on the feelings of the past, the yin and yang of love and hate, but we weren't in high school any more. I bit down on my BLT and chewed slowly.

"You mentioned 'we' a moment ago. I assume you've made a lot of friends in New York?" I said after several minutes of silence.

"Yeah. Guys I work with mostly and some friends from college who moved to New York at the same time. So we go out. And there was Juliet."

I took the bait. "Juliet?"

"My ex."

"Oh." This was where we were headed.

"We broke up six months ago."

"I'm sorry, Nick."

He gave me a rueful look. "I should have seen it coming but I didn't."

"That's hard. How long were you together?"

"Over four years. We met in college."

"Wow." I felt sad for him. Four years is a long time to invest in someone who walks out the door. I thought about James. How long had he and Angelica been together? Maybe longer than four years. I didn't know. I looked back at Nick.

"I'm over the worst of it now."

I tried to lighten the mood. "So you're on the rebound, then? I'll be sure to watch out in case you do something crazy."

"When have I ever done something crazy?"

"The aforementioned Schnapps incident."

"But you and Jake were in on that one."

"Miller's pond." He'd insisted the ice was thick enough to walk on. It wasn't.

"A freak accident."

"The Nikolai party," I said.

A friend of a friend told him about a great party in Stratford. Nick failed to get the address or the complete name of the host. All he knew was that the friend of a friend's last name was Nikolai. Since so many people in the area are related, there are hundreds, maybe thousands of people with the same last name. We drove around for hours and never found the party. We did, however, find a snow covered ditch and had to have a good Samaritan with a truck and a chain pull us out.

"That could have happened to anyone."

"And the hot sauce incident?" Nick bet Jake that he could eat a hamburger with an entire bottle of Tabasco poured over it. After four bites, Nick's tongue was so swollen that he couldn't talk. If only Vince could have seen it.

"Okay, okay. I forgot about that one. Maybe you should worry. But I just wanted to reconnect."

"And see if there was still something between us?"

He hesitated, torn between hedging and honesty. Honesty won. "I was curious. I haven't seen you in so long."

"I'm not the one that got away."

"You might be."

I gave my head a little shake, but a part of my brain wanted to examine the possibility.

"Hear me out, Liz. You don't know how often I've wanted to pick up the phone and call you. Just to talk like we used to."

"Why didn't you?"

"I didn't think you'd talk to me."

"You were very sneaky to get your father to do your dirty work."

"How I got you here is beside the point."

"So what is the point?"

"I've missed you." He made a move to hold my hand across the table, but I shifted it away. I needed time to think.

"I've missed you too," I admitted, "but I don't know if that is enough."

"It could be."

"We had a really rocky relationship."

"But we're older and wiser now."

Nick wanted me back. Juliet must have really hurt him. And, I guess I wasn't as forgettable as I'd thought.

"Look," he said with that persuasive tone I knew so well. "I know this may be too sudden, but I'm just asking that you let me get to know you again."

I remembered a time when Nick could have persuaded me to do anything. "Well —" I hoped that time had passed.

"I've never felt the way I did with you."

"And Juliet?" I said skeptically.

"It was different. We never fought over anything. Then, one day she just walked out."

"I never hesitated to tell you where I stood, even if it was squarely against you."

"It's what I loved and hated about you."

"I could say the same," I replied dryly.

"I know you could." His eyes softened. "I miss that spark we had." I saw the gaze that always made the blush steal up my cheeks. My mind was suddenly overwhelmed with secret memories.

I looked down at my plate. "We were something."

"More than something." He cleared his throat as if to say more, but his cell phone rang. I looked up. He was staring at the number with a stricken look. "I have to get this one. Do you mind?"

I shook my head. The distraction was a relief. I could feel my defenses weakening. Nick used our past as a weapon. A very powerful weapon. I took a long drink of Diet Coke and looked around at the restaurant. Marshfield never seemed to change. That was the problem. In another setting – St. Louis, New York – the connection Nick and I had would seem like nothing. It was this place, I decided.

I thought about Vince. Maybe I just had to get to know him. He was certainly nice and smart. I could overlook the height. Then I remembered James' blue, blue eyes and the way his hands felt on my shoulders as he said goodbye. That was way beyond type. That was chemistry. It was so intense that it felt like a physical presence shimmering in the air around us. Around me. I had to remember there was no reciprocation. No reciprocation at all. Better not to think about James.

Nick reappeared. "I'm so sorry, Liz. It's just —"

"The work doesn't stop."

"You're too good for me."

I couldn't take much more of this onslaught. "I think you mistake me for someone else."

"I was a jerk," he said seriously.

"Are you still?"

He reached across the table and placed his hand very gently under my chin, tilting my head until our eyes met. The feel of his fingers touching my face was achingly familiar.

"I think I shouldn't have let you go."

I took his hand. "You were my first everything. No one can replace you in that."

"So why not try again?"

"We are not the same people we were then."

"Are you seeing someone?"

"You should have asked that first."

He grinned. "I should have, but I figured you would tell me if you were." He paused, seeming unsure. "You would have, wouldn't you?"

"That's not the issue. I don't know what I want. My head is spinning right now."

He pressed his advantage. "But you might consider it?"

"I would consider getting to know you again, then maybe more."

"More?"

"I'm not opposed to more in principle."

"More was always the best part."

I felt my cheeks flush bright red.

"And we're adults now. No sneaking around. We can do what we want," he added.

"Not when we're staying with our parents, we can't," I replied. "And, to be clear, I've only agreed to keep in touch and get to know you again."

"Fine," he said, putting his other hand on top of mine. "But don't be surprised if I try for more. I'd forgotten what you do to me."

I gently pulled my hand away. "I think we should pay the bill."

"Oh yes." He reflexively looked at his watch. "When do you need to get back?"

"I have an hour and a half. Do you want to get coffee?" I said.

"Sure." After a small disagreement, I allowed him to pay for my lunch.

We walked the short distance down the street to the Daily Grind. The cold air helped me to clear my head. We sat and talked as we sipped the strong brew. I knew him well enough to ask the questions about his life that kept him from veering off track. He asked about law school and my classes. I told him about the firm and Janice. I didn't mention the murder or the investigation. I couldn't trust myself in front of him. He might remember me well enough to read my face.

After two hours, we walked back to the car in companionable silence. He opened the passenger door, and I slid onto the leather seat. He got in on the other side and turned the engine on. The seat warmed up suddenly. Definitely a different rental class. As I pulled the passenger door shut, I felt Nick's arm around my waist. He was too quick. I didn't have time to protest. He pulled me to him.

"Remember that first date?" he said softly, his face inches from mine. He kissed me firmly on the lips. A war raged in my head.

The rational brain wanted to pull away and slap him. The irrational brain was kissing him back. The irrational brain seemed to have the upper hand. The feel of his lips on mine brought back all of the joyful memories of his touch, his smell. I leaned in further, closer and closer. Maybe this was what I was looking for. Maybe we were meant to be together. And then it wasn't just memories of Nick that filled my head, but something else. Someone else.

I heard the muffled ringing of his cell phone. I pulled away, disgusted with myself.

"Nick, your cell."

"Let it go to voicemail." He leaned in again. The phone continued to ring.

"It's not going to voicemail."

"Leave it," he said, and kissed me some more. The phone continued.

"Damn." He pulled away. He grabbed it off his belt and stared angrily at the screen. "What the —" He didn't finish. He snapped it open and said, "Yes, sir?"

I didn't follow the rest of the conversation. I could tell that something was wrong at work. Nick's voice vibrated with tension. The cell phone had saved me yet again. I felt relieved. He shut the phone off.

"I'm late. Would you mind dropping me off at church?"

"Liz —" Nick started. He saw in my face that the mood had shifted. He put the car in drive and pulled out into the street. "I'm sorry. That was a really bad way to end."

"You had to take the call. Is everything okay?"

"Fine," he said flatly. "I fly out in a day and half anyway. There's no way I could see you tomorrow, is there?"

"On Christmas Day?"

"It's all I have left."

"Your mom would never forgive you," I said.

"I know." I saw the wheels turning. "In the evening?"

"My mom actually has the day off this year. I promised we'd watch movies. You could come by."

"Would your parents leave us alone for more than a minute?"

I smiled ruefully. "Not likely."

"I've blown my one chance, haven't I?"

"Maybe that's a good thing."

He frowned. "Not in my book."

"I mean, maybe we need to get to know each other again. We can't just pick up where we left off. It doesn't work that way."

He pulled into the church parking lot. It was filling up fast for the Christmas Eve service.

"So this is goodbye for now?" he said.

"Yes."

He leaned over, his face again inches from mine. "Goodbye Liz, but don't be surprised if I catch a flight and show up on your doorstep one day."

"Goodbye Nick." He shifted his head slightly, and I felt his lips against my cheek. If I had turned my head even half an inch, I could have kissed him again. I held back. The spell irretrievably broken. I moved away and opened the door. My feet hit the pavement.

I waved to him as he slowly pulled out of the parking lot. He waved back but didn't smile.

CHAPTER 20

After that excitement, Christmas Day seemed flat. I stayed home. We had more snow, so Ashley coaxed me outside for a snowball fight. Mom and I watched movies, as promised. I caught myself wishing Nick would appear a couple of times. He called me at 9:30 to wish me a Merry Christmas. We chatted for a while, then exchanged contact information, promised to email, and said goodbye. He didn't mention coming to see me again. I couldn't tell if I was relieved.

The next day was Monday. I went with my mom back to Wausau. She wanted to return a sweater Dad had given her that was too big. She also wanted to find some deeply discounted Christmas placemats. We didn't find what she wanted. Nothing was discounted to the bargain basement levels required to tempt my mom. Still, it was fun to wander around with her. I could tell that she was dying to ask me about Nick. I managed to elude her questions. At least Nick seemed to have forced all thoughts of my putative detective career from her mind.

As I listened to her talk, I mulled over the nature of my existence. Perverse was the word for it. I had gone from the Sahara desert of dry spells, to two interested parties. Yet, the one person I really wanted was engaged to someone else. I had secured a job at a prestigious law firm, with a partner I liked and respected, but a murderer was still on the loose and other partners were embezzling from the firm. I was the reverse of lucky. I wasn't Midas, I was Sadim.

I considered the murder investigation. I had a feeling, subtle and indescribable, that my mind was close to putting it all together. I felt that at any moment I might reach out and touch the answer. I needed to use this time to really and truly think.

I spent the rest of the week turning the case over and over in my mind. Nick called me when he got back to New York. His call left me unsettled again. I had to expend some mental energy on that problem, but decided not to decide anything until I got back to St. Louis. I concentrated again on the investigation.

Ashley mistook my contemplation for depression. She made a valiant effort to get me out of the house. Most of her friends had already gone back to school, so having a pet project eased the boredom. She even got me to agree to go with her to a New Year's Eve party. It wasn't a hard choice. The alternative was another night home with my parents. My tolerance of their quirks had reached a tipping point. You can't go home again.

At 9:30 on New Year's Eve, we set off together in her junky old Corolla for a party at a friend of a friend's house in Milladore. Milladore is an excruciatingly small town some distance from Marshfield. Depending on the weather and the number of trucks, it took between forty-five minutes and an hour to get there. Snow had fallen during the day, but the night was crisp and clear in a way only rural areas can be.

We drove on the old Hwy 10 for about fifteen minutes in silence. I was still working the case in my head.

Ashley said, "You'll like this house we're going to."

"Whose house is it, again?"

"Dr. McDonald's."

"I thought he lived over on 6th street in town."

"He sold that house. He bought some land once his kids went to college and built this house. It's like his dream house or something."

"Really? Aren't you supposed to downsize at that point?"

She shrugged her shoulders. "The house is huge. Brian told me – you remember him, don't you?"

"Brian Huber?"

"Yeah. Well, Brian is friends with the McDonald's son, Nate. Brian told me the house cost well over a million to build."

"In Milladore?" That hardly seemed like a prudent investment.

"It's the dream house so I don't suppose they plan to sell."

"I guess not. Is Nate throwing this party?"

"Yeah. His parents are out of town."

"They don't know about it?"

She shrugged her shoulders again. "I'm not sure. Nate's two years older, so —"

"Still." I paused a moment. "Am I going to be the oldest person at this party?"

Ashley hesitated. "You're not that old."

"Thanks. That answers that."

We sat in silence for another long moment.

"Liz, promise me something, will you?"

"What?" With Ashley you could never say yes unconditionally.

"Promise me you'll haul me out of there if I start acting crazy. Even if I don't want to go."

"What's going on?"

"I heard Jason might be coming, and I don't want to give him any ideas. Even if I'm a little drunk."

Jason was the ex boyfriend who had dumped Ashley at the end of senior year and then, to add insult to injury, spread all sorts of rumors about her. Most of which were untrue. The rest should have been kept to himself. I was surprised at Ashley's reaction. I would have hated him with a passion and found my revenge. Ashley turned everything inward. That she could even face seeing Jason again was a triumph.

"Understood," I said.

"Thanks, Sis."

"And I can keep him at bay. I have a whole bunch of nasty things I'd like to say to him."

"You always did have a mouth."

"It comes in handy sometimes."

"Speaking of ex's, how is Old Saint Nick?"

"Very funny. He's fine."

"He's after you again?" Ashley was harder to avoid than my mom.

"Hard to say."

"He's definitely interested in something."

"How do you know?"

"I saw you kissing him, or him kissing you."

"What?"

"You're not going to deny it, are you?"

"Well, no, but —"

"You didn't seem to mind, so I assumed you guys were getting back together or maybe it was just —" She looked at me significantly.

"Stop." I giggled nervously. "You are the sneakiest little spy, Ash. Were you following us?"

"No," she said virtuously. "I was just walking on the sidewalk. You've been in St. Louis too long. Everyone knows everyone's business in this town. You can't just kiss Nick on the street without anyone noticing."

"We were in his car – as you obviously know – not on the street. And he kissed me, so I didn't really have a choice on the location. Was anyone else around? Did anyone else see us, do you think?"

"I don't think so. Hey, is Nick a good kisser? I've always wanted to ask. You seemed into him, but I could never see it. He was so geeky." She paused. "Although I can see it now. He's turned into a hottie. I guess I should give you credit for seeing it before anyone else."

"Thanks," I said dryly. "I'm glad you approve. But we're not getting back together just yet."

"Why not? I mean, if he's a good kisser – which he is, isn't he? You never answered, but I can see by your smile that he must be. So, we've established that he's now hot, although he wasn't before. And is a good kisser – which it sounds like he always was. And he's obviously into you. He was then anyway, and his coming to see you now must mean he still is. And you are now looking so much better than you did a year ago and maybe since high school. I haven't told you that yet, have I? The new hair is awesome, and you look really buff. Okay, so where was I?"

I laughed. "I have no idea."

"Wait a minute, I'm starting to get somewhere. He's hot. He's interested in you. You're obviously interested in him —"

I started to interrupt, but she dismissed me with a wave of her hand. "I saw you kiss him back, remember? You must be interested. So the point is – what is the problem? Other than maybe distance, but you're almost done, so you could get a job in New York. Or he could get one in St. Louis."

I interrupted her. "I think he's still on the rebound."

"Since when?"

"Six months ago, but they'd been dating since college. She walked out on him and he didn't see it coming."

"That's not good." She drove in silence for a minute. "But I'm your sister, so I'm not totally clueless. If that were the only thing, you'd still go for it. You and Nick were tight – even I could see that, and I wasn't paying attention most of the time. The rebound wouldn't stop you. You haven't exactly done much since high school."

"How would you know?"

She gave me a pitying look. "Don't lie to me. I know you. There's something else going on."

I said nothing, hoping to stonewall her. A minute passed, and then another.

"Does it have to do with the investigation?" she finally said.

"How did you come up with that one?"

"Ah ha! I can tell it does. Cough it up. What's going on?"

"It's a long story."

Ashley gestured out the window with her hand. "Look around. We've got time."

I looked out the window. There is no feeling more lonely than a drive on a winter's night. Off in the distance, one light twinkled. Then two. The headlights shone in a pale arc in front of us, reflected back off the snow-covered road. And beyond that, there was nothing. No sign of where we'd been or where we were going. Just the inky darkness spreading out around us.

I took a deep breath and turned back to Ashley. "I think I'm in love with someone who's engaged to someone else."

Her mouth dropped open. "Who?"

I told her the whole story from beginning to end, without missing a single detail. Everything that had happened since I found John Harding's body in the stairwell. It felt so good to talk to someone that the words just poured out of my mouth. I couldn't stop. Ashley listened quietly and didn't interrupt. I noticed that we got off on the wrong road once or twice and had to turn around. Other than that, she showed no sign of surprise or concern.

When I'd finally finished, she didn't say anything for several minutes. I waited in suspense.

"You're in deep," she said at last.

I put my head in my hands and closed my eyes. "I know. What am I going to do?"

"You're asking me?" She sounded shocked.

"Yes."

"You really want to know what I think?"

"You know me better than anyone."

"I just never thought this day would come."

I looked up. "I'm serious, Ash. What should I do?"

"Nothing."

"Nothing? That's the answer?"

"Yes. Look. James either loves you back or he doesn't. If he does, but he marries someone else anyway, he's an idiot. You wouldn't want an idiot. If he doesn't, there isn't anything you can do about it. You'll have to just get over it and move on." She turned to me with an impish smile. "And I'm sure Nick or this Vince guy would be happy to help you out."

"Ash!"

"And for the rest of the mess – you'll just have to solve the murder yourself. It doesn't sound like anyone else has any ideas, so it might as well be you."

"It's not that easy," I said.

"Sure it is. You're the smartest girl I know."

"Be serious."

She her face turned hard. "I am serious. That's why I've always been afraid of you."

"You have not!"

"Okay, maybe not afraid – you weren't that buff before. Jealous is a better word. You see what other people don't. It all comes so easy for you," she said.

"You know I have to —"

"I know. But it doesn't make being your little sister any easier. Following you in school was hellacious."

"Just trying to set a good example."

Ashley groaned. "So that's what that was. Remind me not to have more than one kid."

"Come on, you'll have a dozen and you know it."

"With my luck, they'll all be like you."

"Heaven forbid."

"Well, at least I wouldn't have to worry about their grades."

"Cold comfort, I know."

She laughed. "Liz, what am I going to do with you?"

"I don't know what to do with myself. That's why I asked you."

"You'll be fine. And hey, maybe James will come around. Nick couldn't stay away."

"It only took four years with another girl for him to realize that I'm the one."

"Men." She sighed.

We drove up to an enormous house that was partially hidden from the road by several tall spruce trees. The lights of the house were sharp and bright against the utter darkness of the field beyond. People had parked their cars in all directions. It was hard to tell where the driveway might have been. Ashley pulled up next to a blue Ford truck and turned off the engine. The bitter cold slapped me in the face as I opened the passenger door. I shivered. What a night to be out. I looked over at Ashley. She pulled her coat closer and straightened her spine. She looked ready for battle.

We walked towards the front door, our feet crunching in the snow. Music with a heavy bass pulsated from the house. I reached over and tugged at Ashley's sleeve. She turned.

"Thanks, Ash. You're the best."

She grinned and put her arm around my shoulder. "You're not so bad yourself. And, thanks for this." She gestured towards the house. "I know big parties aren't your thing."

"These are your friends. I can make a fool of myself as much as I like."

"I'll step in before that happens, I promise."

I gave her a questioning look.

"It hurts my image to have a nutty sister."

I laughed. We reached the door. The beat was so heavy I felt my chest thump in rhythm. I could hear the roar of voices from outside.

"Ready?" Ashley said.

"Ready." She opened the door and walked in, and I followed.

The music was so loud in most of the house no one could hear anyone speak unless they shouted. And since I had no incentive to introduce myself to anyone, no one bothered to introduce himself to me. So far so good.

Jason had arrived before us and was in the living room with his new girlfriend, a girl from Ashley's class named Carrie. Carrie was actually Jason's fourth or fifth cousin. As if that wasn't creepy enough, they shared the same last name. Only in Marshfield.

Ashley pointed him out to me. He and Carrie were all over each other in a corner. They didn't look up. Despite my lapse with Nick, I am normally against egregious public displays of affection. This couple was more stomach-turning than usual. I grabbed Ashley's arm.

"Are you okay?" I shouted in her ear.

She nodded and shouted back, "What was I thinking?"

I hoped it wasn't a bluff for my sake and decided to keep an eye on her just in case. I trailed her at a discreet distance for most of the evening, watching from the sidelines. Surely I wasn't this immature in college? Probably. I scanned the room again, trying to distract myself. Jason was still with Carrie. Mercifully, he only had an arm around her. He hadn't noticed Ashley.

Ashley walked into the kitchen and I followed. It was a kitchen, but it could have been most of my parents' house as well. I'd never seen one that big before. Acres of granite and stainless steel stretched out before me. People milled about, eating the food laid out on the island like an endless buffet. The music was less intense in the kitchen. You could converse without shouting. I leaned against the Sub-Zero refrigerator and crossed my arms. My mind went back to James.

I glanced down and noticed someone had left a key ring on the counter. It had a key chain from one of the local car dealerships and another for a Wisconsin beer. During that first coffee, James mentioned that he liked beer. I wondered if he'd tried any of the ones from around here. I'd have to ask him. James. I just needed to get over it. Ashley was so right about that.

I didn't realize that I'd picked up the keys until I heard them clank. I looked down at my hands. I turned the keys over and over, one by one. Something clicked in the back of my mind. Something about the keys on the ring. I put them back on the counter with a clunk. I had to call Janice. I got out my cell phone. No reception, as usual. I'd call her first thing in the morning.

Just then Jason ambled into the kitchen, dragging Carrie along with him. I looked over at Ashley, who was picking at a plate of chips and salsa on the other side of the island. She seemed deep in conversation with Ed Sakaranarayanan. Everyone just called him Ed S. He was a friend of Ashley's from high school who was also at U.W., but pre med. Despite the exotic last name, Ed was a Wisconsin boy and a devoted member of the Packer nation. I always recognized him because, except for jeans, he didn't own an article of clothing that wasn't green and gold.

Ed appeared more than just a little interested in Ashley. At least, that's how it looked from where I stood. Ashley was laughing at something he'd just said. Had she ever considered him boyfriend material? Should I give her a hint? No. That would just make her cross him off her list. Perverse. Maybe it was in the genes.

Ed saw Jason before Ashley did. He stiffened and moved closer to her. She looked to see what he was staring at. Ashley watched warily as Jason approached the island.

When he was roughly across from her, she said "Jason," and then very slowly, "Carrie."

"Ashley," he said.

I edged closer and so did Ed, both ready to step in if necessary. Conversations stopped. Everyone looked over. The room hummed with tension. Ashley stared at Jason without blinking. Time seemed to stand still.

Finally, Jason looked down, defeated. "See ya around," he said.

"Yes," she said, still cool.

He grabbed a beer and started to make his way for the opposite door, dragging Carrie behind him. He was about to cross the threshold when Ashley said, "Loser," in a voice just loud enough for us to hear.

Ed and I laughed. Then, it took off, like a virus spreading from person to person. Soon the whole kitchen rang with laughter. The tension of the moment released. Jason didn't look back, but pulled Carrie through the door with a jerk.

"Good riddance," Ed said when he was gone.

"Liz," Ashley said to me, "do you mind if we leave early?"

"Of course not."

"You're leaving before midnight?" Was Ed counting on a New Year's kiss?

"I'm done for tonight," Ashley said. "I'll see you when we get back, okay?"

"Okay," Ed replied. "Happy New Year, Ash."

"You too." She gave him a quick hug and then yelled "Bye all!" to the room. A bunch of hands waved and then went quickly back to their beers.

"Nicely done," I said to her when we were finally clear of the house and I could hear myself speak.

"I swear," she said, "dating Carrie, of all people. It's practically incestuous!"

"Well, not technically speaking —" and then I stopped cold.

"What's wrong?" Ashley turned and looked at me. "Are you feeling okay?"

"Yes." I swallowed hard and started walking again. "Ash, you've hit the nail on the head again. You're two for two tonight."

"Are we still talking about the same thing?"

"Yes and no." I smiled to myself. I had quite a theory to try out on James. "Yes and no."

We passed into the New Year driving back from the party, the lone car on a lonely road.

"Happy New Year, Ash," I said when I noticed that the clock had hit midnight.

"Happy New Year, Liz."

"I'm glad I'm spending it with you. Thanks for listening to my tale of woe."

"Trust me, I've heard worse."

"And you're right. I'm going to take your sage advice."

"Wow, this is a new year. You ask my advice and take it? Amazing."

"You're an amazing girl, Ash. I'm proud of you." I realized that I'd probably never actually said this to her before.

She didn't speak for a long minute and then, her voice filled with emotion, she said, "You're the best Liz. Thanks for everything."

CHAPTER 21

Leaving Marshfield filled me with sadness and anticipation. I had so much to think about. I'd tried to get a hold of both Janice and James, but without success. The flights and the too short connection between them passed in a blur. Running from one end of the airport to the other, I didn't even have time to check my cell phone to see if either of them had called back. Soon I would be completely free of the investigation. Free of James.

It was better that way. I couldn't lie to myself any longer. My feelings wouldn't change, no matter how many times I kissed another guy. The only way out was time. Time spent as far away from him as possible. Lots of it. A total break. No friendship, no coffee, no nothing. I'd keep my distance and hang in till my heart moved on. And then maybe Nick.

When I reached Lambert International, I had six new messages. I scrolled through the list. One from Janice. One from Vince. Two from home. One from Nick. And one from James. Without thinking, I scrolled down till I got to his. I played it.

"Hope your trip went well. I didn't want to bother you while you were home, but there is a new development. It's blown the case wide open. I want to get your insight, so please call me when you get a chance. Talk to you soon. I hope. Take care." Click.

New development? Maybe I was too late. I dialed him back, but got voicemail, so I left a message. I told him I'd try him again when I got back to my apartment. Janice was also out, so I left her the same message. I called home and got Ashley. She'd left me one of the messages from home and Mom had left the other. Ashley wanted to tell me that Carrie had glared at her in the line at Target. She was happy to be going back to college. We agreed to call each other more often – maybe even weekly. Ashley promised to tell Mom that my plane had not gone down in flames over Illinois. Then we said our goodbyes and hung up.

That only left Vince. I didn't have the energy to call him back until I was actually out of the baggage claim. He'd said in his message that I could call him whenever I got the chance. I knew that he secretly wanted me to call as soon as possible. He might even gauge my interest by the rapidity of the call back. That put me in a bad spot. I liked him, but I didn't want to string him along. Once I'd gotten over James and dealt with Nick, maybe things would be different.

I finally saw my beat-up suitcase round the carousel and head towards me. I hauled it over the ledge and wheeled it to the taxi station. The cab driver had a thick Russian accent and smelled like unfiltered cigarettes. How long had he lived in St. Louis? Long enough to know all of the short cuts. He got me to the door in record time.

I ran up the inside stairs and shut the door with a sigh. No awkward small talk with the neighbors, or their son. Thank goodness. I was exhausted. I could have crawled into bed even though it was only 4:00 in the afternoon. I decided to take a shower, change into pajamas, and make it an early night in front of PBS. I stripped off my clothes as I walked to the bathroom. Another bad single girl habit. I'd pick them up later.

I turned the water on and let it heat up. I got in when I could see the steam. It felt so good that I stuck my whole head under the shower and let the water run down my back. I couldn't move. It took me a moment to realize that the phone was ringing. Just my luck. The machine could get it. What if it was James? Distance. Distance. But I had to tell him what I'd come up with. I turned off the tap and grabbed a towel. My wet feet skidded across the floorboards. I made it to the phone just as the machine started to pick up. It screeched when I picked up the handset.

"Hello?" I said breathlessly. I held on tight to the towel with the other hand.

"Hi, Liz." I loved the smoothness of James' voice. Silky and low.

"Hello, James. Good to talk to you again." Distance. I shouldn't sound so happy to hear the sound of his voice.

"How was your visit?"

"Great," I said. I was having trouble holding on to the towel, so I tucked the handset between my ear and my shoulder. I got the towel under control, but the handset slipped from my wet shoulder. It crashed to the floor. I lunged for it and missed. I dropped my towel instead.

"Hello? Hello?" I heard James' voice coming faintly from the handset. So much for distance. I started to laugh. I sat down on the floor, bare backside and all. I spread the towel over me like a blanket and picked up the phone.

"Liz, are you okay?"

I was still laughing. "Fine," I squeaked out.

"What happened?"

"I dropped the telephone. I just got out of the shower, so I'm a little slippery still."

"I can call back."

"No. No. We need to talk, but first, you tell me, what happened?"

"We've got a new suspect."

"Who?"

"Cheri Harding."

"Based on what?"

"The murder weapon."

"You found it?"

"Yes, and it was under our noses all of the time."

"Wait, how is that possible?" I said.

"It was in the garage."

"Where?"

"In a corner on the second floor. Blane Ford found it three days ago. He dropped a folder as he was opening his car door. The papers went everywhere and one landed in that corner," he said.

"That's incredible! Why didn't you find it during the initial search of the garage?"

"I don't know. There's an internal investigation going for that very reason."

"How did you link the gun to Cheri?"

"Two things. First, it's John Harding's gun."

A slow whistle escaped my mouth.

"And second, a piece of necklace was found nearby. We positively identified it as hers. She must have caught it on something and it fell to the ground before she noticed it."

"It could have fallen off at any time."

"True, but how often did Cheri go into the dark corners of the firm's parking garage?"

I turned this information over in my mind. "Wait!" I said, standing up and dropping the towel to the ground.

"What?"

My body was shaking from excitement or cold, I couldn't tell which. I almost dropped the phone again. "I'm going to describe the necklace you found."

"What?"

"Just listen. It has a fine gold chain – I'm sure that's what must have broken – and a charm that's the letter 'C' done in gold filigree and diamonds. It's from —"

"Lane's" we said at the same time.

He chuckled. "Okay, now explain to me how you knew that?"

"John Harding was predictable. He gave the same thing to all of his women."

I heard a slight choking sound, and then he cleared his throat. "Liz, you told me you weren't —"

It took me a split second longer than it should have to comprehend the question. When I did, I burst out laughing.

"What's so funny?"

"You."

"Really." He sounded annoyed. "What's going on?"

I got myself under control again, but I was still shaking. I decided it was the cold.

"Could you hold on a moment?"

"Sure, but you're going to have to explain yourself."

I could give as good as I got. "Right now I'm standing naked in my living room talking to you. I'm shivering from the cold and I need to put some clothes on before I die from hypothermia."

"Oh." I could hear the blush in his voice.

"Do you want to wait or should I call you back?"

"I'll wait."

I hit the hold button, threw the phone down, and ran for the bedroom. In less than two minutes, I had successfully struggled into my jeans and a turtleneck. I wrapped my hair in a towel so it wouldn't drip. I picked up the phone and went to sit on my bed. I hit the "talk" button.

"James?"

"Are you dressed?"

"Yes. My teeth aren't chattering any more."

"You should have told me to call you back."

"My curiosity got the better of me."

"So has mine. Tell me how you know what John Harding gave his girlfriends."

"I wasn't one of them."

"Why the maniacal laughter?"

"It wasn't maniacal, it was absurd. In case you haven't noticed, I'm not the kind of girl men like John Harding go after."

"Because?" He sounded doubtful.

"Because I'm not pretty or docile enough for arm candy."

"I don't know about the —"

"Beauty or docility?"

He laughed. "You're impossible. I might be trying to say something complimentary."

"If you're going to say I'm arm candy worthy, I don't think you should really go there."

"You're certainly not docile."

"That's more my speed."

"So how do you know what John Harding gave his lovers if you weren't one of them?"

"He was having an affair with his personal trainer, Kendra. I told you that. She has this lovely necklace – like the one you found, but with a 'K.' I figured John must have given it to her. I spoke to Cindy at Lane's. They are now selling the design to the general public, but they used to be on special order only. I think John ordered a number of them." There was silence on the other end.

"James?"

"Impressive. How did you know he bought it at Lane's?"

"Chance. I noticed it in the case when I was looking for something else. I have a good memory for those sorts of things."

"You do," he said. There was another pause. "Why did you go to Lane's?"

I'm so demented that I went to see where you bought an engagement ring for another woman.

"I was looking for a gift for my mother, but everything was above my budget. So, it was John's gun, but were there any fingerprints? Or anything else that would connect it with Cheri?"

"It looked clean, but it's been sent to the lab for tests."

"And you're officially back on the case?"

"Yes. It's all hands on deck."

"You don't mind if I still pursue my own investigation, do you?"

"What are you not telling me?"

"I just have a theory. Nothing concrete. I'd like to keep it to myself until I've firmed things up." Or until I could assimilate the new evidence. My theory wasn't looking so hot at the moment. I felt deflated.

"You're not going to do anything dangerous, are you? You should tell me —"

"It's all in my head right now. When I start confronting murderers, I'll give you a call."

"Thanks," he said sarcastically.

I heard a call waiting beep. "Is that on your end or mine?" I asked.

"Mine, I think. I'd better go. Liz —"

"Yes?"

"I still owe you a real meal. Maybe when the investigation winds down?"

"As a token of appreciation for all of my hard work?"

"Something like that. Take care. I'll call you again soon." There was a note in his voice. I might have said tenderness if I hadn't known better.

"Goodbye." His line clicked. I put the receiver back down slowly. So much for distance. My theory was blown to pieces and James had reeled me back in with a single phone call.

Janice called later that evening. At least I could tackle one problem head on. Janice got straight to the point. "So what else have you figured out?"

"The keys on the ring we copied from Tom Green."

"Yes?"

"There are too many keys."

"So?"

"There are keys that don't belong to the file room."

"I wasn't paying attention when we went through the files. Are you sure?"

"Pretty sure."

"What are they for?"

"That depends. Did you find anything in the trust account?"

"You're uncanny. You know that, right?"

I sighed. "I'm sorry. I didn't want to be right this time."

"I know. It took me a while to find the irregularities even though I knew what to look for. They were good at covering their tracks."

"That's always true with an inside job."

"Yes," she said sadly. "I'm not sure we have enough to take to the police, or even the bar, but it's enough for me."

"I'm with you if you want me," I said.

"I'm counting on that, but it takes time."

"When do you think you'll be ready?"

"I'm hoping for March 1st."

"What can I do?"

"Just sit tight. I'll let you know when to strike." She stopped. "What do you mean 'that depends'? What do you think the keys are for?"

"The Lodge has an office, doesn't it?"

"Of course! I should have thought of that myself. Maybe we can track the payments directly through The Lodge accounting statements. Anything to give us enough proof to go to the police."

"I promised James I wouldn't do anything dangerous, but maybe just a bit of burglary. Since he is the police, I'm sure he'd understand," I said.

"No need. I know how to get us in. The firm prom."

"The what?"

"You know. The party at the end of January."

"I didn't know that there was one."

"Look through your mail. The invitations went out between Christmas and New Years."

"Why does the firm have a party in January?"

"To invite the spouses."

"So they won't ask about the Christmas party?"

"You catch on quickly," she said. "The prom is at The Lodge this year. Convenient, isn't it?"

"Very," I said.

"We should still confirm that we have extra keys."

"And figure out which are which."

"So what night will work for you?"

"I'm free whenever you are," I replied.

"Thursday?"

"Sure. At 5:00?"

"4:30. I have some other projects I want you to look at. I'll order us dinner."

"Paperelli's?"

"It wouldn't feel right without it. Speaking of which, why don't you invite him to the prom? We might need the backup – and the cover if someone finds us."

"Wouldn't it look like a date?"

"It's one night. He can't read too much into that. Not when we're on official business."

"He has a fiancée."

"But this is undercover work."

"Hmm."

"Think about it. Not that we're going to be in much danger, unless the fraud was the reason for John's murder."

"I'm not sure that the fraud was the reason. It doesn't fit with my other theory."

"You have a theory?"

"I did a lot of thinking over the break. Now I just have to do some research." And get a handle on the new evidence.

"Well, see you on Thursday."

When we hung up, I steeled myself to call Vince. Fortune smiled on me in the form of voicemail. I left him a noncommittal message and went to bed. The next morning, I awakened full of purpose. I dressed and ate quickly and then drove over to school. I wanted to catch Kat before someone else sent her on a wild goose chase. I needed help with my goose chase, and she was the only one who could do it. It is not widely known, but research librarians are invaluable allies in the war on crime.

Kat's office appeared empty, but I wasn't fooled. She couldn't hide out in the stacks forever. She arrived ten minutes later, carrying some papers and a Styrofoam cup of coffee.

"Liz, what a pleasant surprise. Need some help with your note?"

"My note is no more. Someone got to the topic first."

"Too bad."

"Not really. I've got another research project that may turn out to be more meaningful."

"What is it?"

I got up and shut the door to her office.

"So much secrecy," she said with a smile. "This should be good."

I took a deep breath. "It's just a little murder investigation I'm involved in."

Her eyes got very big. I gave her a synopsis of the murder and my theory. She understood immediately what I needed and why.

"That may be hard," she said. "Those records are old enough that they're probably still in paper format."

"I don't have the money or the time to travel."

"Then I'm glad you came to me. I've got some people I can call."

"I knew I could count on you."

"At least it's something for all of those ALA conferences." Kat's stories about the American Library Association conferences were hysterical. It's difficult to really appreciate the idiosyncrasies of the average reference librarian until you see them *en masse*.

I got up out of the chair. "Thanks again," I said.

"I'll call you as soon as I know something."

"And I'll let you know if anything else turns up."

"Be careful Liz. If you're right, you're dealing with people who have nothing left to lose."

"I know."

On Thursday night, Janice and I confirmed the existence of six keys that did not match anything in the file room. We had to play cat and mouse with the cleaning staff and three attorneys who stayed late, including Blane Ford. I also saw Chester skulking about. I don't think he saw me.

I spent the next week waiting for word from Kat and avoiding the office. Maybe it was just paranoia, but I was starting to feel watched. Was someone on to me? I began looking over my shoulder and taking different routes to school. In between the cloak and dagger, I also mulled over whether to invite James to the prom. Awkwardness hung in the balance against our need for police protection. And police protection was starting to look pretty good. Plus, it might be my only chance to go out with James, even if it was a pretend date. I'd never be the Other Woman.

I spoke with both Vince and Nick. I tried to keep the conversation light and friendly. Vince was an easier sell. Nick knew me well enough to get me off the friendly track way too easily. I resisted his verbal advances as best I could. He mentioned a visit, and I pled a singular devotion to my law school studies. It seemed to work, but I wasn't sure how long I could maintain the holding pattern. Now I just had to forget about James.

CHAPTER 22

A week before the prom, etiquette forced my hand. I picked up the invitation and realized that I had to RSVP. There was a check box to bring a guest. It was the moment of truth. James and I had been playing phone tag about the investigation, so I had the perfect excuse. I just lacked the nerve.

I dialed his cell phone and got voicemail as usual. I left a message. "James, it's Liz. Janice and I are doing some breaking and entering. Thought you'd want to know. Give me a call, no matter how late." If that didn't get him, nothing would.

I heard the phone ring within the hour, but it wasn't James. It was Kat. "Jackpot," she said when I picked up the phone. She'd found the proof I needed. Now, I just had to confirm one more thing and my theory was back up and running. Not perfect, but compelling enough. All that was left was a little field trip.

I pulled a flashlight out of the drawer, threw on my coat, and ran out the door. It was just getting dark. After driving around for a while to make sure I wasn't being followed, I pulled the car up and waited. I watched her leave and then the coast was clear. When I got back to my car, I hummed the theme song to Mission Impossible. I was good. Only some minor loose ends remained, and who really cared about those? I looked at my cell phone. James still hadn't called me back. I needed to talk to him now that everything was falling into place. The Lodge was still an outlier, but maybe a look around their files would pull it together.

I got home, microwaved dinner, and did some school work. At 10:30 the phone finally rang. I saw the number and my heart sped up. "James!" I said too enthusiastically.

"Liz, I'm sorry I'm calling so late. I didn't check my voicemail until now. It is crazy around here. What are you and Janice up to?"

I explained about finding the fraud and our suspicions about The Lodge. I told him that we wanted to see if the keys fit anything in The Lodge office.

He let out a low whistle. "That's big."

"Janice doesn't think we have enough to go on just yet. We think The Lodge files might just give us the proof we need."

"So you want me to help you break into The Lodge office? That's not really my line of work. And you shouldn't —"

"It's not like that. We've been invited in. No trespassing required."

"I don't understand."

"The firm has a party every January. This year it's at The Lodge."

"Another party?"

"Spouses are invited."

"Did the Christmas party live up to its reputation?"

"And how," I said.

He cleared his throat as if he were about to say something.

"But Janice and I got out alive. So the plan is to leave the party at some point and snoop around the office."

"Are you suggesting that I go as your guest?" He didn't seem too upset at the idea.

I let out my breath. "If you don't mind. Or Janice's. It makes no difference."

"I've never met Janice, so I'd rather it was you."

"Well then, me."

"When do I pick you up?"

"Janice is going to drive. I agreed to meet at her house. She lives farther west – closer to The Lodge."

"Janice is the chaperone?"

"She promises to let me do whatever I want."

"I like her already," he said.

Then I thought of something. "Do you have a tuxedo? The invitation said 'black tie.' Sorry, I should have mentioned that before."

"Ye of little faith. I haven't gone to a thousand charity events with my parents without owning several. Do you want the top hat? Maybe tails?"

"No Fred Astaire required. Just a normal tux will do. Although yours is probably Armani."

"You know me too well," he said smoothly.

"Okay. I'm going to have to step up my wardrobe. Thanks for letting me know what I'm in for."

"I'm sure you'll look lovely. Now tell me where I need to go and when. Then I'll have to get off the phone. I have another two hours of work yet to go tonight."

"Sorry to keep you up," I said defensively.

"Liz," he replied softly. "I want to talk to you, but I've been running on no sleep for days."

"Can I ask one more question before I let you go?"

"Shoot."

I laughed.

"I mean, go ahead," he said.

"Apropos of that – did John Harding have a concealed weapon's permit?"

"Yes. Is that important to you?"

"Possibly. I have a theory."

I would have said more, but he said, "Maybe you can tell me when we meet?"

"Maybe. Good night. Get some sleep if you can."

"You too. Sleep tight."

"Don't let the bed bugs bite," I replied before I could stop myself.

I heard a peal of laughter as I hung up the phone.

Perhaps it was just my perverse nature, but the prospect of sneaking into The Lodge office caused me less panic than trying to find a dress equal to James in an Armani tuxedo. He was already out of my league. The vision of him in a tuxedo made me feel weak with inadequacy. I needed to do some smart shopping. Fast.

In St. Louis, if you want fine quality on no budget, second hand is the only way to go. St. Louis has the two components that make second hand shops a going concern: a class of wealthy women who won't wear anything past its season, and another class of women who know quality but can't afford it. Supply and demand. I decided to make some forays between classes.

It took five trips and at least fifteen hours of trying anything and everything on before I finally found something that might be worth the loan money. It was a rose red silk sheath dress, with a corset bodice. Simple, elegant, and designer. I wasn't going to do any better on my budget. I found a pair of silver stilettos and a silver clutch to match. In total, it cost a little more than my expensive haircut. A steal. I started to feel more optimistic.

The night of the party, the weather suddenly turned cold. We had had a week of warm weather, so the cold was a shock to the system. I drove over to Janice's house in Creve Coeur wishing I had something more elegant than my old overcoat to wear with my new dress. The shoes looked good, and I hoped I could make it through the evening without breaking an ankle. There was no going back now.

Janice met me at the door. She looked very refined in a long black silk dress and pearls. "Come in, come in" she said, ushering me into the living room. "I like your hair done up like that. Now, take off the coat and let me see the dress." I'd given Janice a blow-by-blow description of my shopping expeditions. I pulled the coat off with a flourish.

"Wow, that fits beautifully. You really got that second hand?"

"We'll call it 'vintage.' It doesn't sound so desperate."

"Whatever you call it, I clearly need to go shopping with you."

The doorbell rang. Janice walked out of the room to answer it. I hung back, holding on to the back of the sofa for balance.

I heard her open the door. "You must be Detective Paperelli," she said.

"It's a pleasure to finally meet you, Ms. Harrington."

"Janice." I could hear the smile in her voice.

"Janice, call me James."

"Come in, James. Liz is already here, waiting in the living room."

I heard their footsteps in the hall. I suddenly remembered that this dress looked better if I stood up straight and sucked in my stomach. I smoothed the dress down with my hands. They shook a little, so I rested them on the back of the sofa behind me.

James walked into the room. I felt my heart skip a beat and then another. He looked magnificent standing there with a smile spreading across his face and lighting his eyes.

"Liz," he said.

"James." My voice came out in a whisper. I swallowed hard.

"You look great." He took a step forward, his hand outstretched. I couldn't move. My hands gripped the sofa, my nails digging into the plush fabric. I forced myself to breathe.

"The tuxedo suits you," I said. I willed my hands to unclench their death grip on the couch. I clasped them together in front of me.

Janice appeared in the doorway. She had a strange smile on her face. "Can I get you both something to drink? Or we can leave right away."

"We can go if you want," he said. His hand was back at his side. He looked at me.

"Fine," I said, reaching behind and grabbing my coat from the sofa.

He came up. "May I?" He pointed to the coat in my hand. I gave him the coat, and he held it up. When I got the second arm in, he leaned very close to me. I took a deep breath. The sweet smell of his skin filled my head. I blinked.

"I love the dress," he said into my ear. "You shouldn't have worried."

I smiled and turned my head slightly. Half an inch more and our lips would touch. I controlled myself. "Thanks for coming. You'll make all of the women jealous of me."

"You don't need me for that. We shouldn't keep Janice waiting."

We followed Janice to the garage where her Mercedes sedan was parked. James opened the passenger door and gestured for me to climb in the front seat.

"Won't you be cramped in back?" I asked.

"No, I insist." I slid into the seat with as much grace as I could muster. He closed my door, and put his hand on the back of the passenger seat. I felt it give slightly as he slid in with ease. I heard his door close. Janice backed the car out. I leaned against the headrest and froze. James' hand rested on the back of my seat again, his fingertips accidentally touching my neck. I didn't know what to do. But I didn't want to move. I felt a shiver of excitement and thought of that night in my apartment. This must be how other women became the Other Woman.

"You're awfully quiet, Liz," Janice said.

I jumped forward like a shot. "What?"

She chuckled. "Lost in thought?"

"Something like that." I leaned back very slowly. The hand was gone. I took a deep breath and let it out. "So what is the plan for tonight?" I asked. My heart still pounded a tattoo in my chest.

"Appetizers and drinks till 7:00 and then the seated dinner. We'll be trapped at our table until that's over. We need to wait until 9:30 or 10:00 to get away and search the office." She looked over at me. "Assuming you're right about the keys."

"I am. I have a sixth sense about these things."

"And no one will notice us slipping away?" James said.

Janice raised her eyebrows. "At a firm party? Half the guests have slipped away by 9:30 to do goodness knows what. We're lucky it's turned cold or the golf course would be wall to wall couples."

"In various states of undress?" he said.

"You put that so politely," Janice said.

"What is it with this firm?" he said.

Janice barked out a laugh. "You'd like to think it's just this firm, wouldn't you? Unfortunately not. It's every big firm. Too many lawyers in one place creates an overload of testosterone – or some other chemical imbalance. I sure can't explain it."

"Interesting," he replied.

The rest of the drive, Janice and James kept up a lighthearted flow of inconsequential conversation. I made few remarks. It was easier that way. My phone buzzed and I flipped it open. A text from Nick. He was in Chicago at a meeting and wanted to know if there was any way we could meet. I decided to ignore the message. One problem at a time. Instead, I leaned back in the seat as far as it would go. The hand never reappeared.

CHAPTER 23

We pulled up in front of the enormous façade of The Lodge, the building that was the hub of the development and the origin of the name. The building contained an expanse of meeting rooms, offices and a ballroom space made to look like an English hunting lodge decked out in weathered stone and timber. I wondered how much money had been spent to make the new look decrepit and old.

The valet rushed up as Janice opened her door to get out. I grabbed the handle of mine, but James was very quick. He guided me out of the car with his outstretched hand. And he didn't immediately let my hand go. I looked up at him questioningly.

"Can you walk in those? This pavement is uneven."

"By all means, keep me from falling on my face."

"Not that I have a problem with the shoes." He looked down at my feet. "I'll tell you what I think of them at some other moment."

I wasn't sure what to say to that so I said nothing. I leaned on his arm as we traversed the cobblestones. We walked into the great hall. A roaring fire in the immense stone hearth made even the large room seem stuffy. I analyzed the décor.

There were coats of arms and tartans everywhere. The walls were festooned with one English hunt scene after another. Someone couldn't decide what part of the British Isles we were supposed to be in. I looked up. The chandelier was made to look like sets of antlers fused together. I stared at it a moment.

"What?" James said.

"Those are not real."

He laughed and slipped an arm around my shoulder. I looked at him.

"I'll help you off with your coat."

"Right."

He checked our coats and then turned to me. "Something to drink?"

I nodded. We moved with the herd to the bar.

"What would you like?" he said as the line inched forward.

"A Diet Coke."

"Ah yes, we may need your little gray cells this evening."

He ordered a Diet Coke for me, and a whisky and soda for himself. We milled around and lost Janice. Or Janice lost us, I'm not sure which. I introduced James here and there whenever someone approached me, which wasn't often. Part-time pre-bar exam associates don't merit much interest. A couple of astute partners made the pizza connection when they heard James' name, but most people shook his hand without comment. No one seemed to notice he was the same detective who'd interviewed people on the night of the murder.

So we mostly talked to each other. I started to relax. He was fun to be around. Even when we didn't speak, I could tell what he was thinking. Sometimes it would just take one look from him, and we'd both laugh. And there was plenty to laugh at. Attorneys are at their most absurd when they try to be sophisticated.

Janice reappeared right before the dinner started and guided us to our assigned table. She had been snooping around and told me where the offices were. We sat down. I knew most of the attorneys at the table since we'd been seated with the estate planning and tax group. The conversation was deadly dull – estate matters. One of the attorneys gave a line-by-line account of the provisions he'd drafted for some client's will. My ears perked up. Then again, that might just be the reason for the hired gun.

I introduced James to the other members of our table, but received the same mild interest or indifference. The young wife of an old partner was seated beside James. She tried to engage him in flirtatious conversation. He parried her verbal advances with a skill I'd never seen before. Too much practice.

The chicken with mushroom cream sauce, overdone asparagus, and a potato concoction arrived. Wine appeared, so I took a sip or two, but not enough to impair my judgment. I looked around the room, trying to pick out the people I knew. James saw what I was up to. He asked me in a low voice to tell him who was who. I did what I could. Fortunately, James had a good memory for faces. He even recognized some people he'd previously interviewed.

I showed him where Blane Ford sat several tables away. His wife sat to his right. And Beth, it must be Beth, was on his left. I hadn't seen her arrive. Then I heard a commotion. I turned my head, but couldn't see around a group of people at the other end of the room, by the door. There was a sudden collective intake of breath and the room went quiet.

"Oh no," I whispered. My sixth sense told me that something was going to go down – and soon.

James asked, "What's wrong?" I pointed to the door.

The crowd parted. Cheri Harding stood there, perched on incredibly high heels and dressed in a skin-tight black gown that shimmered in the lights of the chandelier above. The huge diamond on her finger threw sparks in all directions. She measured the effect of her entrance, her expression calm and malignantly confident. The black widow watching her prey twist in the web. I saw her glance at Blane's table, but I resisted the urge to turn and see who looked back.

"I thought she was under arrest," I whispered in James' ear.

"Suspicion," he whispered back. "We've held off on the arrest to gather more evidence."

"This is bad."

"You don't really think she's going to kill someone in the middle of a party, do you?"

His voice was so low that I had to lean even closer to him to hear. I shook my head, pulling back. I was too close. I didn't want to do something stupid.

Tom Green waddled up to her on his short legs. He smiled ingratiatingly and offered her his arm. She wrapped her hand in his and serenely walked with him to his table. He sat her next to Grant and then shuffled in on her other side. She smiled at Grant and then gazed around the room. Her eyes rested on our table for a moment and moved on. Her expression never changed.

Once she'd sat down, the conversation came flooding back.

"That was an entrance," James said to me.

"The black is a nice touch. Very dramatic."

"What is Tom Green up to?"

"Trying to curry favor. Cheri's got a reason to talk now."

He leaned in again. "Plea deal?"

I smiled. "You'd know more about that."

"What a tangled web we weave —"

"Exactly."

The dinner finally wound down. The band started up. I kept waiting for a signal from Janice, but she continued to hesitate. The attorney droned on about his client's will. I didn't push. I had my own surveillance. So far nothing out of the ordinary. James noticed my distraction.

"Do you want to dance while we wait?" he said.

"Sure," I said mechanically, my mind still on surveillance.

He took my hand and pulled me up on my silver shoes. My mind shifted gears abruptly. What was I doing? We walked to the dance floor. He didn't let go of my hand, and I didn't ask why. A fast number had just ended. A slow one started.

"Good," he said.

"What?" I fought the dreamy haze that set in when I stood close to him.

He smiled. "You won't break your ankle with a slow song."

"Oh."

He put his arm around my waist and pulled me close to him. My pulse raced. I tried to steady my heart. He moved closer still and whispered in my ear. "Who are you watching?" I felt his breath tickle my earlobe.

I willed my brain to work. "Cheri," I whispered back.

The sweet smell of his skin was overwhelming. I pulled away, trying to clear my head. Space. I needed space. We didn't speak for a moment.

"Thank you for coming with me," I finally said.

"You're a fun date, despite the breaking and entering."

"And your fiancée doesn't mind?"

"My what?" He stopped. We stood very still for one long second and then two. I felt his grip tighten convulsively on my waist, his expression inscrutable.

"Your fiancée, Angelica?" I looked him in the eye. "I read about the engagement in the *Ladue News*."

He groaned. "That —"

Janice came up to us. "It's time. Come. We've got maybe half an hour."

James let go of me. "We'll talk later," he said.

"Come on," Janice pulled on my arm. I turned and caught sight of Beth, getting up from Blane's table. I followed Janice out, trying to think of a way to cut back to the ballroom. And I needed a moment to pull myself together. My head started to throb. I was finally at the end of the line with James.

"Janice," I whispered, "you go with James. I need to run to the ladies room. I'll meet you at the office."

"Okay," she said. "Let's go James."

I didn't look at him, but turned and ducked into the bathroom. The door was incredibly heavy. The bathroom seemed deserted and quiet, not even the noise from the ballroom filtered through the walls. I went to the farthest stall and closed the door. I put my forehead against the metal door. It was smooth and cool against my skin. I took one deep breath and let it out. Then another. The pain at my temples had subsided, but I still felt dizzy. More deep breathing. In and out. Another second and I'd go back out to the ballroom.

I heard the door open and the rustle of long dresses and the clack clack of heels. It sounded like three women. They paused, clearly preening in front of the mirror. I hesitated.

"This is such a magical evening," one said breathlessly. I heard a lipstick snap open.

"I feel just like Cinderella," said the other. She was serious. I had to hold my mouth to keep from laughing. Some people need to live a little. Perspective. That's what I'd been missing. I gave myself a mental shake. Whatever James had to tell me, I would handle it.

I was about to open the stall door when the bathroom door creaked again. There was a sudden silence and then a hurried shuffle of silk and a murmur of voices. The women at the mirror seemed to be leaving. I heard the door close and the firm click of stilettos on the marble tile. I had a sinking feeling. The walk sounded familiar.

I peeped through the crack in the door. I saw blonde hair, black shimmering fabric and diamond sparks. Cheri. And there was a woman still at the sink. She turned and flipped her dark hair out of her eyes.

"Oh, No!" I screamed inside my head.

CHAPTER 24

"Great. First she brings that fucking detective and now you," Beth said, her voice like ice.

"Forget about her. I came here to find you. We need to talk. Come to an understanding," Cheri said.

"Yeah sure. I'll do whatever the hell I feel like."

"Haven't you done enough already?" Cheri's voice had a hysterical edge to it.

"What would you know about enough?" Beth remained cool.

"All I'm saying is that these games have got to stop."

"This is so not a game."

There was a pause. I imagined that each was trying to stare the other down.

"I haven't done anything but tell you the truth, you fucking whore," Cheri said in a low voice.

"Whore? Look in the mirror, bitch. You wanted it all, didn't you? The fucking money, the fucking house, your fucking freedom. You just wanted everything. No matter what. But you're not going to get it, are you?"

Of course, The Lodge suddenly made sense.

"That's not true. I loved him!" Cheri cried.

"Like hell you did. Did he even know?"

I heard Cheri take in a breath. It seemed to catch in her throat.

"I didn't think he did," Beth continued. "You set me up so perfectly. God! I can't believe I've been so stupid. But I'm not stupid now. I know what a lying cunt you are."

"You thought I was lying?" Cheri screamed. "I told you the truth! I did you a favor and look at how you pay me back! You took him from me. You!"

"How can you lie with a straight face, even now?" Beth said.

I heard her take a step. Towards Cheri? I didn't know. Despite the fear of discovery, part of me leapt for joy. I was good. Damn good.

"Unbelievable!" Beth continued with barely suppressed fury. "He was not my father. And I'm not your fucking tool."

"My tool? How dare you – and he was your father. I should know. I knew what your mother was!"

Beth's voice dripped contempt. "Don't go there. You'll do what I say from here on out. I'm the one running the show." And then she began to laugh, a low rumbling sound, full of menace. It gave me goose bumps. I wedged myself even farther between the wall and the toilet.

There was a growl like that of a wild animal. Then a scream. I heard Beth cry out, and the thud of a body hitting the floor. Then a knocking sound, a skull smacking against marble. I sprang forward from my hiding place. I pushed and pushed on the door of the stall, but it was stuck. It finally came free and the door flung open.

Cheri was on top of Beth, who struggled to pull Cheri's hands from her throat.

"Stop!" I screamed. I got on Cheri's back and tried to pull her off. She jumped up, stronger than seemed possible, and knocked me backwards to the floor. She grabbed her purse and then hurdled over Beth's body. She pulled the door open and disappeared.

It took me a moment to catch my breath. I didn't know if Beth was dead or alive, but I couldn't stop to help. I scrambled over her and pulled on the door with all my might. It flung open, and I caught a glimpse of Cheri's dress, running down the hall. I screamed. "Help! Help!" Two men and a woman ran over to me. I showed them where Beth lay. "Call an ambulance!" I screamed as I ran. I had to catch Cheri.

She was out the door and on to the golf course before I could reach her. It was the shoes. I couldn't run like I needed to. I ditched them as soon as I reached the grass. I noticed hers a little way ahead. The golf course was a patchwork of floodlights and pools of darkness but her dress caught the light for a moment. I increased my speed.

My bare feet pounded the frost-crusted grass. I ran down the fairway. I saw her once more. She seemed to be heading for the green. I caught sight of her dark silhouette. I gained ground. Thank goodness I had joined a gym. I gave it one more push. I pumped my arms. I heard my dress rip as I lengthened my stride.

And I was upon her. She'd stopped and turned to face me. I couldn't understand. Then she stepped into the light. The gun in her hand glinted ominously.

"Stay right where you are," she said, panting. "Don't move or you're dead, Elizabeth Howe."

"You don't need to do this," I said, taking one more step towards her.

"Back off!" she screamed.

I stopped. "Now Cheri, calm down. We can talk."

"I'm not talking to you." I heard her wheeze as she took a breath.

"Cheri, I know you didn't do it," I said calmly. "If you give yourself up now, no one is going to blame you – no one thinks you killed him."

"I didn't kill him!"

"Of course you didn't. Now just put the gun down."

"You don't tell me what to do. No one tells me what to do!"

"I'm just saying – take a deep breath. Think this through. Hurting me isn't going to help you."

"Maybe I don't care," she hissed.

I heard a noise to my right, off in the darkness. I focused on Cheri. "Cheri, this can all be worked out. You'll see. Everything will be just fine."

There was the noise again, only this time Cheri heard it too. She turned her head to look. I saw my chance.

I sprang forward and lunged for her feet, toppling her backwards. I heard the gun go off. My eardrums throbbed, but I didn't care. I struggled to hold her. There is some advantage to weight. I used what I could to pin her down. I got completely on top of her, pressing down on her chest with all my might. She finally stopped struggling.

"For the love of God! What did you do that for?" a familiar voice said behind me.

"Just help!" I replied between clenched teeth. James came up. He picked Cheri's gun off the ground with his left hand and held another gun in his right. His gun didn't look large enough to be a police issue. How had I missed that?

"I was just getting into position. You could have been killed!" he said angrily.

"Well I'm not dead," I spat back. "What should I do now?"

"Get off of her. You're going to crush her chest like that."

"Thanks." I got to my feet and glared at him.

"Hold this," he said, handing me Cheri's gun. "And don't drop it."

"I know how to handle a gun." It was a little semi-automatic. I slipped the safety back on. He put his gun into a holster that fit neatly under his arm and then held out his hand for the other. I gave it to him. His eyes held mine a moment. They were filled with white-hot rage. I looked away. He pulled Cheri up by one arm. She seemed as limp as a rag doll. He started to walk away, dragging her by the arm.

He turned to me once more. "Don't move. I'll be right back."

I nodded. I didn't feel like giving him the benefit of a real answer. I was too angry.

He was gone for what seemed like an eternity. I shivered in my thin ripped dress and bare feet. Maybe abandoning the shoes wasn't such a good idea after all. I saw flashing lights off in the distance. The ambulance had arrived. Or perhaps it was the police backup. When I'd just decided that I wouldn't stay there another minute, I saw James' tall silhouette. Now I'd give him a piece of my mind.

"Liz," he said as he got closer. I saw he had my shoes in his hand. He gave them to me. I put them on the ground. My feet felt numb. I almost fell over trying to step into them. He took my arm and steadied me. I pulled away, glaring at him.

"You have some nerve. After all I've been through tonight!" I could feel the tears running down my cheeks.

"I have some nerve?" He grabbed my shoulders. "You could have been killed. Killed! Why didn't you let me handle the situation?"

"I didn't know you were there. I thought I was on my own."

"Well you're not, Liz. You never were."

"Sure."

I felt his grip tighten. "So this is it?"

"What?"

"I should have known," he said bitterly. "It's Vince, isn't it?"

"What? I don't understand a word you're saying."

"You don't understand anything." He pulled me to him and hugged me. "I couldn't live with myself if something happened to you."

I looked up. He had the strangest expression. Tender. Angry. Confused. I couldn't tell.

"Forgive me."

"For what?" I said, brushing away the tear that slowly dripped down my cheek.

Then he kissed me. A tender sweet kiss, full of longing. I couldn't help it. I put my arms around his neck and pulled him closer. The feel of his skin next to mine, the soft pressure of his lips, it was almost too much. I felt like I was melting into him. My heart raced and yet we moved as if in languorous slow motion. The world fell away. It was just the two of us.

He shifted first. Slowly, like someone exercising supreme force of will, he separated himself from me. I clung to him, unwilling to let go.

"We should stop. I don't want to, but we should."

I stepped back and looked up into his face. "What do we do now?"

"I don't know. What a mess!" I couldn't tell if he meant the case or us. He studied me closely. "You've figured the whole thing out, haven't you? I can see it in your eyes."

"Most of it," I said modestly. I shivered from the cold.

"I'm sorry. Here." He shrugged out of his jacket and put it around my shoulders. I put my arms through the sleeves and pushed them up. He crossed his arms in front of him. I wondered if this meant that we should now keep our distance.

"Tell me." He stepped back. "I'm pretty sure Beth killed John Harding, but Cheri was the one with all of the obvious motives. What I don't understand is the connection between the two women. They were both sleeping with Harding, but what else? I need to know what you know before I go back to that madhouse." He pointed in the direction of the lights. There were more now. "Or someone finds us here."

"Okay." I took a deep breath of the cold night air. "It all started a long time ago in John Harding's home town, Poplar Bluff. John and Blane Ford grew up there. They knew each other as boys. They also knew another family, the Millers. The Millers lived close by, and Blane was distantly related to them. The Millers had two daughters, Amy and Cheryl, otherwise known as Cheri. Both John and Blane moved away before the Miller daughters were grown, but the families must have kept in touch, because when John Harding's first wife died in a car accident, he went back to Poplar Bluff and reunited with Amy. She was eighteen at the time."

"They were together and then he went back to St. Louis. Amy found out she was pregnant. But Amy was also seeing Blane on the side. Probably she didn't tell anyone about Blane because he was her cousin, and that might have caused trouble in the family. So Amy ran as far from Poplar Bluff as she could before anyone found out about the pregnancy. She got to Las Vegas. She had her baby there and then worked doing things I probably don't want to know about. At some point, she met a wealthy businessman, Hank Jones. They married and moved to Texas. He adopted her daughter as his own. Beth Jones."

"Can I ask how you got all of this information?"

"Random comments Beth made to me and to Vince and some careful research into birth certificates and census records by my reference librarian friend, Kat." I paused. "And the fact that Blane Ford got Beth's DNA sample at the firm's Christmas party."

"Okay," he said slowly. "You're going to have to explain the last part."

"I had to go to a really dull party with my friend Holly. At the party, I talked to a Ph.D. student who told me about the Fords. It turns out that the family has donated a large amount of money for research on a familial gene that resembles ALS. Every member of the family has been sequenced. Blane swiped Beth's glass at the party and put it in a plastic bag so he could take it to the lab. He got someone there to do a DNA analysis for paternity. Blane told Beth he was her father over the Christmas holidays."

"I think I'm seeing where this might be going."

"Beth moved to St. Louis to go to law school. Her wealthy adoptive father got her a high-end apartment in Clayton. She joined the gym closest to her apartment, which is where I also go. She met John Harding there, and they started sleeping together. She was John's usual type – thin with dark hair. John gave Beth one of the letter necklaces, just like he did all of his women. At the same time, Beth also started dating her official boyfriend, a student at UMSL."

James touched his forehead. "Oh, of course, the MetroLink stop at UMSL. That's why you asked me about where the credit card was found."

"Right. But you're getting ahead of me. I'm sure that Beth got the summer associate job at Ghebish and Long because of her relationship with John. She certainly didn't fit the summer associate mold. It probably seemed very convenient for John to have his mistress at work. It meant that they could meet at any time – in any place."

"Like the third floor stairwell of the parking garage?" he said.

"Of course. In the blind spot of the surveillance cameras."

"They knew that area very well."

"Well enough to avoid being seen arriving or leaving," I said.

"And Cheri?"

"John married Cheri before all of this happened. Cheri was originally a brunette, by the way, just like all the others. My guess is that she went prematurely gray and decided blonde was the best route to go. Anyway, I'm not sure if John knew Amy had gotten pregnant or not. But Cheri did and when she saw Beth at one of the firm functions, she figured out who she was. Cheri also realized that John was having an affair with her. Now, this is where it gets tricky. I don't have all of the answers, but I think Cheri committed one crime to avoid being implicated in another."

"You've had quite a few answers so far," he said.

"Cheri knew John was heavily invested in The Lodge development. She also found out he was embezzling from the firm to keep the investment afloat. She didn't want to have anything to do with it. Probably because she was smart enough to know that a Ponzi scheme will always fail. To add to this, John cheated on her, with Beth and others. Eventually, he would want to replace Cheri. She knew that Maddie got very little in the divorce settlement. So, Cheri decided to get rid of John before he could take her down financially or by divorce. How to do it?"

"Get someone else to pull the trigger."

"Right, but there is a small problem with hiring the assassination of your husband."

"A small problem?" he said dryly.

"Okay, a big problem beyond the obvious one. It's called a tortfeasor limitation. They show up on both life insurance policies and wills. If Cheri were even suspected of involvement in the murder, even if her involvement couldn't be proved in a criminal case, she might lose out on all of John's life insurance and anything else he left her in the will. So she had to find someone else with a reason for murder and nudge her along."

"Beth."

"What would you do if you found out that a man started an affair with you knowing that you were his daughter? Because I'm sure that is what Cheri told Beth. I don't think Beth knew anything about her family until Cheri confronted her."

"I'd be in therapy, but I don't know if I would shoot him," James said.

"Well, Beth did shoot him, and with his own gun. I think she actually loved him. That would make her hate him all the more. On the night of the murder, she drove out of the garage at her usual time and parked her car at one of the city lots. Then she walked back to the building. She came in through the unlocked door of the parking garage and made her way back to the firm floors without being seen. I would go back through those key card records again. I bet she couldn't cover up all of her entries and exits."

I paused, thinking it through. "She sneaked into John's office and got his keys and his wallet to make it look like a robbery. She went down to the garage and hid the wallet in a corner at the bottom of the stairs along with some sort of trench coat and her handbag. She took off her shoes. She'd previously talked to him about meeting her in the stairwell. That's why when I went down to the kitchen, he'd already gone off to the bathroom."

"To the bathroom? How do you know that?"

"There was an empty glass in the kitchen sink. John Harding had drunk a full glass of something while he smoked his cigar. A sixty-something man, going to meet his twenty-something mistress. Prostate issues. I don't think I really need to explain further."

"No," James said tersely.

"Beth took the keys and opened John's car, which was always parked in his same reserved parking space. She got his gun out of the car, probably the glove compartment. She knew where he always kept it. She set the keys down and waited for him."

"The concealed carry permit question – I wondered why you asked that."

"Now you know. I'm not sure if they exchanged words or if she shot him as soon as she saw him. One shot from underneath him – Beth is a petite woman – and one shot standing over him, to make sure he was actually dead. He could identify her, after all."

"Cold," James said.

"Then she grabbed the keys and was down the stairs to where she had hidden her things. She put her shoes back on, threw the gun and the wallet in the handbag —"

"Must be some handbag."

I looked at him. "Giant purses are in right now."

He grinned. "Go on."

"She cleaned her face and hands, probably with wipes from the purse, and then put the trench coat on to hide any splatter stains. Finally, she threw the keys into the bag with the rest. I heard the rattling sound when I opened the door to the stairs. As I was freaking out over the body and running back upstairs, she walked out of the stairwell. She exited the building through the unlocked door of the parking garage and walked down the street to the MetroLink."

"Wouldn't it be odd to wear a trench coat in August? Someone must have noticed her."

"It got cool that night. You had your leather jacket on, if you remember. Besides, have you ridden on the MetroLink late at night? She would have been the least odd person on that train."

"Point taken."

"She took the train to her boyfriend's apartment. I assume he wasn't home that night, so she could wash up without a problem. Then she rode the train back into town the next morning and retrieved her car. Really, if she hadn't started avoiding me, I might not have been so suspicious of her. Probably she thought it was a good idea since I'd found the body and might notice something if I spent any time with her."

"What do you think about the credit card?"

"I think that was on purpose, to make it look more like a robbery, but I don't know for sure. Otherwise, it was a happy accident."

"Very happy. I assume Beth planted the gun and the necklace to throw suspicion on Cheri?"

"Yes. When Blane told her he was her father, she knew Cheri had set her up. So, she set out to get Cheri at Cheri's own game. She knew about the necklaces. She had one. Cheri had been sleeping with John while he was still married to Maddie, so she knew Cheri must have one also. It was just a matter of getting it. She had John's keys, but Cheri had changed the locks after his death. Well, all but an unused back door off of a little patio at the back."

"Wait. It sounds like you have firsthand knowledge of this door."

"I did some snooping," I admitted. "So Beth got into the house, found the necklace, and then created the set up with the gun. Blane made the call to the police. He wanted to protect Beth by implicating Cheri. I don't know how deeply he's involved."

James didn't speak for a moment. "So all that stuff about The Lodge and the embezzlement was just a smokescreen you put up while you uncovered the true motive."

"No, I'm not that clever. I thought the embezzlement could be the motive, and in a way, it was. But women don't kill men just because a deal goes bad. Women kill men for personal reasons. I know that because I'm a woman."

"There aren't many women like you," he said gently.

"I'm glad the trick pony is a crowd pleaser."

"You're so much more than the trick pony." He moved closer. "Liz. Tell me I still have a chance with you."

I took a deep breath. Who would have thought it? Ashley was right after all. "There is no one else."

He smiled boyishly. "Good."

"And you?"

"That engagement ended long before the invitations could be sent."

"You want me even though I can't pick you out of a crowd?"

"I can pick you out. We'll find each other." I felt a lump in my throat.

"So, maybe we should walk back."

I nodded. He interlaced our fingers and took a step forward. "You're going to be okay in those shoes?"

"You can catch me if I fall."

"I will if you let me."

"I'll let you."

We started back.

CHAPTER 25

It was almost a month after the firm prom before James could finally buy me the dinner he had promised so often. That night we walked into the din of sirens and people. I handed him his tuxedo jacket. He squeezed my hand and then let me go, drifting back into the maelstrom of police procedure and the investigation. I saw him once more, right after I'd given my statement about what happened in the bathroom.

He leaned over and said, "I'll try to keep your name out of the rest of the investigation if I can."

I nodded.

"I'm going to be really busy, so don't forget me."

I smiled. "You can send me an email now and then if you like."

"I will, I promise."

I found Janice, who took me home and held her questions. There would be plenty of time later to fill her in. We met the following day. I told her as much as I felt I could. She told me she was starting the escape plan. I called Nick and told him I would not be traveling to Chicago and asked him not to come to St. Louis, but chickened out on telling him why. It still didn't seem real. James called that day and every so often afterwards. But there were emails – like the love letters of old – sweet, almost reverential, but with a style that was all his own. I treasured them.

The night of the dinner, I felt giddy with anticipation. Holly had dragged me out to purchase yet another little black dress. She convinced me with a detailed analysis of cost per wearing and the maxim that you can never have too many l.b.d.'s. I also had to splurge on new lingerie. My mother was right as usual. What I owned was not fit to be seen. It took a couple of hours, but I even found some bras. While they didn't make me look like a model – nothing could hope to do that – they also didn't look like something from the former U.S.S.R. One of the bras was even black, not the usual white or industrial tan. It managed to combine a certain sex appeal with actual support, a feat I had yet to see a bra perform. Maybe tonight was the night. One had to be prepared for any eventuality.

Holly wanted to come over and help me dress, but I refused. Although I could have used the make-up help, I knew she really wanted to hang around long enough to see James' reaction to her handiwork. There is something wonderful and delicious about the wait itself. I didn't want to share it. And I certainly didn't want to share him.

I got ready with time to spare. I slipped on my silver shoes. Use what works. Then I wandered around my apartment straightening one thing and putting away another, filled with a nervous energy I couldn't satisfy. I heard his footsteps up the stairs, and his firm knock on the door. It took all my restraint not to run across the room and fling the door open. I couldn't anyway because of the shoes. Instead I took lady-like steps. I removed the chain and turned the deadbolt with a measured flick of the wrist.

I opened the door. "Hello."

"Hi." He took one step towards me and then another. He had dressed as carefully as usual. A precisely cut blazer, a tailored white shirt, expensive-looking slacks, and those Ferragamo loafers. He looked more handsome than I remembered. Tired though, the fatigue of the investigation etched around his eyes. His smile was as brilliant as ever. I caught sight of the elusive dimple in his cheek. I noticed all those details in the two seconds it took for him to take my hand and pull me to him. I wrapped my arms around his neck. He held me tight. In one smooth move, he shut the door with his foot. Then he leaned down. I turned my face up. His mouth found mine. I kissed him back, feeling a wave of searing emotion. Nothing compared to it. Time seemed suspended. My only thought, my only focus was the touch of his lips on mine. I seemed to be falling, falling, losing myself in the intoxicating feel of him. I realized my knees were shaking.

I started to pull away, my head still buzzing with the electricity of the moment. "I think I'm going to have to sit down," I said.

"I know. If we don't stop now, there won't be any dinner." He kissed me again.

"Does there have to be dinner?" I said after a moment.

"No, not if you don't want to." He leaned in to kiss me.

"No." I pulled away, my mind clearing. "No, I've been promised dinner for over four months. We should go to dinner."

"Whatever you want. There is always dessert."

I grabbed my jacket and my purse from the back of the couch. I wasn't going to let him have it that easy. "Play your cards right and there might be dessert."

"I'll play them very carefully." He handed me into my jacket. It was unusually warm for this time of year. Spring seemed to have come early, and I could finally skip the overcoat.

"You look beautiful tonight. I should have said it before."

"Thank you. And the shoes? You had some opinion."

He grinned. "Better not go into that now – maybe over dessert."

I laughed.

He opened the door and waited beside me while I locked it. I felt his arm creep around my shoulder. Then we walked down the narrow stairs side by side, pressed together in a familiar way.

"Where are we going, by the way?" I said.

"You'll figure it out before we even park the car."

"You know me that well, do you?"

"I'd like to know you better." He leaned down and kissed me on the cheek.

"The cards, remember?"

He laughed ruefully. "I haven't forgotten."

We reached the bottom of the inside stairs. The door to the Henderson's flung open. Joe stood there staring at us.

"Oh. Hello Joe." I pulled away from James. "Joe Henderson, this is James Paperelli – my – ah – friend." I looked over at James. James looked at me and then extended his hand to Joe. They shook hands stiffly.

"Pleased to meet you," James said.

"Same here," Joe replied. I could tell he didn't mean it.

They stood there in silence for several interminable seconds.

I jumped in. "Well, good night, Joe."

"Good night, Liz." Joe turned and gave James a hard look. "Good night, James."

James gave him back stare for stare. "Joe," he said. James nodded his head in Joe's direction and then put his arm around my shoulder. He pulled me out the door. We started the walk towards his car.

"You never mentioned your neighbor is in love with you."

"He's not my neighbor. His parents are. He just comes over to help them out."

"And to see you?"

"I keep telling myself that's not the case."

"Okay," he said.

We reached the car. He opened the passenger door to let me in and then slid behind the wheel. I'd never ridden in his car before. It was a silver Infinity, one of the small sporty models that sat low and sleek. The dashboard seemed to be all dials and gauges. There was leather and burled wood everywhere. I noticed it was an automatic. He put it in reverse and then pulled out, headed to our mystery destination.

"Your car is very nice," I said, wanting to start with a safe subject.

"Thank you. It handles well in city traffic."

"Don't you prefer a manual transmission?"

"Yes, normally, but I hate driving stick in the city. All the stopping and starting makes me nuts. This car was a compromise." He looked over at me. "How did you know that?"

"Your hand on the shift. You're like a parent of a teenage driver who finds himself pressing an imaginary brake at every stop. You want to shift but you can't."

He chuckled. "Nothing gets by you, does it?"

"Not usually, no."

He reached over with the hand that was on the shift and took my hand in his. "I have a question."

"The parlor trick?"

"Maybe. It depends on your methods. How did you know I live in Lafayette Square?"

"Simple process of elimination. You have to live in the city as a requirement of your job. You have money to spend on a very expensive piece of property. Plus, you like quality, so you are going to spend money where it counts. You are young, so you want to live close to the action. That leaves three areas – the Central West End, Lafayette Square, or the lofts downtown."

He smiled and nodded.

"I knew from your taste in clothes that your style overall is more traditional than modern. That eliminated the lofts. So I was left with two options. But you knew about the beer selection at a bar that's known for chocolate. That's odd. You must go there often. And that place is close to Lafayette Square. Ergo, you live there."

"Very impressive. And all of that without an Internet search?"

"That was only for confirmation."

"Cheater."

"But I know where we're going."

We turned on Hanley Road. Fitting. I could now check it off my list. We pulled up in front of Pomme and the valet walked up to meet us. James handed him the keys. Then he opened the door for me. I was still struggling with the seatbelt. I'd gotten it caught in my jacket.

"Trapped?" he said.

"Yes. You can't take me anywhere."

He leaned over me to work the buckle. I could smell the scent of his skin, and the familiar overlay of soap and cologne. Maybe my subconscious had engineered the problem. Maybe he thought the same thing. He bent his head and quickly kissed me on the neck as he released the seat belt.

"Dessert," he whispered in my ear.

"Cards," I whispered back.

He pulled me out of the car and steadied me on my silver heels. I held his arm as we walked into the restaurant. Pomme did not disappoint. It had the same exposed brick walls and wooden floor as the café, but the ambiance was elegant and intimate – dark wood and candlelight. At James' direction, the hostess guided us to a small private table at the back.

I sat down and spread the cloth napkin across my lap. The waiter appeared promptly with water and menus. He presented the wine list. I don't know much about wine, so I let James make a selection. The waiter returned with bread, butter and some sort of nibble. Pâté perhaps. I took a small bite. Delicious.

James and I talked little nothings. The wine appeared. It was red with a deep dark flavor, a hint of sweet at the end. By the second sip, I was hooked. The waiter took our orders. I ordered the filet, James the short ribs. Then the waiter disappeared, leaving us to more substantive conversation.

"I don't mean to talk shop, but can you tell me how the case is going? Oh, and Janice told me to tell you that the keys were for The Lodge office. She's been in touch with the county investigators. They seem to be focusing on Tom Green and the other members of the management committee, so I guess none of the IT staff have been implicated. Maybe Chester was replacing mice all over the building." I smiled. "And Grant quit the firm right after the party, so I don't know if he's been questioned at all."

"Doubt it. Would you trust a guy like Grant with a role in your embezzlement? Tom Green and his cronies are not that stupid."

I shook my head. "He did have a tendency to talk."

"And as to your first question, our case is going better than it was. Blane Ford is still not talking. Cheri's not talking. But Beth finally regained consciousness."

"Today?"

"I got a call this afternoon. We'll see if she has any memory of anything."

"It's going to be a hard case," I said.

"You don't need to tell me. If Beth or Cheri don't roll over, it will be hearsay and circumstantial evidence from start to finish."

"But how to prove Cheri intended for Beth to kill John?"

"We'll leave it to the prosecutor to figure out."

I shook my head. "Love does strange things to people."

"What a thing to say on a night like this," he said lightly.

I smiled. "I didn't mean to imply anything."

"I hope not."

"However, I have a question along those lines. If you don't mind?"

"I don't know if I like the sound of that, but go ahead."

"What happened to your fiancée?"

"All the gory details?"

I nodded.

"Well, you have a right to know." He took a sip of wine. "It involves you."

"It does?" I sat back.

"How to begin? We'd been dating for a long time, off and on. We'd break up then get back together. The last time we got back together, we faced serious pressure from our families to get married. Her family in particular."

I gave him a look.

"I'm not saying I just went along with it for my family or anything like that. I really thought I loved her. And, to be honest, I hadn't met anyone I liked better. I'm not getting younger – as my mother likes to remind me. I thought – maybe this is it?"

"So you proposed?"

"I proposed. Although the details her mom put in the *Ladue News* were exaggerated. It wasn't that dramatic. She said yes, so there we were, planning the wedding. It was set for this October."

"What happened?"

"We started fighting almost as soon as we announced the engagement. She'd moved in by that point. Everything was a drama with Angie. The smallest thing could set her off. On most days you could have cut the tension with a knife. I couldn't stand it, so I spent more time at work."

"But you stayed together?"

"I kept thinking it would get better."

"I totally understand," I said.

He smiled. The smile reached the depths of his eyes. "Then I had the brilliant idea to ask you to help me with the investigation. I knew when I met you that you were someone special." He leaned in.

"I probably put off calling longer than I should have. And seeing you just made dealing with Angie even harder."

He took my fingers in his own across the table. I felt his thumb gently sweep across my knuckles. His touch was like no one else's. "Every time I talked to you, I was more and more attracted. You're different – I can't explain it."

If I hadn't been sitting, my knees would have buckled under me. "So what happened?"

He looked down at my hand and then back at me. "Would you believe Mark?"

"Mark?"

"He made me see what was going on."

"How?"

"After the night we ran into you and your friend, he said that it was obvious that there was something between us. He told me to break my engagement before it was too late."

"Did you break it off then? We'd hardly spent any time together." No need to mention that I'd already fallen hard.

"No. I couldn't own up to it. I told him he was wrong. That we were just working on the case together. But it planted a seed. As time passed, I could see he was right. I just didn't know how to get out. I felt trapped. It was a mess." He shook his head.

"And?"

"You forced my hand."

"Me?"

"When I went over to your apartment with the photos, I wasn't expecting to stay very long. I'd promised Angie I'd be home to go out for dinner. I thought we would just look at the photos, identify the people, and then be done."

"But I couldn't do it."

"And I made you cry." He held my hand very tightly. "You don't know how sorry I am. When you burst into tears, I didn't know what to do. I thought you'd never speak to me again, and I couldn't let that happen. I realized that Mark was right. I decided to stay and make it right with you."

"And Angie?"

"She was furious when I got home. Like I'd never seen before. And then it hit me – this was my chance. I told her where I'd been."

"She assumed the worst."

"Of course. She told me she was leaving, and I didn't argue. In fact, I watched her pack her bag and fly out the door. She went to her mother's house."

"Your family thinks I'm the Other Woman?" The irony was too great.

"No," he said firmly. "I told my family that nothing happened between us. I just couldn't stand the fighting any more. I told Angie the same thing when she wanted to make up." He paused. "I think my family has come around. They see how much happier I am now."

"I'm curious," I said shyly, lowering my eyes. "Did you want something to happen that night?"

"You have no idea how much. When you put your head on my shoulder, it took all my will power not to —"

I looked up. His gaze nearly made my heart stop.

Fortunately for my cardiac health, the food arrived. We sat quietly for a couple of minutes savoring our dinner. The filet was perfection. Holly certainly missed out as a vegetarian. I mulled over everything he had told me.

"How is your filet?" he said.

"Wonderful. And the short ribs?"

"Delicious. What is it you're afraid to ask me?"

"Am I that obvious?"

"You are to me." He gave me a sly smile.

"It's nothing."

"Come on. It can't be that bad."

"Well, it's just – I've seen a lot of rotten things with this case, and you say you were wrong with your fiancée. So, are you sure you're right with me? I mean, if you're not sure, I'd rather know now. It would make it easier."

"There is no guarantee, of course. But I can say I've never felt the way I feel with you. That instant connection – I can be myself. That's the thing, just me."

"Oh." I took a bite of filet and chewed slowly.

"You?"

I took a sip of wine. "It's been like climbing up a rock face, knowing you were engaged and trying not to want you for myself." I smiled sheepishly. "Lately I've done nothing but fall off the mountain."

"And the other guys?"

"There are no other guys."

"I thought I was too late, you know. That you were already with Vince."

"Mark. Of course," I said.

"He's my younger brother. He had to rub it in that you were off the market."

"It was one date."

"Glad to hear it."

The waiter returned to ask how we liked our food. We told him it was wonderful. Our plates were clean. James signaled to him and he nodded. I wondered. The waiter reappeared in a moment with a small bottle. Even I could tell it was a very expensive dessert wine.

"You shouldn't have," I said to James.

"It's just a little something I had tucked away."

"I won't be able to walk out of here with that much alcohol in me."

"I'll carry you."

"I'd like to see you try. I'm not the lightest girl in the world."

"I can carry my own weight and then some."

"How complimentary. You're supposed to say I'm as light as a feather."

"You would have laughed in my face."

"You do know me."

The waiter poured the wine and then discreetly removed himself. James picked up his glass. "A toast," he said.

I picked up my glass. The wine had a wonderful amber color. I caught a whiff of plum and honey. "What are we toasting?"

"A beginning. I can now in good faith spend as much time with you as my job and everything else will allow."

"Assuming I don't get tired of you?"

"With your permission then. To a new beginning."

"To a new beginning," I said. We clinked glasses. I took a sip. It was liquid ambrosia. "Tell me what you mean by 'good faith.'"

"I thought you'd catch that."

"It was a lawyerly toast."

He looked at me over the rim of his glass.

"Well?" I said.

"It's taken me a while to disentangle my affairs."

"Angie just moved all of her things out of your house?"

"That, and we finally worked out an arrangement for the wedding down payments and everything else. I just wanted it to be done, whatever it cost, but she dragged things out."

"She hoped you'd reconsider. That's what I would have done."

"I'll remember that."

"It shouldn't be a surprise. I'm tenacious. It's one of my few virtues."

"Begging for a compliment? I'm shocked. You know you have many virtues, and no vices I can discover. At least none of the bad ones."

"Give it time."

"You want to ask something else – I can see it on your face."

I nodded. "It's mere curiosity. What happened to the ring? It got quite a write up in the *Ladue News*."

"That announcement is going to haunt me till the day I die. Do you really want to know?"

"Sure."

"Angie threw it at my head the night of the big fight. She almost took my eye out. I couldn't find it for about a month afterwards."

I laughed. "You're lucky it didn't get sucked up by the vacuum or something."

"I worried about that. Every time I heard a clunk, I had to open the thing and sort through the dust. I finally found it under a chair. It's in the safe deposit now."

"So you can move on in good faith. I still can't get over the use of that phrase."

"You are rubbing off on me with your lawyer speak and your inverted grammar."

"I'd like to think it's an improvement, but please go on."

"So I want to spend time with you, if I have your permission."

"You've always had it," I replied.

The waiter reappeared. "May I refill your glasses? And, would you like to see the dessert menu?"

Our eyes met across the table. James gave me a wicked smile. "About those vices. Cards?"

"Dessert." I nodded.

James turned to the waiter, who looked perplexed. "Please send the wine back to the kitchen with our compliments. I think we'll skip the dessert this time. Just the check. Thanks."

"Shall we?" he said, reaching for my hand across the table. I felt the sparks jump across our interlaced fingers.

I gripped his hand more tightly. "Yes," I said. "Yes we shall."

ACKNOWLEDGMENTS

I would like to thank Jaime, Lillie and Jaimito for all of their support. I would also like to thank my parents, brother and sister-in-law for their editorial suggestions and willingness to read this book in between diapers and general mayhem. Dara, Cindy and Kajal deserve special praise for their unstinting encouragement, constructive criticism and their ability to make me laugh at constant rejection. I couldn't have done it without them. Praise also for Dana and Chinell for their invaluable assistance and infectious enthusiasm. And I send a heartfelt thanks to my book club, and in particular Dave, for acting as my beta testers. Thanks also to Eric for appreciating **Nerdy Girls** when others did not. Finally, no acknowledgement would be complete without mentioning the great debt I owe to St. Louis, Missouri and Marshfield, Wisconsin – two welcoming and quirky places I have had the privilege to call home.

ABOUT THE AUTHOR

L isa Boero is a practicing attorney who lived for many years in St. Louis, Missouri, but now resides in Marshfield, Wisconsin with her husband and children. Legal experience combined with a strange neurological condition inspired her to write **Murderers and Nerdy Girls Work Late**, the first book in the **Nerdy Girls** series. For more information about Lisa and all things **Nerdy Girls**, please see Lisa's website at *www.lisaboero.com*.

Made in the USA
Lexington, KY
14 August 2013